SKINWALKER MEDIUM

G.G. Collins

CHAMISA CANYON
PUBLISHING

Chamisa Canyon Publishing

chamisacanyon@live.com
Attn: Rights & Permissions

Book Cover by Vila Design
Editing by Jay Terre

ISBN 978-1-7354282-5-3 (Paperback)

AUTHOR'S NOTE

In *Skinwalker Medium* I have fictionalized the belief in skinwalkers, known to the resident Nations in the Four Corners region as evil witches. They believe if you say the word it draws one to you so they prefer not to speak about them. Are they real? After researching this subject I will never again drive through any of the reservations without a black obsidian arrowhead.

The Navajo live primarily in Arizona on their reservation of more than 27,000 square miles including parts of New Mexico and Utah. Several highways crisscross their home.

The Santa Fe Penitentiary riot of February 1980 was real. There are descriptions of what actually happened in this work of fiction. I've tried to use as many factual elements as possible while leaving out the worst of the atrocities. You can find this information online if you are interested. Please do so with reverence. Lives were snuffed out in the most barbaric ways.

Acknowledgements
& Gratitude

My thanks to Sharon Kepford Ogan, weaver and stargazer, for her assistance in explaining the art of weaving. Otherwise, I wouldn't know the difference between a weaving fork and an egg beater. Her weavings are beautiful works of art.

And to Stephen J. Hanan, assistant director, for enlightening me on the ins and outs of filmmaking and explaining what a video village is. His description of a film set was beyond helpful. He is best known for his work in *Reservation Dogs* and *Minari*.

My gratitude to Tony Hillerman, who paved the way for Native American stories to be told.

To the people of the Navajo Nation whose beliefs and ways I find fascinating and worthy of sharing. I try to treat all Native American stories with respect and honor.

Lastly to my husband, and soulmate, who died unexpectedly last autumn. God, what to say? He was my best friend, traveling companion, dinner date, pet co-parent and partner in crime. That made him first reader and editor. He could brainstorm with me to all hours. To say I miss him is an understatement. I loved his sense of humor and our conversations over dinner. Best of all, he let me be me. I will miss him for the rest of my days. Wherever you are in the cosmos, I love you. Meet you at the Rainbow Bridge.

For Sharon
In memory of Lacey

"There are two wolves fighting inside all of us.
The first one is evil; the second one is good ...
Which wolf will win is the one you feed."

—Native American Proverb

SKINWALKER MEDIUM
BY G.G. COLLINS

Old Main looked ominous as Rachel approached it from the parking lot. Paint peeled from its skin like a bad sunburn. One of the deadliest prison riots in United States history took place there February 2, 1980 at the Santa Fe State Penitentiary. After 36 hours of blood-soaked terror, it ended. Thirty-three people lost their lives in the most heinous ways imaginable and more would be traumatized for the rest of their days.

Rachel stood outside trying to get her feelings under control. Even many feet away from the entrance she was impacted by the suffering that had taken place years before. Reports of hauntings were frequent and believable. Film crews experienced clanging cell doors at night despite no electrical power to operate the doors. Mysterious human-like shadows had been described. Paranormal investigators who sat vigil swore never to return.

She walked past watch tower No. 1 and into Santa Fe's ugly past, far from the tourists enjoying themselves while shopping for turquoise jewelry and sipping margaritas in the downtown plaza. The glitz of the City Different was only fifteen miles from this world: one of barbarism.

Inside, she waited notebook and recorder in hand for her guide.

Shaking the dread was impossible. She observed the gift shop and couldn't quite comprehend T-shirts from a penitentiary – even a closed one. A yellow T read "NMCD STATE Prisoner." As Rachel explored she saw weapons on exhibit. Prisoners fashioned them from glass shards. The metal objects she thought to be shanks. All were on display in cases, the type one usually associated with trinkets. It was confounding to her to see these deadly shivs put on view but the prison was more of a museum now: a place to learn about what happens when the worst of humanity goes on a rampage. Black and white photos showed scenes before and after the riot.

"Hello, I'm Ernesto Pacheco," a man said.

Engrossed, Rachel started.

"Sorry, to surprise you," he said. "I understand you are here to tour the facility for an article your magazine is publishing."

He looked kindly. Rachel guessed him retirement age. His tanned skin had the lines of a lived-in face. His eyes were deep brown and his hair was mostly silver. She liked him. While she couldn't always judge a person on first impression, her reporter's intuition had become reasonably dependable.

"Yes, I'm Rachel Blackstone with High Desert Country Magazine," she shook his hand. It was a good handshake, not too strong, not wimpy. Sincere. She handed him her card, which he slid into his shirt pocket without reading. It was plaid – the shirt. Cream and burgundy and it topped a pair of worn jeans. His feet were outfitted in hiking shoes, a frequent foot covering in the Santa Fe area.

"I don't think your magazine has covered the prison before," he said. "Most visitors are young thrill seekers who don't fully grasp what happened here. They tour the facility, ask questions and go back to the plaza for drinks and burritos."

His voice was slow and soft. Rachel warmed to him. He had a gentle, calm way about him. He seemed to sense her unease.

"You're correct, we haven't done a story on the riot before," Rachel said. "I've been with them almost from the beginning."

"You'll probably prefer to pass on the *mug shot*?"

Rachel was astonished and horrified.

"Really?" she asked.

"Most of the tourists like it." He shrugged his shoulders.

Let's begin the tour," Ernesto gestured. "If you'll follow me."

"Okay," she mumbled.

"You've seen our shop," he said. "Some people find it off-putting. I don't blame them. We'll bypass the courtyard and get straight to it."

He showed her the administrative offices first.

"This is where the rioters destroyed all the records," Ernesto pointed to an office with crime scene tape across the door opening.

Rachel followed him as he made a left turn. They passed two cellblocks and several dormitories. Near the end of the hall, he stopped.

"This is Dormitory E," he said. "It was 1:40 a.m. when inmates high on prison-made hooch – consisting of water, sugar, fruit and yeast and mixed in a garbage bag – accosted two guards, took their guns and keys. The two guards were inexperienced. In those days prison officials tended to give them a uniform and tell them they were guards. With those keys, the prison became the inmate's playground.

"To make matters worse," Ernesto continued. "The most dangerous offenders – those who spent most of their time locked up in individual cells had been moved to this dormitory while their Cellblock 5 was under renovation.

"You'll notice," he pointed to the clock. "At each place we stop the clocks have been permanently set to the time an incident happened in that area."

Ernesto reversed and showed Rachel back down the corridor.

"At 2:02 a.m. rioters broke through the reinforced windows of the control center," he said. "At that point, they were in command of the entire penitentiary. From there, they pillaged the pharmacy and added drugs to their already drunken state. Within a short time, prisoners had found cutting torches and set fires in the gym and administrative offices. Then felons were released from Cellblock Three."

"How were they able to breach the control center?" Rachel asked. "Was there no bullet-proof glass to protect the staff from this kind of thing?"

"The glass was bullet-resistant, but despite that they were able to break through in less than five minutes using fire extinguishers to smash the glass.

"The atrocities that occurred next were inhumane by anyone's standards," Ernesto continued. "The rioters opened neighboring Cellblock 4 where the snitches, child molesters and those in protective custody were housed.

"Normally we don't show Cellblock Four. Since you're working on a legitimate story, I've been given permission to take you in there. No photos please."

Rachel agreed. Julian, the High Desert Magazine publisher and her employer had insisted she carry a cell phone for her safety, but she wasn't sure she knew how to take a photo even if she wanted to. Yes, she was tech-challenged.

As they approached Cellblock 4, the feeling of dread took on a whole new level. Her legs wanted to run and blood pounded in her head. Ernesto stood aside the door. She was hit with what felt like wind. Only this was the collective rage of inmates driven to kill. It was primitive and palpable. She could hear the screams of those being assaulted and murdered. Some begged for their mothers.

Rachel slipped her recorder into her jacket pocket. Her notebook fell to the floor. Ernesto picked it up and held it out to her.

"Are you okay?" he asked.

"Uh, yes," Rachel replied. "It's overwhelming."

"Not everyone feels that," he said. "Most come here as a result of what we call dark tourism. They may not respect the loss of life or the deplorable conditions that led to the massacre. It's just another sight to see.

"Do you still want to go in?" he asked.

"Yes," Rachel heard herself say it but she had to force her feet to move inside. It was stifling. The air was acrid and felt thick with death. Her lungs resisted. It wasn't oxygen that could support life. The stench of smoke and blood remained.

Ernesto showed her the marks cut into the floor where an inmate was killed and the permanent burn marks where another met his fate.

"When it was over, about 36 hours of brutality," he said. "Thirty-three men had lost their lives in the most awful ways. All were 40 or younger. One was nineteen."

The agony and weeping continued to emanate from the cellblock as if the horror was occurring in that moment. She did a partial turn to take it all in. The bodies, burned mattresses, and blood-soaked cellblocks had been cleaned of most of the evidence that remained after the massacre. Only the scarred floor contained the visible proof that something horrific had occurred here. Otherwise, everything had been thrown away. It was empty, but it didn't feel empty. Thirty-three souls remained forever in this place. She could envision all of it. Inundated with ghastly emotions, she turned away. A shadow moved near the end of the cells.

"What was that?" she asked her hand to her mouth.

"What did you see?" Ernesto said.

"Looked like a shadow. Human-shaped, and wearing something bulky, maybe a cape."

"We, the Hopi and other Indian Nations, call them shadow people," he said. "They are frequently malevolent. They exist all over the prison. The worst are here where most of the bloodshed took place."

"I have to leave," she said. As quickly as she stepped out of the Cell-block 4 the screams lifted and she was able to steady herself.

"Most people aren't so viscerally affected," Ernesto said. He reached to touch her shoulder. "But I am one of them. A couple of the guides have similar reactions to this particular block. I understand what you're feeling."

"What is that breeze I feel? Is there a draft?" Rachel asked

"No, it is a *dark wind*," Ernesto explained. "The Navajo define it as 'out of control.' It destroys judgment. We mustn't stay here long.

"This way to the entrance," he added.

When they reached the lobby, Rachel was relieved.

"Let's go outside," Ernesto opened the door for her.

They stepped out into the sunlight. Rachel felt the heaviness lift from her body.

"About what you saw; the one you described as wearing a cape," Ernesto said. "Now that we are safely away from it, I can explain."

"What do you mean, safely away?"

"Cellblock 4 is haunted as you witnessed," Ernesto said. "These en-tities are dangerous."

"What is it?" Rachel asked.

"It is called *yee naaldlooshii*." Ernesto said.

"Is that Navajo?" Rachel was puzzled.

"Yes, if you would allow me?" He asked for her notebook. "It is spelled like this and pronounced thusly." He returned the tablet.

Rachel looked at what he had written: *Yee naaldlooshii; yee-nahld-loo-shee.* He'd added the phonetic pronunciation.

"What is it?" she asked.

"In English, it is called a skinwalker," he said. "Skinwalkers are mali-cious witches. They have much power to do evil. Most American Indi-ans have their version. Some call them a wendigo. In the Southwest we know them a skinwalkers. Most Navajo, Hopi and Ute will not even speak the word. It is inviting trouble. Bad trouble. I tell you this now only because you saw it.

"It would be prudent not to include this in the article," Ernesto continued. "It could bring down the power of the beast onto you and those you love."

"I promise you, I will not write about it," Rachel said. "Thank you for the warning."

Rachel knew it couldn't be a part of the story anyway. Julian kept to fact-based stories. She had left out things before when writing stories for the publication. The last thing she wanted was to endanger anyone.

"What is one doing here?" Rachel asked purposely not saying the word.

"I would say one of the family members of the prisoners killed or the guards who were traumatized have become one to exact revenge," he said.

"Wait please." He walked back into the lobby and returned a few seconds later. "Since you saw it, I think you should have this."

He placed an arrowhead in her palm.

"This is black obsidian; it will protect you. It is born of volcanoes deep within the Earth. Keep it on you at all times."

Rachel thanked him for his time and the protective crystal. Once in her car, she sat still and tried to shake off the trepidation. It wasn't happening again. It wasn't.

CHAPTER 2

That evening as Rachel walked east on Palace Avenue she thought about how unsettling her interview at the Old Main had been. Usually the blue *portal* she passed beneath was cheery, but not tonight. Tonight, she felt haunted by her past as well as the spirits left in the accursed prison.

Across the street sat the Museum of Contemporary Native Arts with its colorful columns. It was often photographed. The real treasures, the art of Indigenous peoples, remained inside.

Opposite it, stood the St. Francis Cathedral with its unfinished towers; money had run out during the building and so it remained incomplete. It was beautiful outside with its rose window and brown adobe facade, but its interior was a wonder. Graceful arches lifted the congregation's voices as they sang. Even for the nonreligious, it was a spiritual place. On occasion, Rachel would light candles for her friends who were facing life's difficulties. On their birthdays, she would light one for her family members including her brother, who had recently been released from prison.

Rachel's father, Ian Woods, had been a reporter for the *Albuquerque Journal* after writing for the *New York Times, Washington Post* and *Los Angeles Times*. When they added children to their family, her parents moved back to New Mexico. Her mother died when Rachel and her brother were young. She couldn't even bring to mind what she looked like – only memories of old photographs she had seen.

Her father's investigative skills brought fear to those whose criminal acts he revealed. It was his ability to ferret out diabolical details that ended his life. He had been run off the Santa Fe ski basin road and died.

Brother Chris had gone in another direction, one with underhanded deals and easy women. He had talked a good game and became Santa Fe's mayor but had mixed with the criminal underworld. He'd paid for it at the new Santa Fe pen. The last Rachel knew, he'd been headed for southeastern New Mexico. Maybe it was better not to know.

She thought of Anthony Blackstone and how their marriage dissolved over time. He was a producer of documentaries for PBS. When Hollywood blockbusters didn't come through for him, he became melancholy and began to drink too much. She left their relationship one night. She ran away after buying the Mercury Marquis. It wasn't a perfect ending. Endings are hard.

Remembering was both painful and somehow cleansing.

Rachel took a left into the Prince Patio and looked for Chloe Valdez. She had been her best friend for many years. Chloe ran the most successful real estate company in Santa Fe, Sun Dancing Realty, and excelled at finding the right house for the right people. She kept her last name from her first marriage because it helped sell houses in an area of Hispanic traditions. Her friend was clearly not Latino, but born of French parents who lived in Paris where her father did something called international investment banking and her mother ran an art museum.

When she decided to sell real estate, she quickly picked up Santa Fe style and made it work for her. The look prevailed in the crowd of southwestern sophisticates and included turquoise jewelry, broomstick skirts and colors of the region.

Chloe waited at the host stand inside The Shed, a popular dining spot in downtown with staying power. Owned by the Carswell family, the third generation currently operated it.

She flirted shamelessly with the host, whom she had known for years. Her long hair was pulled back and held in place with a turquoise clip. As usual, Chloe was the picture of a Santa Fe woman with a turquoise skirt and black silk blouse. The skirt was tethered with a matching belt and silver buckle, her chest heavy with a squash blossom necklace.

Chloe turned to see Rachel approaching and ran to embrace her. It was her usual greeting. She air-kissed both cheeks and stepped back still holding Rachel's shoulders.

"You look down," Chloe said. "We must change that to happy. We've got two stools waiting for us at the bar. I've already placed our order." She hustled Rachel into the restaurant.

Chloe had a beautiful exotic face she made up accordingly. Rachel was more the mascara and lipstick type. She envied Chloe's together look but didn't want to put in the time on herself. She never knew when she might get a call-out on a story and preferred a more natural look. As they walked out of reception, every eye in the restaurant was on Chloe.

Two margaritas awaited them on the counter: one a house version and the other pomegranate. Chloe was convinced the pomegranate in her pink margarita was healthier than the more common lime drink.

"You might want to start two more," Chloe said to Hector the barkeep. "I think this could shape up to be a three-margarita night." Hector flashed them a radiant smile and obediently went into action. Rachel knew Chloe was a generous tipper and a genuinely kind person and so did Hector.

"If we're going for a three, I want food," Rachel said. "Would you please put in an order for carne adovada and a cheese enchilada?"

"And make it a bleu cheese & walnut salad for me," Chloe added.

Chloe tried to go vegetarian for the most part. The salads were delicious, but came topped with the most delectable blue cheese so not really a calorie saver.

"Okay," Chloe said. "What's up?" She turned toward Rachel and gave her the x-ray vision look. She narrowed one eye and turned slightly. That was meant to get Rachel to open up. Her reputation was to hold things close to the vest.

"I had an interview at the Old Main today," Rachel said knowing it was useless to try to put her off.

"Oh my, that must have been disturbing."

"You have no idea," Rachel said. "The creep factor was quite high and when my guide took me to the cellblock where most of the murders occurred, it got truly alarming."

"Are you saying what I think you're saying?" Chloe engaged further, leaning in.

"I saw something called a shadow person."

"Really?" Rachel didn't like the way Chloe's face lit up at the mention. Chloe had always been interested in the paranormal; Rachel had been drafted reluctantly by the spirit world.

"My guide, Ernesto, didn't call it that however," Rachel paused. She felt uncomfortable talking about things that weren't factual as she knew them in her world. But that world had been expanding in the past couple of years. Her definition of normal was evolving by the day.

"What did he call it?" Chloe asked.

"A skinwalker," Rachel whispered.

"Holy shit! I've read about those," Chloe said. "They're exceedingly treacherous. From what I know many of the Indigenous peoples believe in them."

"Ernesto didn't speak about it until we were outside the prison," Rachel said. "He gave me this because of my reaction to that part of the prison." Rachel removed the black arrowhead from her shoulder bag and handed it to Chloe.

The stone glinted in the lights from the restaurant as Chloe held it in her palm. She felt the smoothness of the cut crystal with her fingertips.

"What was your reaction?" Chloe asked.

"Like I said, the whole experience was creepy. When I arrived at Old Main, I didn't want to go in, but it's an assignment. It was all unsettling, but when we got to Cellblock 4, I could hear ... the screams. The rage and agony were overwhelming. I couldn't hold onto my notebook. When I stepped inside, and saw the, the floor. The marks ... "

"I know what you're talking about Rachel," Chloe said. "You don't have to say it. I've read about the riot."

"Seeing it was more than enough; I had to leave that haunted unit and get out of the building."

They were quiet for a few minutes. Chloe broke the silence.

"What is it made from?" She held out the stone.

"Ernesto told me black obsidian. He said to carry it on me at all times." She returned it to her bag.

"We need to talk with Mari-Lynn and see if she recommends anything else," Chloe said.

Mari-Lynn Alo had been Chloe's pot supplier until she and her partner moved to Santa Fe from Pueblo where she had conducted a pot business, both legal and illegal depending on the Colorado law at the time. She opened a metaphysical shop in Santa Fe and Celeste; her partner ran a legal marijuana dispensary. Mari Lynn knew almost everything about crystals. She was also known to have visions that helped Rachel and Chloe on prior paranormal manifestations.

"Does this mean?" Chloe asked.

"Mean what?" Rachel deliberately misunderstood. She had already reluctantly acknowledged to herself *it* was probably happening again, but wasn't ready to enlighten Chloe. In fact, she couldn't be certain there was anything more amiss than her seeing a shadow in a cellblock – where humans were slaughtered!

"You know I can't talk about the details of a story in the works," Rachel tried. "The prison riot is on record. Anyone can look up the specifics. It's shocking in its cruelty. Now that I think about it, the only thing new I have to report is that shadow. I can't include it in the piece because it is impossible to confirm."

"Then there is no problem," Chloe said.

"Let's wait and see if anything develops," Rachel said. "Caution can't hurt at this point."

The women sat in the festive bar contemplating what might come. For Rachel, it no longer felt welcoming. The conversation had cast a pall over the two friends.

She couldn't help but feel cold. Maybe a front was coming through. Rachel knew better. *It* was happening again, she just didn't want to admit it.

CHAPTER 3

Rachel took an Uber home after the three-margarita dinner. Chloe installed the app on her phone and ordered the ride. Once home, she puttered around her kitchen getting her tortoiseshell cat, Chile Pod, her dinner. The cat was a bit miffed at the lateness of the meal even though she always had kibble to eat. When Rachel placed the canned food on the Saltillo floor, Chile Pod didn't dive in. Instead, her ears went on alert. She leapt to the kitchen counter and stared out the window at the courtyard. Within moments her tail turned into a bottle brush.

"Hey Pod Girl," Rachel said. "What's up?"

Before she could determine who or what was up, a wolf's howl carried on the breeze interrupted her thoughts.

"Oh no." Rachel grimaced.

The white wolf who had been assigned to protect her conveyed a warning. Something or someone was about to put in an appearance. The tiny cat knew the routine and usually sensed it a few seconds before Rachel.

Chile Pod hopped down and jumped on a chair under the table where she cowered behind the tablecloth. She let go with her scariest hisses.

"You stay there," Rachel said. "I'll go see who it is."

She grabbed her yard coat on the way out the back door. It was November and cool at night. The heavy denim kept the chill off.

Soon the city would have their employees out wrapping garland and adding holiday red ribbons to the plaza. Decorating began in earnest after Thanksgiving, usually the first or second week in December. Hotels placed electric farolitos along the flat rooflines.

As she descended the steps from her back porch, there was nothing in sight but her herb bed all tucked in with winter mulch. She paused next to the garden.

In the blink of an eye, the odor of a spent match enveloped her. Rachel waited for what she knew would come. Soon the hissing and rattling followed. The familiar colors began to seep across the gravel. These hues were more vivid than previous comings. They were black, white, yellow and red, the fours colors of Native American directions.

The colorful vapors came toward her crawling along like fog on water, each from their respective direction. When they met in front of Rachel the vibrant vapors rose into a column. While she waited for the spirit to show itself, Rachel remembered the first time this happened. She wanted to speak with her deceased father to question his death. When performing the Hopi ritual to return the dead the wrong spirit returned. Mario was an evil man her brother had known during his days as mayor. Mario was a criminal when alive and after death he created storms that killed people. It was a hard lesson for Rachel. Afterwards, other spirits appeared to her, including the white wolf Kiyiya (key-ī-yah) so named because it meant "howling wolf."

The vertical form was now changing into the spirit who had come to visit her. Usually it was a body, this one was different. Out of the mist stepped Skeleton Man, also called Másaw, the Hopi Lord of the Dead.

Rachel was taken aback. She never expected to see him again after her journey to the Land of the Dead.

His skeleton looked even more tattered than when she met him the first time. It was badly discolored. His joints crackled as they rubbed together when he moved. He still had the presence of a leader despite the breechcloth and white tunic he wore. His chest was heavy with many necklaces made of vibrant beads.

"Hello." She wasn't sure what to call him. "How can I help you?"

"You are Rachel?" His broken jaw threatened to come apart as he spoke. Each word caused his ribs to shake. She watched, mesmerized by his eye contact even though he had none. The empty sockets looked directly at her. His *gaze* held hers. Rachel was afraid to look away for fear it would seem disrespectful, but it was difficult to look upon this ancient one because he was so frightening. There was no doubt he had the kind of power reserved for only a few. At the same time, she admired him for his longevity and endless knowledge. He seemed to adapt to his new surrounds and stood straighter. He was all business.

"You will encounter one of the most evil entities," he said. "You must see it through."

"See what through?" Rachel asked.

"The journey," he said. "You were successful stopping the Fifth World coming, were you not?"

"Yes, but ... " Rachel floundered. "I have no idea what journey."

"You will know it." Másaw waved his hand from right to left. Rachel noticed the bone spurs attached to his knuckles hinting at arthritis in the life before this one, or maybe he had led many lives.

Rachel had been exasperated at their first meeting with his cryptic messages. She wanted to know more.

"I must go." Before he disappeared into the haze, he said: "Beware the *wùuti*." He vanished.

Rachel was left bewildered. "What journey? And what is a *wùuti?*"

She took a step and heard something crunch. Looking down, she noticed five kernels of dried yellow corn. She scooped them up and dropped them in her jacket pocket. From her experience in the Land of the Dead she knew they represented the Five Worlds of the Hopi. It was official; a calling card of sorts. Másaw had really been there.

That meant whatever was coming was grim. She hoped it wasn't a near cataclysm like last time.

CHAPTER 4

Rachel walked into the High Desert Country offices the following day. What had been a small building doubled in size after Julian Brazos, the publisher and editor, recently added a second floor. To Rachel's delight it included an office for her upstairs with Julian and a title on her door: *Rachel Blackstone, Editor & Senior Writer*. With it came a view of the Sangre de Cristos. She no longer dealt with office gossip in the bullpen.

Stella Dallas, the administrative assistant, sat typing on her keyboard. Yes, her mother was a Barbara Stanwyck fan and she wore the name proudly; proclaiming she had viewed all of Stanwyck's movies and The Big Valley TV series. She and Julian were the original staff. Rachel came along a short time later and began working as the primary reporter while Julian and Stella ran the show.

Stella was the only snappy dresser in the office, her vintage Chanel suits were one of the things Rachel liked about their quirky office. The office fashion plate, every hair in place and every bit the stylish 60-something. The rest of the staff chose jeans and tees. Rachel dressed hers up with a jacket. One black outfit hung in her closet reserved for art gallery openings and other upscale events. Chloe had helped her choose it, Rachel being the opposite of a trendsetter.

Ever efficient and relentlessly courteous, Stella was the resident non-swearing staff member. The only time Rachel heard her swear was during their escape from the Lemurian Dracs after Stella's kidnapping.

"Good morning," Stella said with a big smile. "Jules wants to see you, something about the prison story."

"Thanks Stella. On my way."

When she reached the second floor she made a hard left and walked along the balcony. Jules left it open so he could keep an eye on the bullpen. She passed the restrooms on the way to Jules' corner office. If one continued on, there was another staircase to the roof where they had outdoor meetings. Jules was threatening to put exercise equipment up there too, but the response had been lukewarm so that remained to be seen.

Jules' door was open so she knocked on the door jamb.

"Hey boss?" He hated it when she called him that so she did it on occasion to annoy.

"Hey subordinate," Jules answered.

"Ouch," Rachel replied. "I hear you wish to see me?"

"Yeah, come in. Have a seat if you can find one."

Rachel looked around. Any and every flat surface had something stacked on it: old copies of *High Desert Country*, ancient paper manuscripts, paid bills. She had no idea what else might lurk there. She scooped up the shortest stack in a visitor's chair and sat down crossing her legs and swinging one foot slowly while Jules smoothed his grey beard. Jules looked around for a note and found it under several files lying on his desk. Rachel opened her notebook and waited for the pertinent details.

"Okay." Jules cleared his throat. "Word got out that we were working on a story on Old Main. Got a call this morning from a former guard who would like to share what he remembers. He may have a bone to pick, but it might be one that needs picking. His name is Oswaldo Delgado. The man was about 20 when the riot occurred. The reports I've read indicate that the hiring of guards was quite lax so we need to know what the process was when he was hired."

"That confirms what Ernesto Pacheco told me during his interview," Rachel said.

Jules gave her the address and phone number written in his nearly indecipherable handwriting.

"Got it," she said. "Anything else?"

"Be easy with him," Jules said. "He was practically in tears on the phone. It's likely he has PTSD and regrets. We want the story, but not at the risk of him having a psychotic break."

"I will," Rachel said.

"I know. Don't even know why I said that."

"You know what PTSD is like," Rachel said. Jules had been in active fighting in the military. He was being careful of brethren in arms.

"Yeah," he whispered.

"I'll give him a call."

With that, she left his office and walked down the catwalk to hers. Her office was a little bit of heaven after working in the bullpen for years. No more overhearing the constant phone calls and the tapping of computer keyboards. And then, there were the various smelly snacks. When Shorty opened the sardines, Rachel had to flee outdoors.

Her hand-crafted desk came with the office and had the Zia sun emblem engraved on the front. The sun rays represent the four directions or seasons. Four is a sacred number to the Zia Nation symbolizing the Circle of Life. Many had misappropriated the symbol for T-shirts and mugs by filling in the circle. The circle must be open to be properly put on view. Julian had asked their permission to make use of the desk and had donated to the Zia student scholarship program.

Rachel sat down and took a moment to admire the Sangres from her window. Winter had its own kind of magic and snow covered mountains definitely fit the description.

Because of her propensity to become involved in metaphysical mysteries, her friend Mari-Lynn insisted she grid her office and house with black tourmaline and selenite to protect from spirits and hauntings. She also equipped her car with a selection of protective crystals.

Rachel pulled out her research file on Old Main. One source said in 1956 the penitentiary was state of the art containing better recreational and rehab facilities than most high schools in New Mexico, even going so far as to add it had no peer with any institution in the U.S. But 25 years later, one of the worst prison riots in the country's history erupted.

What had gone wrong? Maybe Mr. Delgado could enlighten her. Rachel picked up her phone and called his number. He was anxious to speak with her, "before he lost his nerve." She agreed to meet him in an hour. She had a feeling this would be a tough but memorable interview.

CHAPTER 5

O swaldo Delgado didn't share the lifestyle depicted in the tourism brochures. He lived in an older area southwest of downtown. There was a dilapidated truck, formerly orange, parked in front of an equally dilapidated adobe house. Stucco on the exterior walls had fallen off in small chunks. Cracks connected the holes like a puzzle. The lintel above the front door hadn't been painted in decades but a few Taos blue flecks remained. It appeared the other houses populating this neighborhood were in uniformly bad shape.

The condition of the house was good compared to the health of Mr. Delgado. Rachel had about given up knocking on the door when he answered. He used a walker and pulled an oxygen tank.

"Mr. Delgado, I'm Rachel Blackstone."

"Come in." He reached out a frail hand to her. One of the few chivalrous gestures he could offer. He hobbled to an ancient recliner with time-worn cracks in the leather. Tables graced both sides, one with a built-in lamp. There was an assortment of prescription meds and a pitcher of water with some snacks. She assumed he didn't want to make frequent kitchen runs. The remaining table had a small stack of books and well-read catalogs.

He offered her a place on an old leather sofa. Likely it was a match to the chair but it was covered with rumpled blankets and a pillow, hard to tell. She figured he must sleep there too. Rachel felt badly having to sit on his bed and tried to perch on the edge. A glance around the living room revealed peeling paint on the walls and a dirty rug over the Saltillo floor to catch him if he fell. It had once been a lovely house.

"Thank you for talking with me." She pulled her notebook out and set the recorder on the coffee table. "I'm going to start the recorder now. Are you ready?"

"Yes," he acknowledged. "I'm ready. Call me Ozzy."

"Okay Ozzy. Thank you. I understand you contacted our office with an interest in being interviewed regarding the Old Main riot story we're doing?"

"Yeah. I'm only 63, but I feel my time is limited and I want to get what happened off my chest."

Rachel was stunned he was sixty-three. Had he told her he was 83, she would have believed him. Life had been unkind to this man.

"Tell me about your job at the prison," Rachel prompted.

"I were a guard," he scoffed. "If you could call it that."

"What do you mean?"

"I mean I were 20 years old and never been a law enforcement officer of any kind. I read an ad for the job and answered it. Hell, they barely interviewed me. But they gave me a uniform and a gun so I was a *corrections officer*. No training. Nothing. High school dropout. What did I know about guarding prisoners?"

"Why did you take the job?"

"It paid $9,000 a year. Not much, but better than the nothin' I was makin'."

"Were you on duty the night of the riot?" Rachel asked.

"Hell yeah. 'Scuse me miss."

"It's okay," Rachel assured him "I'm not offended by profanity."

"What happened that night?" She tried again. It was obvious he was getting to something.

"It were cold. I weren't supposed to work that night, but someone called in sick. Probably didn't want to get out in the freezing weather."

"Did the cold have anything to do with the riot?" Rachel asked.

"Naw. I don't think so," Ozzy said. "The situation were the most dangerous criminals in the prison had been moved to the dormitory while their cellblock were worked on. You have to understand. They put hardened criminals from Cellblock 5 in the same dorm as forgers, thieves and addicts. Normally, they was allowed one hour a day out of their cells. You see? That's why it happened. They was out of their cells and into the general population in a dormitory with open sleeping. That dorm was supposed to hold 50 to 80 prisoners. That night there was more than 200 inmates there."

Rachel remembered from her research that originally the design of the dorm included single beds, but as the population increased bunk beds were added and later inmates were sleeping on the floor.

Ozzy started coughing, a deep cough the kind that comes with COPD. He clapped on his chest with a cupped hand, and tried to reach around and do the same to his back. Rachel sat by feeling helpless.

"Would you like me to pour some water?" Rachel asked.

"No," Ozzy said. "It's passing.

"I don't know who made the hooch," Ozzy continued. "I heard it were made with raisins and yeast. Got it from the kitchen. They brewed it in a garbage bag and hid it in a shower.

"It was hell in that room," Ozzy continued. "Noise all the time. Radios blaring. All on different stations. The emergency lights went out and left them in total darkness. I heard screams. Sometimes those sleeping on the floor would get kicked, accidentally or uh purpose. Fights would break out. Sex would happen and I don't think it were wanted.

Those maximum types were animals. No, monsters. We was too afraid to go in there. Sometimes we pretended to do the headcount rather than take the risk."

"So the dormitory was overcrowded," Rachel said. "How did the riot begin?" She already knew, but wanted it in his words.

"Them dormers got smashed," Ozzy said. "When the guards went 'round at 2 a.m. the inmates pretended to sleep, then rushed them, 200 men against two guys. Who you think won that?

"You have to understand, it weren't just prisoners, some of the guards would beat inmates in their cells at night, kick'em down stairs. The inmates returned the favor. They put a belt 'round the neck of a guard after overpowering him. They kicked and shoved him to the control center.

"Someone found a fire extinguisher and bashed in the control center windows. I were told it took less than five minutes to get in. In 'bout 20 minutes the inmates had total control over the prison."

"Where were you during the takeover," Rachel asked.

"I were ... hiding." His voice choked. "Couldn't move. Didn't believe what I were seeing." He was breathing hard as his chest rose and fell as if he'd been running.

"Where were you hiding?" she asked.

"I was assigned to Cellblock 5 to guard the construction materials. I seen the mob coming, dragging and kicking one of the guards. He weren't recognizable for so much blood, swelling. I done went to the stairwell to hide while they stole blow torches. When they crossed the hall, I sneaked out and seen them cutting the door open to Cellblock Four. They started hauling prisoners out of cells after cutting through the bars. When I seen what they was doing to the prisoners with the torches – it weren't purdy – I ran down the steps and hid in the basement."

Ozzy began coughing again, trying to catch his breath. It had all come out too fast for his lungs to catch up. Tears rolled from his eyes. Rachel didn't know if it was grief or part of the COPD symptoms.

"Ozzy, do you want to continue?" she said gently.

"Yeah, yeah. I need to get through this."

"What happened next?"

"There were *pandillas*, uh, gangs of them. They broke off chair legs, pipes, anythin' for a weapon. Some wore gas masks or bandanas. Don't know where they found the gas masks. Don't know if it were to hide their face or because of the smoke. They set fire to anything that would burn. They busted up bathrooms and radiators. Soon the hallway was flowing water. It were mixed with blood, sewage, papers, mattress stuffing.

"That's all I seen happen, but when it was safe to come out, hours and hours later. I were told it were late the next day. I seen what were left."

"What was left?" Rachel asked.

"Bodies. Blood everywhere. The biggest mess I ever seen." He stopped again to regain his composure. "They won't let anyone into Cellblock 4 anymore, but I saw it. I saw it before it were cleaned up. That's where the snitches and rapists was kept. They made them wear different clothes, a jacket, so everyone knew who they was. Even if they didn't inform, they could be made to wear the jacket. It were a game with some guards, 'snitch-jacket game,' they called it. Marked a prisoner for beatings or worse."

"What did you see in Cellblock Four?" Rachel asked. "If you are up to telling me. We can stop the interview at any time."

Ozzy adjusted his oxygen and placed a pillow against his back. He coughed again, but it was less intense.

"There were so much blood, it were hard to know what I were lookin' at. But I saw the marks on the floor where they hacked off one guy's head and the burns on the floor where they set fire to another.

Can't take pictures of it, but they is online. The monsters raped a bunch of them." Ozzy's breathing became labored.

"Haven't held a decent job my whole life 'cause I have PTSD from that night. Any little thing can kick it off and I have to come home: seeing blood, loud noises, fires, crowds. Employers don't cotton to that. Smoked too much. Drank too much. Now old before my time."

"Ozzy," Rachel said reaching for her recorder. "I'm going to stop the interview now. I can get this from other sources and you won't have to relive it."

"Okay," he said obviously tiring. "But there is one thing. The thing I have to get off my chest."

"Go ahead." Rachel left the recorder running.

"The thing is," Ozzy said. "I were a ... coward." The tears came again. He wiped at them with his hands. "I didn't lift a finger to help nobody. I just watched the whole horrible thing like it were a movie. I couldn't move. Barely breathed. I'm ... so ... sorry."

He gasped and Rachel was afraid he would collapse. She hurried over, gently held his shoulders and settled him into his chair.

"Do you need to adjust your oxygen again? Or need medication?"

"Naw. I'm good now. Needed to say it," he replied. "Go on the record, I think you say."

"Ozzy," Rachel squatted at the side of his chair. "Please remember, you were a very young man, a boy really. You shouldn't have been there in the first place. Nothing prepared you for what happened that night. No one could have been prepared."

"Doesn't 'scuse it." He said. "I ... accept my responsibility."

Rachel was certain it was time to close the interview.

"Ozzy, I'm going to go now. Are you sure you want all of this in the story?"

"Yeah, all of it. I reckon I can die with a clear conscious now." His face was tear-streaked but his breathing seemed to have stabilized.

"Okay Ozzy. Thank you for sharing this with me today. I promised to tell it the way you told it to me."

"Thanks miss."

Rachel gathered her recorder and notebook. On her way down the cracked and broken concrete walk she ran into a young woman, dressed in rumpled blue hospital scrubs. Her red hair was pulled back into a tight bun. Rachel guessed her to be about 20 years old. The scrubs didn't indicate a doctor, but more likely a nurse aide or tech. She was wearing a hospital lanyard. Rachel glanced at it long enough to see her name: Melinda Harris.

"Who are you?" she demanded.

"I'm Rachel Blackstone with *High Desert Country* magazine." Taken aback. "And you're ...?"

"What are you doing here?"

"I spoke with Mr. Delgado," Rachel replied. "At his request."

"He can't be tired out. He'll have nightmares." She quickly turned a key in the front door and burst into Ozzy's house. "Grandpa, are you alright?" The door slammed behind her.

Rachel got in her car and headed back to the office. She rarely had family members of interviews get upset. No doubt, caught her on a bad day.

CHAPTER 6

Rachel raced into the High Desert Country office and ran up the stairs, barely nodding at Stella. But Stella knew the look, somewhere between cheerless and tears. Certain stories took a toll on reporters, something she felt the public didn't realize. Only a few journalists had no compassion or integrity. Most cared a great deal about the tragedies and violence they reported including the people who carried the burden of the consequences.

Stella needlessly pushed her blonde hair back in place, sighed and returned to work.

At the end of the catwalk Rachel slowed and entered Julian's office.

"Rachel, I didn't expect you back so soon. Did the interview go badly?"

"Jules it was awful. No, the interview was good, but that poor man. Reading about what happened is different from being there." Tears threatened.

Jules handed her a box of tissues and closed the office door. Opening the small refrigerator next to his desk, he pulled out a bottle of water and opened it.

"Here," he said. "Drink. Doing something ordinary can help you feel more normal."

Rachel took a sip mostly to make Jules happy, but found the act of swallowing the cold mineral water brought her back to the present. When she finished telling him about Ozzy, she said, "Forty-four years have passed. I thought the passage of time healed. Mr. Delgado hasn't healed. It's as if it happened yesterday. His granddaughter says he has nightmares."

Julian tented his fingers and leaned back in his chair. Rachel often thought he would tip it over, but thus far had avoided that outcome.

"When you had your first encounter with the spiritual – is that the word you prefer?"

"Close enough," Rachel said. She didn't feel comfortable with any of the descriptive words: psychic, medium, diviner, soothsayer, mystic, clairvoyant, and telepathist. Spiritual, intuitive and empath weren't awful, but they still felt strange and unnatural when applied to her.

"How do you remember 9/11?"

"Like it was yesterday," she said knowing he was right.

"When what happens is as heinous as this prison riot, a horrific historical event. It barely heals over, the scab ready to come off at any time." Julian said. "The truth is, history gets heavier with time."

* * *

A few minutes later, Rachel sat in her office looking at a message Stella texted her. She hadn't gotten used to the cell phone yet and found this way of communicating to be one more chore to cope with in her everyday busy work life. After a few narrow escapes, Jules had insisted she carry it with her at all times.

Rachel couldn't help it; she was just an analog woman. She still used an old micro-cassette tape recorder. Her lower drawer was filled with dozens of the things. They were labeled, kept until the interview was published and then for several months should a question or issue come up. That was her proof of what someone said. Her notes could back that up; the tape was substantiation.

Computers had made writing her stories easier – but email! The bane of her existence! Now texts. Oh well, only the office had her phone number – and of course, Chloe and Mari-Lynn. And, she didn't have to pay for the damn thing. Jules was footing the bill. Apparently, he had a "family" deal for everyone in the office; unlimited calls and texts.

Stella had typed a woman's name, Iris Phillips, and her number. "Jules wants an interview with this woman. Her son was an inmate during the riot. Suicided recently according to Jules' contacts. Cold call."

That made it touchy. Rachel picked up her desk phone and dialed the 505 number.

"Hello?" said a woman's voice.

"Hello, this is Rachel Blackstone with *High Desert Country* magazine. You're not expecting my call but I'd like to talk with you regarding the prison riot if you would feel comfortable doing so."

"Comfortable?" she said. "Are you kidding? Do you know my son killed himself?"

"Yes ma'am," Rachel said quietly. "I do. I'm very sorry. It's entirely up to you if you want to talk about such a tragedy." She waited wanting to give her time to think without pressure.

"How'd you get my number?"

"I imagine my assignment editor found it through online public records. Would you like to think about it and get back to me?"

"No! Bloodsuckers!" The line went dead.

These kind of calls always left Rachel feeling drained. She never wanted to inflict pain on anyone. It wasn't worth it to cause stress in another's life for a story. The woman was grieving and Rachel didn't blame her. She returned to her research.

About an hour later, Stella buzzed her.

"Mrs. Phillips is on the line for you," she said. "She's contrite. She's checked you out."

"With whom?"

"Someone she knows did an interview with you, Mr. Delgado. And I reassured her you were okay to talk with."

"Thank you Stella. Ring her in."

"Mrs. Phillips? How can I help you?"

"Well, I'm sorry I was rude. I don't trust the media, but a friend of mine, Ozzy Delgado, told me you are okay. I just spoke with him."

"That was very nice of Mr. Delgado," Rachel said. "I did speak with him earlier. How do you know him?"

"Uh, we're in the same support group. Of course, he can't always attend."

"No, I suppose he can't." Rachel waited. She wanted this to be Mrs. Phillips idea.

"Look," she said. "My boy Jeffery was in that prison the night of the riot. What he saw cost him dearly. And he finally took his life."

"Are you telling me you'd be willing to talk with me?" Rachel asked kindly.

"I guess I am. People need to know what happened there."

"Okay. Can you meet with me tomorrow?" Rachel asked.

"Yes." Mrs. Phillips gave Rachel her address and agreed to talk the next afternoon.

Rachel buzzed Stella.

"I don't know what you said to her, but thank you."

"I told her we send you to do all the delicate interviews. Mr. Delgado did the rest."

"Thanks Stella. And I'm sorry I ran past without saying hello awhile ago."

"Sweetie," Stella said in her best mom voice, although she wasn't a mother. "I know what you're working on. I was here and I've read the news stories. Not to worry."

Rachel's cell phone chimed. When she picked it up there was a GIF from Stella: a virtual hug.

CHAPTER 7

After work, Rachel turned the key in the Merc and nothing happened.

"Oh crap," she said. "What a day." She pulled the cell from her escape pouch – also called a purse on rare occasions – and called Chloe.

"Don't tell me that claptrap you call a car is going dicey on you," Chloe remarked.

"Please save the editorial for later over margaritas," Rachel replied. "Juan's Auto Casa is on the way to pick it up but they don't have a loaner just now."

"Not to worry. Chloe is here. See you in a few." She hung up.

While Rachel waited for the Auto Casa to send a wrecker, she thought about how she had met Juan Hernandez and his bonus brother Chad from a very different *madre*. During her first venture into the bizarre world of the supernatural she had been driving – hurriedly – to escape the bad guys she was certain were following her. In the process she drove the Grand Marquis through a rather large patch of prickly pear somewhere north of town and crashed into a low spot in the desert.

Turned out it was Juan and Chad who were following her, not the bad guys, and they kindly rescued both her and the car. Juan owned the

Auto Casa. He felt so bad about scaring her; he'd had her Merc towed to his garage where he fixed it free of charge. There she met Lloyd Loretto, an American Indian healer, who blessed her car in a smudging ceremony. That was the moment Rachel pledged to patronize Juan's Auto Casa for all her days.

By the time Chloe arrived, the wrecker had tugged her car onto its flatbed and was on the way to Juan's competent hands.

Chloe pulled into the magazine office parking lot in her little red Lexus. She got out and handed Rachel a fob. Rachel had been a passenger in it but never driven it.

"What the hell is this?" Rachel asked watching it carefully should it expel a toxic gas.

"That my dear friend is a key fob," Chloe said.

"Okay. Where's the key?"

"You don't have a key. You carry this on you and the car will let you in and will start. Go ahead, get in."

Rachel was accustomed to sliding into her car seat but these were bucket seats with rather tall bolsters on each side.

"You know, if a guy wasn't careful getting into this car he could injure the family jewels." She settled into the seat.

"We don't have to worry about that," Chloe said.

"How do I start it?"

"Oh Rachel, you've watched me often enough. Depress the brake and push this button that says 'Start Stop Engine.'"

"And no key?"

"Nope, it's safer than a key."

The engine purred quietly to life.

"What's this?" Rachel pointed to a flat spot on the console.

"That's the touch pad," Chloe side-eyed her waiting for the tech outrage to follow. "It's the same as on your laptop. Oh, I forget, you don't use it and instead hook up a mouse. You likely won't have to use it because all the programming has been done. See this button with the face?"

Rachel eyed it suspiciously. "You mean the person who is spitting?"

"It's not spitting, it's speaking. You push that and wait for the car to ask you what channel you want to listen to."

"Really! A talking car!" Rachel scoffed.

"Right now, I'd settle for a button that smacked the driver," Chloe muttered.

"I heard that." Rachel pondered all the dials and gadgets. "Are you sure I can drive this thing?"

"Yes Rachel." Tired. "Even you can drive it. At the end of the day, it's just a car."

"This is the last of my tutorial," Chloe continued. "If you hear a beep, look at the screen in front of you on the dash; it will tell you what's up. Sometimes it's as simple as alerting you that it's freezing and there might be ice. If the steering wheel vibrates, it means you've crossed a traffic line and you need to move back in your lane. Don't panic, it's there to be helpful."

Rachel rolled her eyes heavenward.

"Now put it in reverse – that's R," Chloe said with a smile. I'll show you how to use the camera.

"I have to take pictures too? Of what?"

"Just put it in R."

"Okay, okay."

"You can see everything behind you." Chloe pointed to the dash screen. "I still turn around and look, but for the most part the camera gives you a wide-angle view that covers the blind spot and avoids collisions. Be sure to check for oncoming vehicles from the other direction."

"Do I have to pass a test to drive this thing? I mean, it's cute but geez."

"Nope," Chloe said. "You have insurance; I have insurance. We're good.

"See if you can get us to The Shed. I alerted Hector to expect us."

"You what?"

"You've heard of reservations?" Chloe raised a perfectly plucked eyebrow.

Rachel slowly backed out of the empty lot and made her way downtown. She parked several blocks away from the restaurant after an exhaustive search for a parallel parking space big enough to avoid hitting another car.

"There was one right down the street," Chloe said. "Now I have to walk in these heels for three blocks."

"I've always told you to wear shoes you can run in," Rachel remarked.

"That's ridiculous."

They exited the car and stood on the sidewalk. Chloe rubbed her ankle as if she had already walked the three blocks.

"Click the button on the fob to lock the car," Chloe said.

Without looking, Rachel pushed on the fob. The trunk lid opened.

"Oops," she said.

"Don't touch the red one."

Too late, the alarm went off. People out walking on a nice evening turned to look. One guy called Rachel a *turista* thinking the car was a rental she didn't know how to drive. Rachel frowned at the fob as if it would give her instructions.

"Give me that," Chloe turned off the alarm. "What am I going to do with you? It's like dragging you kicking and screaming into the tech century. Here, keep this in your purse, or whatever you're calling it this week and keep things simple."

"I should have called the place that rents wrecks," Rachel commented. "Bet I wouldn't have needed the driving lesson."

"Try to have fun with it," Chloe said. "It's a sweet ride."

Chloe's heels clicked in annoyance as she walked Palace Avenue. Rachel trailed a step behind. She knew she'd be buying the margaritas tonight. Maybe next time too. She silently vowed to be really, really careful with the car.

CHAPTER 8

Revenge was necessary. It had been a long time coming. With so much suffering, this was the right thing, despite the high price. Although it was known that whites should not perform the rituals of the American Indians, it would be done. Knowledge of medicine and healing easily paved the path to *adishgash*. Witchcraft in Navajo culture is something best avoided. In the worst case, one must stop it.

One particular witch, the *yee naaldlooshii* or skinwalker is never mentioned by Native people. To speak the word acts as an invitation for one to materialize. In order to become a witch a person is required to practice dark magic and breach tribal taboos such as killing a family member, committing incest or handling a dead body. They are almost always male. Some have a score to settle, others are just wicked.

Skinwalkers are powerful, can keep up with the fastest car, fly, shapeshift and mimic animal and human voices. They can also get inside the human mind and trick them. One must never look into the eyes of a witch.

Removing the fingerprints, palms and skin of the feet had been the most difficult, even more so than the killing. In order to make the powder from the flesh with the identifying marks must be flayed from the body. Once done, the flesh is left to dry. After a ritual, the dehydrated skin is pulverized into a powder known to the Navajo as *anti'l* or corpse powder. It is used to make another person sick or die.

The person placed the flesh inside a dehydrator. When cured, the mixture was often dropped through the smoke hole in a hogan, used in a dart gun or added to pellets in a shotgun. Blown into someone's face, it would be potent black magic capable of killing.

CHAPTER 9

R achel drove to Española about 25 miles north of Santa Fe for her appointment with Mrs. Phillips. Española has the distinction of having one of the highest crime rates in the country, whether looking at small towns or big cities. As the most dangerous city in New Mexico, your chances of property or violent crimes were one in fourteen. This also made it a more affordable housing alternative to Santa Fe. Unfortunately, drug trafficking was so bad the mayor asked for more officers to combat the issue in a January 2023 letter to the governor.

Of course, there are those who don't agree with the designation and have lived safely and happily in Española for decades. Some say that most of the crime is committed by outsiders.

As an aside, sometime during the 1980s the city declared itself the Lowrider Capitol of the World.

Rachel asked Chloe if it was safe to drive her car there. Chloe assured her the catalytic converter was painted green and the car's serial number engraved on it. Stealing catalytic converters continued as popular sport in many areas of New Mexico, the Española Valley was one.

She located the neighborhood where Iris Phillips lived. It was quite downtrodden. Disparity was a country-wide issue, but in New Mexico where the tourist brochures were glossy and expounded on the three peoples living in harmony, reality could be disappointing. In this community, whites could be as poor as Indigenous and Latino. Poverty is an equal opportunity circumstance.

Rachel parked in the street. It was something she always did. She felt it was discourteous to park in someone's driveway. Having mastered the fob, she locked the doors.

Across the street was an aging pickup. A bumper sticker, although partially worn off, had originally read: "If it's Tourist Season Why Can't We Shoot Them?" Not the entire population of New Mexico appreciated tourism, including some benefactors of the state's visitors.

The house, like many in the neighborhood, lacked a new paint job. Flecks of white paint remained. The peeling shiplap exposed rotting wood where the occasional rain had infiltrated the siding. The front door had been blue or green, hard to tell at this stage.

Only the two wires protruding from the door frame attested to the doorbell's former existence. Rachel knocked. Shortly it was answered by a woman who was 80-ish. If poverty was the new smoking, this woman wasn't long for this world. Although she could move freely the lines on her face told the story of a life gone tough. Her white hair was long and held with a single braid. Worst of all, pain oozed from her being. Despite what her life had become she was heavy with jewelry. Her neck, wrist and fingers were wrapped in turquoise and silver. Maybe wearing it made her feel better. She motioned Rachel to an arm chair. The room may have been elegant when new. The area rug was wool and she thought from India. Although worn, a good quality brocade fabric covered the sofa and the chair where she sat. There was nothing, not even in the home accessories that said New Mexico, only the jewelry she wore.

Rachel held her notebook. It was something she did so when an interviewee looked out their peephole they knew she was the reporter they were expecting and not a salesperson going door to door. She set the recorder on a side table next to Mrs. Phillips.

"I'm required to tape this Mrs. Phillips, for accuracy. I hope you don't mind."

"As long as I don't have to listen to it," she said. "Hate the sound of my own voice."

"Almost everyone does, me included." Rachel said and pushed the record button. She had already noted the date, time, name of interview and subject on the tape so it was queued.

"I understand that your son Jeffrey recently passed." She wasn't going to use the words suicide or killed himself. His mother was more than aware. If she chose to use those terms, it was okay.

"Sixty-two years old," she said. "Lots of life left. But he couldn't live with what happened any longer. It's like with so many Viet Nam vets. There may have been more die of suicide after what they saw in Nam than were killed during the actual war. People can only live so long with evil stuff in their heads."

"Did you know it is estimated between 50,000 and 100,000 Viet Nam vets have died at their own hand?" Mrs. Phillips asked. "War dead exceeded 58,000."

"Those are painful numbers," Rachel said. "You know better than I." She paused to give Mrs. Phillips time to make the transition to the interview.

"Do you feel comfortable telling me about his experience at the prison and his life after?"

"Yes, I want people to know what happened from his point of view," Phillips said. "He got picked up for dealing drugs for the third time and that time he was sentenced and sent to Old Main. Of course, we didn't call it that at the time." She sighed and searched the room for what to say. "He was in Cellblock 5 the night of the riot, across from Cellblock 4 where most of the murders took place."

Rachel nodded.

"He told me he was at the back of the block. The cell next to him was empty. He heard the prisoners yelling and coming his way. At first he wasn't afraid because a key would be needed for entry. But they, as we have known for a long time, had keys. They took them from the guards after overpowering them. He slipped under his bunk and pushed himself against the wall. He could see a lot, more than he wanted to.

"Death squads had formed. They came to Cellblock 4 where they systematically tortured, raped and killed 33 people. My son ... " Mrs. Phillips rubbed her temples fighting tears. "My son flattened his body against the wall and watched until he no longer could. He covered his eyes with his hands and wished for two more hands to cover his ears. He said it seemed to go on forever and he wanted to die so he'd never have to see that massacre again."

She stopped. Rachel waited for Mrs. Phillips to pull herself together. This was a story that needed to be told by this particular woman so she could heal. Rachel held back tears with sheer determination. That anyone could be so cruel to another human being was beyond her, but it occurred everyday somewhere in the world.

"When it was over and 33 men and boys were dead, he was terrified to come out. He stayed there for hours waiting for help that didn't come until way too late. He had to close his eyes because when they were open all he could see was bodies and blood. Mattresses were soaked with it. The inmates had torn the place apart. They came after the prisoners in Cellblock 4 because the some guards told them they were snitches, and snitches deserved to die. The violence was so abhorrent he couldn't speak about it. But I read the papers and the subsequent books. I know the vile things done, the marks and burns on the floor. I know what they mean. And my baby witnessed it.

"He told me every night when he closed his eyes, it would play out again. He had severe insomnia from that time on. No drug would allow him to sleep. We tried them all. I was a pharmacist so I knew which ones were most effective, but none would give him rest."

"You were a pharmacist?" Rachel asked. "Did you leave that profession?"

"Yes, my son needed me and I had to leave work once too often. I was let go."

"What kind of work did you do after that?" Rachel asked.

"Cleaned houses, delivered pizzas, poll worker at elections," she said. "I couldn't have a job that required daily attendance. The house deteriorated because I didn't have money to fix anything. Nor did I have money to keep him in therapy. Everything fell apart."

"Was your son affected in other ways?" Rachel prompted. Mrs. Phillips was nearly spent.

"Jeffrey couldn't work. He'd get a menial job, suffer a flashback and come home. The flashbacks were so frightening to the other staff they couldn't continue to employ him. I understood; I've seen them. He would fall to the floor and relive it covering his eyes and crying uncontrollably. Jeffrey said many times it was unbearable. One day I came home find him dead. He'd gotten some heroin and overdosed."

"I'm sorry to ask Mrs. Phillips, but did he leave a note? Is it possible it was an accident?" Rachel asked.

"Yes, he left a note," she said. "It was simple; I remember every word. 'I can't go on. Thank you for all you did for me. I love you.'" She buried her head in her hands heavy with rings.

It was one of those moments Rachel would have preferred to be most anywhere else. Carrying this much pain was too much to expect of anyone. She sat quietly for a few moments. The words "I can't go on" would stay with her forever. How bad does it have to be that you simply cannot go on with living?

"Mrs. Phillips, is there anything I can get you? Anyone I can call for you? I really hate to leave you when you're so sad."

"No, but thank you," she said. "Please add to your story that my boy felt guilty the rest of his life because he wasn't Superman and could do nothing to stop the monsters who did this. He even bought one of those Superman action figures. He said it gave him courage that he would be braver should he ever need to be again. Childish I know, but he often reverted to childlike ways to cope.

"He blamed himself for their deaths!" she grabbed a tissue and mopped her tear-stained face. "I told him over and over he was not responsible, but even with copious amounts of therapy he always blamed himself. It was not my baby's fault!"

Rachel knew it was time to go. She picked up the recorder.

"Thank you Mrs. Phillips. I'm so very sorry for the loss of your son and what you've both been through. I hope you can someday be at peace."

CHAPTER 10

M ari-Lynn Alo was doing her afternoon meditation in her spiritual garden. It had grown from a medicine wheel to something more elaborate yet in keeping with the sanctity of her Hopi heritage. Her last name Alo meant spiritual guide and she had made it her business to help in this way whenever possible. She learned about crystals from her father. He was a Hopi who believed in the benefit of things like *tádídíín* or corn pollen which he used for protection especially when outside his homeland.

She and Celeste, Mari-Lynn's partner, grew their own yellow corn and harvested the pollen from it. The couple had a large garden but grew mostly the Three Sisters: corn, squash and beans. They planted them together in hills because the growing patterns complemented one another as their nutrients fed the soil and the human body. Pole beans and squash were planted at the base of the corn. The corn stalk provided a place for the beans to climb while the squash vines spread across the ground. The nitrogen from beans leached into the soil making them hold fast in the mountain winds. After planting, she and Celeste would create small dams around the hill to hold water, filling the interiors with lava stones that released water slowly as the Ancestral Puebloans had done.

When she harvested the corn pollen, Mari-Lynn would then bless it, package it and sell in her metaphysical store, Chrysalis. She sold them with leather pouches and always carried one with her.

When she and Celeste moved from Pueblo, Colorado to Tesuque they'd paid a pretty penny to have the meditation wheel moved too. It didn't break the bank. Mari-Lynn had been a pot dealer when it was illegal and always managed to be a step or two ahead of the law. She'd been successful in hiding and investing the profits.

Now that pot was legal in New Mexico, she had opened the two stores in Santa Fe including Celeste's marijuana dispensary New Harvest. They grew the cannabis on their property in a large greenhouse and employed local workers to care for it. Thus far, business was smokin'.

The medicine wheel was made with granite blocks and sandstone pathways leading to the center of the wheel. The four quadrants around the center represented the four cardinal directional colors each filled with stones of varying color. Outside of the circle, desert flora had been planted to provide privacy from any curious eyes the nearby forest might have. On this late November day, the chamisa held onto its spent blooms. They had been frosted with snow several times during the autumn.

Mari-Lynn sat on her meditation cushion in her usual sinuous garb. Today, layers of light airy chiffon in lavender ebbed and flowed in the breeze. Although difficult to imagine its construction it wasn't ruffles – much more subtle.

She pushed back long silver hair and closed her eyes. At first she used alternate nostril breathing to settle into a meditative state. Once there, she waited for the pleasant thoughts that came to her most days.

Mari-Lynn felt the change coming before the vision. Dread enveloped her like a lowering cloud. There was movement, but she couldn't determine what it was. Pieces of something seemed to float through the air, streaks of red. The bump against her back was alarming. She turned, but saw nothing. With closed eyes she again tried to return to the tranquil place.

The next bump was more of a blow. It rocked her hard. The vague kinetic images were larger. Fear gripped her. Mari-Lynn took evasive action and began to levitate in order to see more clearly what was happening around her. As she lifted, she recognized their house with its rounded brown corners and the screened porch on the back. It served as her meditation room on rare rainy days. The ubiquitous hot tub was covered in their backyard. The wind chimes swayed in harmony as the mountain breeze picked up. It was her house.

Cautiously she looked downward and could not believe what she saw. In her medicine circle two wolves fought: one pristine white and the other black as a Santa Fe night. The most alarming feature? The red eyes of the dark one. It appeared to be a struggle that went beyond a pack's fight for rights to breed. The snarling animals were intent on killing one another. Each wolf carried bleeding wounds. The floating objects she had witnessed were fur tufts as each wolf ripped at the other.

Mari-Lynn didn't know what to do. Was this occurring now or a vision of the future or even the past?

There was something else: an onlooker, a woman observed the ongoing battle. Mari-Lynn floated in the woman's direction and recognized Rachel. She stood somewhere between indecision and defeat. The terror on her face said it all. She feared for the white wolf. Behind her, Chloe and a man she didn't know crouched on the ground, closer to Rachel, another man watched, wanting to help and not knowing how.

Mari-Lynn knew it was Kiyiya, Rachel's spiritual guardian. Although this white wolf was a master of disguise and ingenuity, it looked to Mari-Lynn like he might not win this fight.

* * *

Kiyiya had been the only white wolf in his pack. His parents were the alpha couple but because of his color he was eyed suspiciously by the others. When he observed his refection in a stream, he asked his mother why he was the color of snow. She told him he would play an important role in the spiritual world and would someday know what that entailed. But for now, he should enjoy being a wolf. And for several years that is what he did.

One day, as he hunted he felt a quick but sharp pain in his chest and began falling. The plunge into clouds and darkness was more frightening than the subsiding pain. The farther he fell, the slower his descent. When he landed lightly on all four feet, he confronted a ghostly spirit who bullied a lone woman on a deserted highway. She was frightened.

Kiyiya knew instinctively she was to be protected. This was his purpose as told him by his mother. Once he growled the spirit recognized him as a superior and disappeared. He turned to the woman. She feared him, but he made no move to be aggressive. Her face expressed confusion, but she was grateful. At that moment he understood his mother's words. This was his spiritual job, to protect her. Kiyiya would learn he had special powers to change shape, glow and become invisible when necessary. His howls would alert her to danger. And he would give his second life to protect her.

* * *

As Mari-Lynn continued to watch, she felt something exceedingly wicked about the black wolf. It seemed to be super powered. Its muscles were massive. At times, it would stand on two feet like a human, roaring. Red drops fell from his canines, the blood of the white wolf.

She slowly came back to rest in her medicine wheel and opened her eyes. No wolves fought in her midst. Mari-Lynn was alone. It had been a vision, an unusually vivid one.

She had to call Rachel. Evil had returned.

CHAPTER 11

Rachel's landline was ringing as she unlocked the kitchen door from the garage. The interview with Mrs. Phillips had been disturbing but instead of taking a few minutes to recover, the damn phone was ringing. She saw it was Mari-Lynn. Mari-Lynn didn't call to shoot the bull. And Rachel wasn't a bull-shooter either. Reluctantly, she picked up.

"Rachel, I had a vision a few minutes ago. I don't understand it all, but I feel you need to be aware."

"What was the vision?"

"Kiyiya may be in danger."

"Kiyiya. Really? But he protects me." Rachel found this news perplexing.

"The vision showed him fighting with another wolf. A black wolf," Mari-Lynn explained. "The reason I think it's Kiyiya is because you and Chloe were in the vision too. There was blood and fur in the air. Kiyiya was tiring. The black wolf is powerful. If Kiyiya can't fight it off, I fear for you too."

Rachel didn't want to dismiss Mari-Lynn's vision out of hand. She had been right before.

"Was there anything else?" Rachel asked.

"No sweetheart, not this time, but I thought you should know. There is evil afoot again and this time it may have four feet."

"Thank you," Rachel said, but Mari-Lynn was already gone.

The second she replaced the receiver, the phone rang again.

"Good grief," she muttered. "Can't a girl get a little respite?"

"Hello?"

"Rachel, it's Stella. We got a strange email for you. It came through Proton Mail so there is no way to trace the IP number. And it came to the main email address for the magazine. Jules thinks that means the person didn't have your private email.

"Do you have your email set up on your cell?" Stella asked.

"Uh, I think you set it up for me," Rachel starred at the icons on her home page. She pressed the one that said M, hoping that meant mail.

"Yes, I think this is it." Rachel puzzled over the image that appeared. There were two solid vertical lines. Each had two circles: one open at the end and the other intersected the line about halfway, as though the line was going through the sphere.

Typed below strange artwork was a short message: "Paths can be dangerous."

"Do you know what it means?" Rachel asked.

"Jules thinks it might be a Native American petroglyph."

"Thanks Stella. I guess I've got some research to do."

Before doing a search for Native American petroglyphs, Rachel dialed the number for Dave Chee, a ranger at Bandelier National Monument. She met him while investigating the Fourth World of the Hopi when the Dog Star was threatening all of Earth. He'd told her that his mother could do some of the things Rachel could. It made her uncomfortable at the time, but both of them could be helpful in identifying the symbol.

"Hello?" Dave answered.

"Hi Dave, it's Rachel Blackstone. We met a couple of months ago at Bandelier."

"Oh yes, I remember," he said.

"I'm working on another story for the magazine," she said. "I've received an email from an unknown source. It looks like Native American rock art. I wonder if I might send it to you and see if you can tell me what it means. I don't know what nation."

"Of course. You can send it to my cell via email if you want."

"Uh, can you tell me how to forward it to you?"

There was a short silence.

"It's a new phone," Rachel said not wanting him to think she was a total computer illiterate. "Don't know if you remember, but I'm not the cell type, yet my boss is insisting I carry one for work. He thinks I get myself into trouble too often."

She could hear the muffled chuckle, but didn't know if he was amused at her for her lack of IT skills or that Jules worried about her.

"Open the email and look for three dots.

"Which three dots? There is a set up top and in the middle."

"The middle," Dave said.

"Now choose forward. When I get it, I'll answer you by text."

"You'll need my number," Rachel said.

"No problem, it's already on my phone."

"Uh, oh yeah," she mumbled, embarrassed. She'd really like to make a good impression.

"Thanks Dave," she said. "I appreciate it."

Rachel sat down at her desk. Chile Pod was on her lap before she could settle into the chair.

"Hey girl, where did you come from?"

She gently scratched Chile Pod's head. The tortie looked up with wide green eyes as if to question what's up.

"Yes," Rachel confirmed. "I'm afraid we are once again on a new adventure."

Chile Pod blinked telling her she understood.

Rachel hoped it wasn't an adventure to doom, but didn't share it with her diminutive companion. Only problem with that was the cat had great instincts. She knew her human was worried.

Her phone chimed again. She looked at the email icon. Nothing there. Checked the messages and saw a new one. Clicked to find a text from Dave.

"Don't recognize. Seeing Mom tonight. I'll ask her." He ended it with an emoji of a little man waving. Rachel wasn't sure how she felt about emojis. Guess she'd have to learn that language too.

Chapter 12

The next morning Rachel arose to her cell chiming. Unaccustomed to it she had to figure out why it beeped. It was a text message from Dave Chee.

"Spoke w/Mom. Wants to see u. Can u meet at Bandelier?" Another waving man.

"Okay," she replied. She hesitated to use an emoji. Crap, who was she kidding? She'd pick the wrong one and insult someone. Chloe had teased her about never using eggplants or peaches, but Rachel, in an attempt to seem more tech savvy didn't ask why.

"Today?" Dave queried.

"Yes. When?"

"One-ish?"

"That's affirmative," she replied.

Rachel had time to finish the transcription on the interview with Mrs. Phillips. She would proof it later. By noon, she was on her way out of Santa Fe. She quite liked Chloe's car. She had to admit that satellite radio was rad but a talking car appeared a bit suspect. The vehicle had get-up-and-go her Merc didn't possess and the comfort level surpassed hers. Maybe she'd write enough stories to save up for one of her own. Maybe. Nope, she was certain she could get a few thousand more miles from the Mercury.

Chloe would probably offer to buy her one, but she'd already turned down her offer to install a safe room and other alarm features in her house. Chloe thought she needed them, but Rachel was convinced the spirits who showed up at her house could move right through reinforced steel walls and sliding bunker doors.

A perfect autumn day in New Mexico, she happily kept driving. The mountains were snow covered, pierced by green pines. The sunlight was bright under a cloudless sky. Rachel felt the warmth on her face, grateful for its daily appearance and the moon roof. Walt Whitman had said, "Keep your face always toward the sunshine – and shadows will fall behind you." Probably, she thought, he wasn't speaking of the type of shadows she encountered.

She still marveled at how the light played on the piñon that dotted the desert backdrop. The mix of green, brown and pink colors of the buttes and rock towers in the ancient land were gorgeous, worn by wind and water into unique shapes. Each layer of rock represented another era of challenges that humans and animals alike had braved along with the rewards of good harvests and joyful benchmarks.

It was no wonder artists came from around the world to paint and photograph New Mexico's high desert. Writers flocked to northern part of the state too. The legends and history made for good storytelling. She often used the state's history in her stories for the magazine. Lilian Whiting, a journalist and author, first referred to the American Southwest as the Land of Enchantment in her 1906 travel guide. Oddly, New Mexico was originally called the "Sunshine State," but after the state adopted its new slogan, Florida picked it up even though it receives several times as much rain. Somehow Land of Enchantment stuck to New Mexico.

No wonder, its topography alone was amazing. The state boasted glistening White Sands, majestic mountains, astonishing caves, hot springs and canyons carved from powerful water. And then there's the food, dishes swimming in green or red chile, margaritas to chill over and *tres leches* cake or flan for a delectable finish.

By this time, Rachel was approaching Española. She took the exit to Los Alamos, driving west and then south to Bandelier. Some of the highway was exhilarating where the edge of the pavement met the sky. The closer she came to Bandelier the road became curvy and descended into Frijoles Canyon where the Ancestral Puebloans had built their city, tended crops and raised families. Gratefully, in 1916 it had all been preserved in 33,000 acres of rugged beauty by President Woodrow Wilson.

Dave was waiting for her in the car park. In summer, parking fills quickly but this time of year there were spaces available.

Rachel shook hands with Dave remarking, "I thought your mother lived on the Navajo Reservation. Is she visiting you?"

"I moved her to White Rock," Dave said. "She wasn't crazy about it at first. I had to promise to bury her on the rez. Navajo believe that where you are born is where you should be buried. She has joined a group of Native women here and makes regular trips to the rez to visit family and friends. Translation: I make regular trips there to take her. But I don't mind."

"Do you live nearby?"

"Yes, I live in Los Alamos," he said.

"Come," Dave opened his SUV door for her. "It's not far."

When working on a story, Rachel always let the office know where she was going. It was a safety thing and although she had no reason to mistrust most of the people she interviewed, Jules insisted it was prudent. She quickly texted – at least for her – to let Stella know she would be in White Rock and with whom. Her thumbs wouldn't cooperate. She could only hope that Stella too had some interpretive powers and could understand the gist of her message.

Dave drove back the way she had just come.

"Welcome to the home of the Big Enchilada," Dave said.

"Are we talking food or something else?" Rachel asked.

"People like to climb a rock face called the Big Enchilada," Dave said. "Most climbers rate it a five out of ten, so not very exciting from their point of view."

White Rock had a rural feel. It was a town of about six thousand. Rachel noted several restaurants and thought most people would do their shopping in Los Alamos.

Mrs. Chee lived in a small frame house, painted brown with white trim. The paint looked new. Rachel wondered if Dave had a hand in that. The front door was a darker brown and flanked by flower pots bursting with purple and orange pansies.

"Let's go around back," Dave said. "She's nearly always in her garden."

Dave followed the path and opened the gate for her. Rachel took one look at the world of purple plants in lovingly tended flower beds. In the gardens she saw purple sage, lavender and echinacea mixed with white chamomile, herbs and orange mums.

"Wow!" Rachel exclaimed.

"I know. I call it the 'Purple Haze' garden. Mom likes to grow medicinal plants as well as food," Dave explained. "Almost all of these have healing properties. And she's wild about purple."

"That we have in common," Rachel said.

In the center of the yard were the leavings of a bountiful garden. Today, only a few pumpkins and dried corn stalks remained.

His mother sat in a white swing seat near the garden. She rose as Rachel and Dave entered. She was a lovely woman with sun-kissed skin and dark hair pulled back in a traditional bun and tied in place with buckskin. She wore a pale blue dress with a striking turquoise orange blossom necklace.

"Rachel, this is *shimá,* my mother, Doba Chee," Dave said in Diné. "Mother, this is Rachel Blackstone, the reporter I told you about."

"*Yá'át'ééh.*" She pointed to her heart and then waved her hand away from her chest. "It is a pleasure to meet you. Please be comfortable."

"*Yá'át'ééh* is hello in Diné," Dave explained. "It translates to 'it is good.' The movement of the hand is the greeting in sign language."

After the introductions, they all sat in the yard enjoying the warm fall day. On a table between the swing and the two periwinkle chairs that Rachel and Dave sat in, was a tray filled with a clay tea pot and cups. Blue cookies placed esthetically on a platter were topped with colorful sprinkles. Everything was lovingly laid out on a woven Navajo place mat. Doba poured tea for everyone and passed around the cookies.

Rachel noticed the tea was herbal and delicious. It tasted of pine with a few drops of honey. She once drank sweet grass tea and it reminded her of that.

"It is cota tea," Dave said by way of explanation. "It is a wild grown medicinal plant. It's reputed to boost mood and aid digestion. And the pot is Navajo made."

"It's lovely," Rachel said of the brown tea pot with the large purple flower painted on the side.

The cookies were delicious. The texture was much like cornbread in that one crunched the corn meal bits, but in and around those was a delectable sugar cookie. Rachel liked the yen and yang of textures and thought they could be addicting. She made herself slow down and enjoy each bite rather than scarf it.

"These cookies are wonderful," Rachel said. "I've never had them before."

"She doesn't make them often," Dave said. "They are special occasion cookies."

"I've never asked for a recipe in my life," Rachel said. "Is it something you would care to share?"

"I will gladly send the recipe to you," Doba said.

"My son says that you have the vision," Doba continued without skipping a beat.

"Yes, I guess," Rachel stumbled. "I'm uncomfortable with it. Nor do I know what to call it, but vision is so much better than psychic or fortune teller. I don't really do that anyway."

"I was uncomfortable with it too," Doba said. "But you learn to live with it rather than at odds. How long have you had the sight?"

"I did a stupid thing," Rachel said. "I missed my father and wanted to talk with him so I tried the Hopi ritual to return the dead."

"And did it?" she asked.

"The wrong person came back, a wicked man," Rachel explained. "And suddenly I could see – and talk with – the dead."

"You're the one?" Doba asked.

"I don't know," Rachel said.

"The spirits talk and they have spoken of you, but I didn't know your name."

"The spirits talk?" Rachel asked.

"Oh yes, about people who are important."

"I wouldn't go that far," Rachel said.

"You underestimate your worth," Doba said.

"What did you do about the evil spirit?" Dave asked.

"It took a while but with the help of a Hopi shaman I sent him back. Unfortunately, he killed Joseph, the shaman."

"And you still communicate with him?" Doba asked.

"Uh, yeah," Rachel said. "How did you know?"

"Like I said, the spirits talk. Cherish your contacts in that world.

"Try to look at this gift as a victory," Doba continued. "It is very unusual for a non-native to be entrusted with these abilities. You must continue to use these gifts to help people. The Great Spirit sees something in you. It is an honor."

"I'll do my best," Rachel said feeling confused and unqualified.

"I believe you have a symbol you need translated," Doba said.

Rachel pulled the single white sheet of paper from her purse pocket, unfolded it and handed it to Doba.

Doba dropped the paper as if it had burned her hand. When it fell to the ground, the edges of the paper began to turn black and fall off as ash. They all watched in amazement as the paper continued to smolder toward the center.

"Son," Doba said. "Take a photo before it's gone!"

Dave was startled but pulled his cell from his jacket and quickly took several photos.

Although it seemed safe in this magical yard, Rachel felt frightened. Why had it not burned her hand?

In an instant the paper exploded causing a rain of sparks that transformed into blackened ash floating in the air. One by one they landed on the grass.

"I can tell you this," Doba said. "The figure means prophecy. In some cases it can mean the good that comes from far-reaching wisdom – seeing what is to come. But with the added message and what just happened I would say it is a warning. This could be from a potent source. Only the most powerful witches can do what we witnessed. You must be careful. Your life and people you care about could be in danger."

After the worrisome event, Dave and Rachel left to return to Bandelier. Dave didn't immediately start the SUV once they were inside; instead he turned on the accessory. Rachel looked at him in question.

"Roll down your window," he said as he did the same thing. "I want what I'm about to say to flow out of my vehicle. He pulled a black arrowhead from his visor."

"I have one of those," Rachel said. "The guide at Old Main gave me one. Said it would help keep me safe from skin ... "

"Don't say it," Dave interrupted her. She thought he would touch her lips with his hand but he stopped short. "Never say it to a Navajo or any Native person."

"Okay," Rachel stumbled. "Is that why your mother called it a witch?"

"Yes, we don't use the other term. Our belief in them is ingrained from childhood. I myself have seen several."

"Am I in real trouble then?"

"I'm afraid you could be," he said. Dave reached across her and opened the glove box. He removed a small leather pouch. There were several others among the maps and papers crowded into the space.

"This is corn pollen," he said. "I want you to carry this with you as well as that arrowhead.

"It's the real thing," he continued. Grown on the Navajo Nation, the pollen is harvested from the yellow corn stalk. It is then blessed and dispersed among the members. It's difficult to get if you are … "

"White?" Rachel asked.

"Yes," he said. "Promise me you will carry it on you. We are usually safe inside a house or building, but if you are on the road, they can appear and believe me, they can run as fast as your car. Please be vigilant. They are dangerous. They can kill."

Rachel sat in Dave's car on the warm afternoon and could not shake the chill she felt. What had she gotten into this time?

CHAPTER 13

Ensconced at The Shed's bar, Rachel and Chloe read the latest copy of High Desert Country. The place was full, most of the restaurant tables as well. Thanksgiving was a week away. The city had begun to fill for the holiday.

"It's great Rachel," Chloe gushed. "It lays out the events as they happened. Mr. Delgado's experience comes across quite strong, how frightened he was and unprepared to deal with anything like this. I almost felt like I was there beside him. I teared up when he said he was a coward. Poor man."

"Thanks," Rachel said. She always felt embarrassed when someone praised her, but it was nice that Chloe was such a supporter. "He was a good interview despite his impairments. His memory seemed just fine."

"This is the first part?" Chloe asked.

"Yes, we have three planned," Rachel said. "The next issue will include memories of a young man who witnessed the brutality of Cellblock 4 as told by his mother and finally an expert on prison incarceration. The last will include improvements made at prisons in general to prevent this kind of thing from happening again. Not that I delude myself in thinking it can't happen again. There are still prisons in this country that are considered the worst of the worst, concrete fortresses where humans are locked up 22 to 23 hours a day. Some have no windows; others have a four-inch window."

"But what can we do?" Chloe said. "These prisoners are locked up for a reason. They murdered people, sometimes a lot of people. The prisoners are the worst of the worst too."

"And therein lies the quandary," Rachel said. "I don't think this series will resolve that."

Chloe signaled Hector. He quickly made two fresh drinks and set them down on the bar. He saw the open paper.

"I read that," Hector said. "I've only lived here a few years, didn't even know about the prison riot. Grim stuff, but good article."

"Thank you," Rachel said. "I agree, it is quite grim."

Hector pushed back against the bar and hurried to help another patron.

"You ever notice he's gorgeous?" Chloe asked.

"I noticed he makes good drinks and is always friendly," Rachel said.

"What is *wrong* with you?" Chloe shoved her arm playfully.

"Guess I'm more interested in storytelling now. And you know, I haven't been all that successful in the relationship department."

"How about your ranger friend, Dave is it?" Chloe asked.

"He's a friend who is helping me with this story. His mother interpreted the petroglyph symbol for me."

"If you say so," Chloe gave a self-satisfied look.

"What does the symbol mean, if you can tell me that much?" Chloe asked.

"I think I can tell you this much," Rachel said. "Mrs. Chee said it meant prophecy. She also said that it could come from a powerful source and I should be careful."

"Rachel!" Chloe exclaimed. "Shouldn't you have told me this from the get-go? How does she know it's a powerful source?"

"Now don't get upset," Rachel said. "But the piece of paper with the symbol kind of exploded."

"Exploded!" Chloe said alarmed. "Who did that?"

"No one," Rachel said. "When Mrs. Chee took the sheet of paper from me, she immediately dropped it on the ground smoldering, and it burst into flames."

"Are you saying it was spontaneous combustion?"

"I guess that's the answer, but we don't know what made it burn and why I didn't detect it," Rachel said. "But Mrs. Chee said it was likely a witch."

"And what kind of witch could it be? Are we talking skinwalker?"

"It sounds like it," Rachel replied. "I'll admit I'm concerned. I have no idea how vast or strong my vision is, but I'm betting not strong enough."

"Rachel, you have to stop doubting your, uh, skill set," Chloe said.

Rachel could imagine the wheels turning in Chloe's head. She knew what was coming next.

"You and the Pod are moving in with me until this is over," Chloe said. "This is a new trick in the paranormal realm we haven't experienced before. Geez Rachel. What's going on?"

"I expect we're going to find out," Rachel said.

When they had finished their drinks, they left by way of the courtyard. Neither noticed the person sitting on a bench with more than a passing interest.

Chapter 14

Rachel packed her bag with a couple of outfit changes, the few cosmetics she used and her laptop. She hesitated as she looked at the jar of retinol cream she had recently purchased. It was her first indulgence in anti-aging. She was a bit embarrassed to own it. She was a pro-age type having allowed her silver strands to highlight her hair, but was it different than applying sunscreen to protect her skin from the New Mexico sunlight? She was going with no, and accepted there was a bit of vanity in her.

Next she picked up Chile Pod's bag. The tortoiseshell had been watching her person's activity from the comfort of the bed. Now, she was interested. This was *her* bag. It meant they were going somewhere.

"Yes Miss Pod," Rachel said. "We're going to visit Auntie Chloe. Where, I'm sure she has new ways of spoiling you." Chile Pod recognized Chloe's name and squeaked in anticipation.

Rachel ran to the kitchen to grab Chile Pod's favorite food and treats. She wouldn't need any bowls because Chloe had personalized bowls for the tortie and everything her cat could possibly need or want.

She'd received a phone message from Juan's Auto Casa. He said it would take a few days to get parts for her Merc. Mercury had gone out of business and since her Marquis was a 1986, it was getting difficult to make repairs. Most had to come from salvage yards now. Rachel could see into her future and she was going to be buying a new car sooner than later.

Once their bags were in Chloe's car, Rachel came back through the door that had been added to the kitchen from the garage so she could safely come and go without exposure to the elements, both earthly and ethereal.

Chile Pod was waiting in her carrier, determined not to be left behind. She knew Auntie Chloe would have treats for her.

"You little dickens," Rachel said. "When did you learn that trick? I can't get you in the thing when it's time to go to the vet."

Chile Pod's green eyes were questioning at the word "vet." Had she misinterpreted her person's activities?

"Yes, were going to Auntie Chloe," Rachel said to reassure her.

With that, she double checked all the doors and windows were locked, shades drawn and lamp timers working. As was her habit, Rachel always checked to make sure the stove was off, twice in spite of the fact she barely used it. Setting Chile Pod down, she set the alarm and stole out of the kitchen.

Once they arrived at Chloe's new gate, Rachel was relieved when her card once again opened the high-tech security gate. Her first attempt at opening the gate had been a fiasco. Chile Pod had witnessed the whole mess of button pushing and swearing at the voice inside the gate control. It was mortifying.

"At least we can be somewhat certain, Auntie Chloe can't throw anymore tech stuff at us, right?" she asked the tortie. "I mean, what else could there possibly be?" But Rachel thought to herself that was a bit like asking what else could go wrong?

When they reached the garage, Chloe was waiting for them.

"How did you know we were here?" Rachel asked.

"The gate told me – there's a camera you know. Thank you for not swearing at the little man in the box. The last time you did that was embarrassing."

Rachel grimaced. Cameras were everywhere these days. One couldn't throw a hissy without someone seeing.

"Hello Chile Pod," Chloe cooed as she picked up her carrier. Rachel followed with the two bags. Inasmuch as Chile Pod weighed about eight pounds, Chloe was getting off easy. The cat's canned food she was lugging likely exceeded that weight. Rachel wished she'd left more of it behind. One never regrets packing less.

By the time Rachel clambered into the kitchen, Chile Pod was out of the carrier daintily eating something that looked good enough for people.

"It's human grade cat food," Chloe said all smiles. "Miss Pod likes it."

Rachel could only wonder how much it cost and if it was imported from France? The can on the kitchen counter had a picture of the Eiffel Tower on the label with a crowd of cats below it.

"I've got a surprise for you two," Chloe said.

"Oh not again," Rachel said, resigned.

"Come." Chloe beckoned. Rachel followed a few steps behind Chloe down the hall to her room. Chloe being quite successful and a generous person had added a dedicated suite for Rachel and Chile Pod. The room was large enough for a bedroom with an office area. The bathroom integrated a secluded area for the tortie's litter box which worked automatically. Rachel wasn't sure where things went but the litter was always clean and fresh. There was an eating area for the Pod's food and water, and a small refrigerator where Evian water and baby food were kept. If Rachel was a good girl she could drink the water too.

"Voila!" Chloe spread her arms for the big reveal.

Chloe had replaced the old bed with something Rachel had never seen before. It sort of resembled a canopy but there was only a frame. It was sleek and appeared space-age worthy. At the foot of the bed there was something that reminded her of a folded mosquito net. The king-sized bed had two independent mattresses.

"Okay," Rachel said. "What on Earth is it?"

"It's your new bed," Chloe said. "You can raise the head or feet or both. It has vibration, color therapy and sleep sounds.

"Give me your phone," Chloe said with authority.

Rachel cautiously handed it over, thinking *what fresh hell is this?*

"Now, I'm going to download the app for the bed. That way, you can work it from your phone."

"What's an app?" Rachel knew intellectually, but didn't realize there were already several on her cell.

After a few minutes, Chloe was satisfied it had downloaded and opened the app.

"Here's how you adjust the bed: head, foot, pillow and lumbar. There are settings for anti-snore and anti-gravity." She swiped to the next page. "This is the reading light and the vibration control. It will even keep track of the number of hours you sleep and a whole wealth of other things. My favorite is all the noises you make at night. Don't know if you snore? Now you will. I don't by the way."

"And this, *this* is the TV control."

"But where's the TV I've always used?" Rachel asked.

"I gave it away," Chloe said rushing to the foot of the bed. "This is your screen." She pointed to the mosquito net. "One touch here and the screen lowers for watching." Chloe waited until the screen was in place. With a nod of satisfaction she added: "What do you think?"

"Uh," Rachel muttered. "I, uh, don't know what to think. I've never seen anything like it. And I mean never."

"Just try it out tonight," Chloe said. "I have one and I love it. It's like a bedroom within a bedroom with all the bells and whistles. It even has amber lighting at the base of the bed near the floor. When you need to visit the bathroom, the lights will automatically show you the way. They're motion-activated."

"Okay," Rachel said certain her friend had finally gone off the deep end. "It looks like some kind of space craft. But, it's a pretty color." It was a calming blue that went perfectly with the walls painted in a tasteful brown.

"You painted the walls too?" Rachel asked.

"Yes. Well, not me, but I had a painter come in and do it. It's chocolate mushroom. How do you like it?"

"It's lovely," Rachel said with honesty, but thought she didn't want to eat that combination.

"And I didn't forget Miss Pod." Chloe was going in for the kill. "It came with a special cat bed. She placed the soft oval kitty bed on one mattress. With a touch of a button, it becomes a cat yurt, but if she prefers her sleep *au naturel*, the top folds away. See, page four of the app has the button for that."

Rachel was close to speechless.

"Can't wait," Rachel choked it out. But she had grave misgivings about Chloe's new high-tech toy.

Dusk came and went. Rachel found Chile Pod still in her bed atop the mattress of the spacecraft she was supposed to sleep in. Rachel put off going to bed choosing to glare at it instead. She didn't know about this contraption. It reminded her of a Venus flytrap, attractive to humans, but waiting to close around the instant one was inside.

Tired of staring at the new furniture, Rachel showered and got into her nightshirt. With nothing more to do, she slipped under the covers, phone in hand. She looked over at Chile Pod who was quite comfortable.

"You little plutocrat," Rachel said with mock distain. "Chile Pod, you weren't born to the good life, but you sure take to it naturally."

Hearing her name, the tortie opened her green eyes and raised her head. Rachel patted her soft fur and rubbed her chin. She was so glad this little girl had come with her house. They had become fast friends, although she wasn't sure how she would measure up next to Chloe and her bottled water, gourmet foods, self-cleaning litter box and now this. Chile Pod was sleepy and snuggled back into the soft fold of her kitty boudoir.

Rachel took her phone and pushed a button. Her feet rose, so she pressed another and her head elevated. It was a bit cool in the room so she touched the temperature. But instead of heating the mattress it began to cool.

"No, that's not what I wanted."

She tried again, but the page had changed and she hit the vibration instead. Her mattress began to gently buzz. The pulsation felt really good on her lumbar. Maybe she could get used to this.

"What page was that?" she questioned flipping through the app again wanting to change the height of her feet.

"Crap. Does this have an undo button?"

Rachel, in a V-shape, couldn't move with both her head and feet in the air. She saw the anti-gravity button and tried it. The floating sensation was quite pleasant, yet it didn't get her out of the bed.

"Would you care for sleep lighting?" A disembodied voice asked.

"Hey, Pod Girl, did Auntie Chloe say this thing talks?" The cat opened one eye and immediately closed it as if to say, does it matter?

"I didn't get that," the voice said. "Would you repeat?"

"Yes, by all means let's add lighting," Rachel said sarcastically.

Lights embedded in the frame began to glow a soft pink. Rachel looked at her cat who was now all sorts of bizarre colors.

"Would you care for some sleep sounds?" The voice again.

"Oh, for sure!" Rachel snarled.

The sound of rain was so lifelike that Rachel wondered if she would actually get wet. And there she was a captive. She tried the app again, but it didn't look the same and she couldn't find how to lower her feet or her head. It continued to pummel her body with increasing vibration.

"Guess we'll skip the TV tonight," she muttered.

With an effort she managed to lower her feet but that left her crunched into an uncomfortable sitting position. She tried the app again and the TV came to life.

"Okay, so we will have a little TV. Probably all night as how will I ever turn it off?

Rachel lunged forward and wrapped her arms around her knees. With one huge effort she rolled herself out of the bed and onto the floor. In a millisecond the foot lighting came on bombarding her with amber rays.

"Oh, for heaven's sake!" Rachel turned her head toward the wall. "Wait a minute."

She reached up and grabbed her pillow and blanket. Rachel found a spot on the area rug, pulled the blanket over her and waited for the lighting to go off.

"Much better," she mumbled before going to sleep. On the TV a rerun of *Aliens* carried on. She knew that Sigourney Weaver got the bitch at the end. Ripley could do it without her help this one time.

CHAPTER 15

Ozzy Delgado watched the sunset from his backyard. The home healthcare girl left him with water and coffee, long gone cold. He wasn't supposed to have caffeine, but no longer felt it necessary to follow doctor's orders. What was the point? His life was crap. He limped through his day and had to start early for a bathroom break or risk an extra load of clothes for his granddaughter. It was demoralizing. His lungs often couldn't pull in enough air to get across the room. He could only blame himself after smoking for decades.

He wondered if he could get back inside the house. He'd left the slider open so at least he wouldn't have to fumble with that. His granddaughter had been expected an hour ago and hadn't showed. Getting to the house was going to be his problem. Ozzy adjusted his oxygen and pushed himself up out of the chair using his walker. He turned toward the open slider and hesitated. The apprehension that descended on him was overpowering – like black smoke. He coughed thinking about it. As he moved one foot forward using the walker, he saw something peripherally. Ozzy turned his head.

"Who's there!" he demanded. It better not be those damn neighborhood kids in his yard again.

It wasn't the children, but a single person. At least he thought it was a person. It appeared to be wearing a hoodie which made it look tall.

The warm lamp light beckoned from his living room, but he couldn't move. Red glowing eyes held him spellbound. The figure had unusually white skin. The contrast of colors made it all the more frightening. What made it so supernaturally white he couldn't imagine? It's presence in his yard was disturbing.

"Whatta you want?" he asked more kindly this time. Ozzy sensed he was in real danger and didn't want to make things worse.

The figure said nothing and raised a shotgun. Adrenalin flooded Ozzy's body in a millisecond. Before he could throw the walker over and dive to the ground, let alone reach the safety of his house, Ozzy heard the blast of the gun and a second later felt searing pain in his upper arm. Instinctively, he grabbed his shoulder and felt the sticky blood accumulating on his shirt. The shock sent him to his knees. The walker fell onto the ground.

He heard someone shout: "You should have stayed quiet. You're responsible."

When he looked up, the shape was gone. If he wasn't bleeding, it could have been a dream. Ozzy managed to pull himself up using his uninjured arm. He righted the walker and hobbled toward his house. Once inside, he locked the door and fell into his recliner. When he caught his breath, he called police.

"I've been shot," he said to the dispatcher. "Help me."

"There is a patrol car and ambulance on the way," the dispatcher said. "Press a towel or something on the wound to control the bleeding."

Ozzy didn't have a towel or anything else to cover the wound so he just waited.

In about 10 minutes the police arrived.

"Your neighbors reported a shot fired before you called us," the officer responding said. "Why did you wait so long?"

Ozzy pointed to his oxygen tank and walker. His labored breathing said the rest. The officer found a towel and pressed it against his wound. Ozzy winced in pain.

Once the ambulance arrived, an EMT rushed in carrying a large red duffle.

"My name is Lawrence," he said while examining Ozzy's arm. "We're going to have to take you to a hospital. This needs a doctor's attention."

Ozzy protested. "I ain't got money for no doctors. *¡Qué lástima!*"

"Mister," the EMT explained. "You've got birdshot in your arm. It looks like hamburger and you're losing blood."

"Okay," Ozzy sighed heavily. "Call my granddaughter, will you? Her name's Melinda Harris. She's on my cell. Works at a hospital. Should've been home already." Ozzy gasped for air. "Not usually late."

The EMT nodded and swiped his phone.

"Is there a code?" he asked.

"Naw," Ozzy replied. "No code."

Ozzy was feeling lightheaded. He felt the black coming.

When he woke up a bright light shone above. A man working on his shoulder was a doctor according to the ID hanging on a lanyard from his neck. He removed shot from Ozzy's arm while a police officer stood observing.

"Glad you decided to join the party Mr. Delgado," the young doctor said. "I've just about retrieved all the shot from your arm. Most of it was superficial but I had to dig a bit for a couple of pieces. That's your x-ray." He pointed at the X-ray view box. Ozzy could see the spots in his arm indicating the pellets.

"You're lucky. The shooter's aim was bad and its only birdshot, much less damaging than buckshot.

"You hang tight a few minutes," he continued. "We numbed up your arm but do you need a shot for pain?"

"Naw," Ozzy lied. "It don't hurt."

The doctor picked out two more pellets, dropped them into the stainless steel container and said as though he had won a race. "Finished!" He poured the shot into a bag, marked it biohazard. He added the patient's name, location of the wound, dated it and signed his name.

"There are a few pellets left. It would do more damage to remove them. You'll get used to them.

"Okay, the nurse will come in and bandage that for you. You're going to live." He patted Ozzy's uninjured arm.

Outside in the hall the doctor spoke with the officers who had responded to Ozzy's 911 call.

"There's something a bit fishy about this," the doctor said.

"How's that?"

"It's birdshot and something else. There are a couple of white pellets or pieces mixed in with the shot. It might be nothing, but you'll want this evidence for your firearms examiner."

The officer nodded and dropped the bag inside a paper evidence sack. He quickly wrote the information the examiner would need on the outside.

"He staying overnight?" the officer asked.

"I'll recommend it," the doctor said. "But he's not insured so something tells me he won't be our guest for the night. He's already refusing pain meds, likely to save money. He's not old enough for Medicare. I hate this insurance situation. People ages 50 to 65 seem to fall through the cracks."

"That's one problem we can't solve," the officer said. "His granddaughter is waiting for him in the lobby." The officer left through the hospital ER doors.

The doctor went back to the treatment room to offer Mr. Delgado a bed for the night, but already knew what the answer would be.

CHAPTER 16

"Rachel. Rachel. Are you awake?" Chloe tapped on the bedroom door.

"What?" Rachel awoke on the floor.

"Rachel. It's Chloe. I'm sorry to wake you, but it's important."

"Okay, I'm awake." Rachel pushed herself up, the bed lights came on and she went to open the door."

"What is it?"

"There is something strange in my back courtyard," Chloe said. "I think it's for you."

Rachel grabbed her jacket. Chloe stepped into the room.

"Is that comfortable?" she asked seeing the bed. "And the TV is on."

"Oh yeah," Rachel said. "Nice and comfy. I sleep with the TV on a lot.

"What's going on?"

"I can't quite describe it," Chloe said. "It's similar to a dust devil and it keeps swirling."

"That's how my visitations start," Rachel said. "Do you want to be there?"

"Will I be able to see it?"

"I don't know. Be prepared for anything. No lights. Let the brightness from the moon and stars suffice."

The women left the house via Chloe's kitchen door to the courtyard. The herb bed's fragrance filled the air and in the distance a wolf howled. Kiyiya was on duty. That meant this guest was important. Rachel immediately saw what Chloe described and walked reverently toward it. A couple of metres away, she stopped allowing her eyes to adjust to the diffuse illumination. The rattling noises commenced and Rachel knew someone was about to make an appearance.

The column transformed slowly into – not a person – but Skeleton Man.

"What is it?" Chloe asked. "The dust devil stopped and I can't see anything.

"Hello Másaw, Lord of the Dead." Rachel nodded her head slightly, trying to greet him respectfully. "How did you know I was here?"

Even in the poor light Rachel could see his damaged bones. Some had been broken; others had suffered maladies such as arthritis. Although she couldn't see them well in the dark he had many bone spurs. His broken jaw was apparent in his speech. Sometimes it jangled dangerously when he spoke. She remembered he had missing and broken teeth that made his speech halting. Rachel didn't need light to know who was speaking.

"The spirits talk," Másaw said.

Next, Joseph appeared. Joseph helped her several times since her night of bad judgment in Tulsa. He'd played an important role in her developing the vision she was so reluctant to use.

"Good to see you," Rachel said to Joseph.

"And I you," Joseph replied.

"He reigns high in the upper world." Másaw's ribs clattered as he spoke. "Be watchful. The *wùuti*," Másaw said in Hopi.

"Beware the *ööqa*," Joseph added.

"What does that mean?" Rachel asked. But she was talking to the empty night. Másaw and Joseph were gone. They had said what they came to say.

"Good god!" Chloe squeaked behind her. "Who was that? I couldn't see or hear anything but you responding."

"It was Skeleton Man and Joseph," Rachel replied. "What does *wùuti* and *ööqa* mean?"

"That's something we will have to research," Chloe said.

"How do you communicate," Chloe asked. "Does he speak English?"

"I hear English," Rachel explained. "There is some sort of spiritual translation going on, but I don't understand it. In Lemuria, they spoke from their mind and I received something like closed captions. This is similar in that it's not a direct translation, but more of a mystical one. They throw in the occasional Hopi word."

"I don't know how you do this. It was terrifying and I could only imagine what was happening from your side of the exchange."

"It appears I have no choice in the matter."

"But how do we know it was real and not some kind of dream or hallucination?" Chloe asked.

"Turn on your porch light," Rachel said. "Look for corn kernels."

Chloe hunted on her hands and knees, moving her hand back and forth. She shrieked, "Here they are!"

On her stone path were five kernels of yellow corn. Skeleton Man's calling card.

CHAPTER 17

It was late afternoon when Rachel walked through the doors of High Desert Country after doing interviews all day. She had the feeling that something was in the offing.

"Afternoon Stella," she said.

"Good afternoon Rachel and how are we today?" Stella asked

"If we are me and my sidekick Chile Pod, we are great. Me, I'm a little stiff."

"Why?" Stella asked. "I thought Chloe had you doing yoga?"

"Oh, it's nothing. Just slept on the floor last night."

"Whatever for?" Stella asked.

"Seemed like the thing to do."

"Jules wants to see you pronto," Stella said, eyeing her curiously.

"Ugh, did I offend someone?" Rachel asked.

"Not this time dear. I think he has information from an informant to share."

"Thanks Stella."

Jules was on the phone when she arrived at this door. She took a step back but he waved her in. He thanked the caller and hung up.

"Well, this story you're working on about the prison just got a lot more interesting."

"How so?" Rachel asked with trepidation.

"A source at the SFPD called me about 30 minutes ago," Jules said. "They found something interesting in the shot they dug out of Mr. Delgado."

"Wait," Rachel said. "Mr. Delgado was shot? You buried the lede."

"Oops, sorry," Jules said. "Yes, he was shot in the backyard of his home."

"Is he okay?"

"Maybe," Jules pulled at his beard.

"What do you mean maybe?"

"Well, the shot was removed and of course they gave him an antibiotic. He refused to stay the night but is back in the hospital now."

"I'm confused," Rachel said.

"The police lab discovered bone pieces in the shot pellets."

"Bone?"

"Yes, and they have identified it as human bone."

"That makes no sense," Rachel said.

"Well, it kind of does," Jules explained. "There is a Navajo monster of sorts. Other nations believe in it as well."

"Monster? Are we talking skinwalker?"

"Yes, Navajo witches, or skinwalkers, use bone, especially human bone, to infect the victim. It usually kills them."

Rachel recalled her discussion with Ernesto Pacheco back at Old Main. He had talked about shadow people and skinwalkers, but not about human bone projectiles.

"What do I do? Drop the story?" Rachel asked.

"No," Jules said sternly. "We do not bow to intimidation."

"I've got a confession of sorts," Rachel said. "I think I saw one of those shadow people at the prison in Cellblock Four. Mr. Pacheco said he also sees them."

"And just when had you planned to tell me this?"

"I was hoping never, but well now ... "

"Guess better late." Jules gave a particularly hard tug on his beard. "This changes everything. You need to talk with Pacheco again."

Chapter 18

Ernesto Pacheco agreed to meet Rachel at the Mine Shaft Tavern in Madrid the following afternoon. Neither of them wanted to be at Old Main when they had this conversation.

Madrid, pronounced Mad-rid, had once been a coal mining town. When that fell out of favor it became a ghost town. But artists found a terrific home for their craft and turned it into a charming village. It was a favorite of visitors with its unique stores and eateries. The mostly frame houses were painted bright colors, often multiple colors. The whole place screamed Bohemian: the kind of place where a zebra standing on top of a porch was expected and no one blinked an eye at a purple pickup. One might even see people riding into town on horseback. It didn't hurt the town was snuggled inside a lovely curvaceous valley along the Turquoise Trail.

For years, there had been persistent stories the Mine Shaft Tavern was haunted. Doors that moved unbidden, a chandelier that swung for no reason and blue orbs were all stories Rachel had heard. But it seemed to her there were more haunted places in New Mexico than not.

The Mine Shaft Tavern had been used as a set in movies and television for decades. No wonder, it was a rustic restaurant with saloon doors and a long bar. Many a fight scene had been filmed here. It also had a stage for entertainment and a huge fireplace at the opposite end. String lights hung along the ceiling that brightened the eating space day or night. Locals and tourists alike came for its Wagyu beef and buffalo burgers. Both were raised locally.

She stopped for a moment in the entryway to read the sign once more: "WELCOME TO MADRID. MADRID HAS NO TOWN DRUNK, WE ALL TAKE TURNS." Good to know.

When she passed through the saloon doors, Ernesto was already at a table near a window. He waved her over. Rachel ordered the Mad Chile Burger and a tea because she was working and driving. Ernesto went with the Wagyu burger and a porter. For a few minutes they ate in happy silence. Rachel felt he was the type to enjoy his food without conversation and she was good with that. With Chloe, it became a totally different meal experience. Rachel adapted. She liked both styles.

When he finished his burger, Ernesto wiped his mouth with a napkin and took a thoughtful drink of his beer.

"Can't put off this discussion forever," he said. "Tell me what you need to know."

"A man I interviewed for the story on the riot was shot at his home. The birdshot was found to contain human bone," Rachel said. "According to my employer, who has a contact at the police department, the victim described the assailant as having red eyes and white skin and seemed to be covered with something. Not a hoodie, higher and thicker. He didn't see it very well. He was trying to escape. Using a walker made him an easy victim."

"Did he just shoot him or did he say something?" Ernesto asked.

"My editor said the man I interviewed heard the perpetrator say he was responsible and should have stayed quiet."

"The bone in the birdshot definitely indicates that an evil witch is involved," Ernesto said. "Has this man sickened?"

"He's in hospital but I haven't heard his condition," Rachel said. "I'm assuming all the fragments and birdshot were removed. Would they still be able to sicken him?

"Most definitely. If that was indeed human bone, the victim almost always gets sick and dies."

"By evil witch do you mean skinwalker?" Rachel whispered.

"Do you have your arrowhead I gave you?" Ernesto asked.

"Yes. It's in my bag. I also have yellow corn pollen."

"That's very good," Ernesto said. "Has it been blessed?"

Yes, it was grown on the Navajo reservation, harvested there and blessed. I received it from a Navajo man. It's the real thing."

"Okay. I'll tell you about these evil witches. This is something most Navajo or Hopi will not speak about. I am of two worlds: Hopi and Anglo. Because I have lived off the rez, I feel a bit more comfortable speaking of it than I might otherwise.

"In order to become a witch with malevolent intent, one must first kill a close family member. This kind of action breaks the most sacred of tribal taboos of the Indian American society. In Navajo culture this is an obscene offense. To become an evil witch, there is usually a ritual that can involve cannibalism or even incest. The body is then mutilated so that corpse powder and bone beads can be made. The skin of the palms and feet are taken because they symbolize the identity of the person. They are dried and pulverized to make corpse powder. It is the reverse of the pollen you are carrying that is blessed and curative.

"The next step is to kill and skin the animal you want to be," Ernesto continued. "Once the skin is removed, the witch wears it. Most smear ash on their body. That was likely the whiteness the victim saw. And the skin, fur still attached, make the witch taller and larger. The transformation is complete."

"What is the corpse powder used for?" Rachel asked.

"It too can sicken people, even kill," Ernesto continued. "Often the witch would go to a hogan and drop corpse powder down the smoke hole. The hogan is a round structure. A fire burns in the center of the building and the smoke hole acts as a chimney."

"Do I need to be watchful for this shadow person?" Rachel asked.

"Yes," Ernesto said. "Make certain your chimney flue is closed tightly. Always keep the arrowhead and pollen with you. On your person is best. And be aware these witches can shape-shift into an animal or even another person. They can also run faster than a car. If you are in the unfortunate situation of having one follow you, go to the nearest building or your home and quickly get inside. Usually they won't follow you inside, but they can. And check the exterior of your house for damage after an appearance.

"I can't say this strongly enough," he continued. "These are highly dangerous entities. They kill. That's why they exist. Be vigilant."

Rachel promised she would and they parted company with a handshake, Ernesto placing his other hand over hers. She felt Ernesto was a good friend to have.

On the way home she stopped by the office.

"Girl," Stella said. "Just read your second story on the prison riot. Excellent." Stella put down the magazine on her desk.

"Thanks Stella," Rachel said. "I wanted to pick up a copy myself."

"There's a stack on the meeting table," Stella said. "The rest are out being delivered. By this time, they're probably all distributed."

Rachel gazed at the cover. The first story had accompanied a photo of Old Main. This one had a photo of the remains of Cellblock 4 after the bodies were removed, but before the gory mess was cleared. Jules had run it in black and white. Rachel knew why. It made it difficult to see the blood.

CHAPTER 19

That evening a phone call came through the Española 911 emergency.

"Nine-one-one," the dispatcher said. "What is your emergency?"

"Someone's on my roof!" the woman whispered frantically.

"I'm dispatching police now," the dispatcher said. "My name is Patty. I'll stay on the line with you until they arrive. Are you in a safe place where you can lock a door? If not, go to one now."

"I'm in a locked room," the woman answered. "Are you sure the police are on the way?"

"Yes ma'am. Has anything else happened?"

"It sounds like they are messing with the chimney. I think I heard the cap removed. They may have dropped it on the ground. There was a crash outside.

"Now someone is running across the roof!" the woman's voice was rising with her fear.

"Ma'am, stay calm," the dispatcher said.

"Where are the police?" the woman said. "I'm a senior and live by myself."

"They should be there any minute. Just stay inside your house. I'm with you."

There was a loud knock at the door.

"Oh my god," the woman said. "He's knocking on my door."

"I've been told that a cruiser is at your house now," the 911 operator said. Go check at your front door. Do you have a peek hole?"

"Yes."

"Check it first. The officer should be holding up his ID."

She confirmed it was the officer and opened the door.

"Ma'am, I'm Officer Pete Adams," he said. "I understand you've had an intruder on your property. Please stay inside while I check it out."

"Yes, I will."

She stood nervously while the minutes ticked away. When the knock came at the front door again, she rushed to open it. A quick check showed it was the officer.

"Did you find him?" she asked.

"No ma'am, but there was a ladder against the back of your house and I found the chimney cap on the ground. There was definitely someone up there, but no sign of them now. It was probably just a prank, but I'll make several passes by your house tonight.

"We have you listed as Mrs. Iris Phillips." He checked his cell to be sure. "Is that correct?"

"Yes, I'm Iris Phillips."

"Was anything dropped down your chimney?" the officer asked.

"I haven't looked."

"Let's check."

Iris Phillips stepped aside to allow the officer entry. He removed the fireplace screen and starred into the ashes.

"I can't tell," Phillips said. "I burned a fire earlier, but nothing unusual is showing up."

"You're right," Adams said. "I can't distinguish ashes from ashes, but I'll take a sample in case anything comes of this." He took a photo and used an evidence bag to collect ashes from the floor of the fireplace.

"You let us know if you have any more problems. I put that ladder out of sight behind your shed after I replaced the chimney cap. You have a good night." He tipped his hat and left.

"Thank you officer," she said.

Iris Phillips sat down heavily. It had been an exhausting evening.

Chapter 20

Rachel checked in with the office before leaving for her next appointment, the last of the three interviews for her story on the prison riot. As an editor, it was her job to go through the emails requesting stories. She was familiar with most of the arts and philanthropic groups having written about them many years. There were twelve promo packs from various businesses and charities asking for coverage. She quickly shunted them off to Moon who was proving to be a good reporter. Luna Moon went by her middle name Moon and to Rachel's knowledge no one but their accountant knew her last name. Turned out she had a journalism degree and Julian was about to make her a full-time employee.

The turning point came when Rachel suggested she do a column called "MoonScape." Moon was having trouble doing staff reporting that entailed stories she thought tedious. Rachel had given her a pep talk pointing out they were not boring, and in fact important, to the people she was interviewing. Even something like a barbeque contest sent thousands of dollars in entry fees to worthy nonprofits. That's how good cities worked with people willing to help orchestrate fun ways to give.

After their talk, Moon had thrived and hadn't complained about "boring" stories since. Her column with all its entertainment interviews and news of upcoming concerts had captured the City Different's attention. Rachel was proud of Moon's turnabout.

She sent the emails to Shorty, High Desert Country's photog, asking him to coordinate with Moon. Sherman Smith had been with the magazine almost as long as Rachel. He wasn't short. At 6'4" he had to stoop to get through most Santa Fe doorways. When not curating the magazine's photos, he could be found perusing comics. His other job had been fixing the old copy machine, but when Julian renovated the office, he included a new state-of-the-art copier. Unfortunately, the staff was not state-of-the-art so he continued to clear paper jams and re-program it. He was quite handy at "hacking" websites when needed, but that duty wasn't written down anywhere. Happily for Rachel, he rode a motorcycle which freed up room for her huge Mercury Marquis in the postage stamp parking lot at the office.

Her intercom buzzed.

"Hey Rach," Jules boomed. "Can you come to my office for a moment?"

"Sure boss," Rachel said knowing how much he hated it.

"And don't call me boss."

"Yes boss. I mean no boss." She disconnected.

"I can see you're in a good mood today," Jules said as she hovered at his door. "Come in, won't take a minute."

Rachel sat waiting for him to clear his messages.

"The woman you interviewed for the prison riot story," he said.

"Yes, Iris Phillips."

"I checked in with my police contact and there was a call from her to 911 in Española. Seems she had a visitor on her roof that dropped a substance down her chimney," Jules said.

"What do you mean a substance?"

"The officer who collected it was about to throw away the sample when one of the other officers, a Pueblo member, looked at it and asked for lab work. It seems he was familiar with the material."

"Are you ever going to tell me what it was?" Rachel asked. Jules loved his mysteries.

"Corpse powder," he said.

Rachel gasped.

"Geez, that's the second time I've heard about corpse powder in the last few days. Has she become ill?"

"Not to my knowledge, but I'm staying in touch with my police and hospital contacts in Española."

"Have you come across this very often?" Rachel asked

"Of course, I've read the Hillerman books and reference texts on southwestern Indian culture, but I've never run across it working on a story. Apparently it is a real thing. How did you hear about it?"

"I spoke with Ernesto Pacheco over lunch the other day. Since we both had our black obsidian arrowheads he felt protected enough to talk about it."

"Who are you interviewing this afternoon?" Jules continued.

"A sociology Ph.D. at UNM," Rachel said. "Her name is Olivia Kanteena and she researches crime including the consequences of incarceration."

"Just based on her last name, I'd like you to inform her of what has happened to our first two interviews so she can decide for herself if she wants protection."

"Will do. Anything else?"

"Be careful in Albuquerque," he said. "You know what's going on there."

CHAPTER 21

The crime rate in Albuquerque had been growing steadily. No one seemed to know why or how to fix it. On one hand, the police department wasn't known for its empathy when it came to the mentally ill. The Justice Department had closed the investigation in the killing of James Boyd after a prolonged standoff. Boyd was illegally camping in the Sandia foothills and had a long history of mental illness. But no formal charges were filed against the APD.

Some blamed the crime on the growing homeless population. Businesses had closed especially those along Central Ave., Albuquerque's segment of U.S. Route 66, where the homeless population had set up tents on the sidewalks and in the alleys. This put off potential customers from entering the stores and made a scary proposition for shop owners to cross the alley to their storage units. It was a problem that was more pronounced as the unhoused became more threatening often using drugs, damaging windows and intimidating customers. Housing had been established in the form of a tiny home village, but sobriety requirements kept the homeless away. The rules were relaxed so more people could take advantage of this transitional program.

It had been suggested that because both I-25 and I-40 intersected in the city that it made it easy to traffic drugs and humans. The interstates made for a fast getaway out of the city. But Albuquerque was not the only city where crisscrossing interstates existed so that didn't clarify the cause of the violence.

Rachel hated the fact she no longer felt safe walking Old Town or driving along Route 66. She kept up with Albuquerque news and looked for crime trends in all quadrants of the city, but murders seemed to happen in all areas.

The University of New Mexico had its share of crime too. Students expressed concerns after hearing occasional gunshots. Some felt unsafe even when walking with others. A new program called Campus Watch worked similarly to Neighborhood Watch. Security was available to escort students to their cars and apartments. Call boxes and the Lobo Guardian App had been created to enhance safety and make reaching law enforcement quicker.

The trip down from Santa Fe seemed to fly by in Chloe's sports car. Yup, she was going to miss this little car and its radio. She wondered how many greenbacks it took to drive one of these off the showroom floor?

She took the Lomas Blvd. exit off I-25 and drove east toward the University of New Mexico. When she reached Yale Blvd., Rachel took a right and quickly found a campus parking lot. The social sciences building looked like stacked boxes. The only New Mexico detail was the brown facade. It wasn't fooling anyone: architecturally, a plain Jane. She parked and placed her media parking permit on the dash passenger side. It didn't guarantee she wouldn't be towed, but thus far no one had bothered. She grabbed her ID lanyard and quick-stepped it across the concrete.

The first door she saw took her inside. She had no idea if it was front or back or had some other designation. Rachel stopped a student and asked where Professor Kanteena's office was. He pointed; she said thanks and walked down the hall he had passed through.

Inside the office a woman sat at reception. She looked quite young but that might be helped along by the two braids that hung against her neck.

"You must be the reporter," she said. "If you can pop into a seat for a moment, Professor Kanteena is finishing a phone call."

The phone on the receptionist's desk buzzed.

"You can go in now," she said. "Right through there."

Professor Kanteena was waiting at her open door.

"Hi, Olivia Kanteena." She shook Rachel's hand. "Make yourself comfortable."

"Rachel Blackstone. Thank you." She handed the professor her business card.

Dr. Kanteena was fortyish and about Rachel's height, had black hair worn long and straight. She wore a traditional turquoise necklace and matching dangle earrings or shoulder dusters. A professional black jacket covered a bright pink T. Her makeup was minimal. She was a natural beauty. Everything about her echoed pride: in appearance, knowledge and her culture.

Behind her desk a credenza held stunning pottery from her Laguna pueblo. Their artisans were known for their geometric designs in predominately yellow, orange and red. Although once the location of uranium mining, the Nation had moved onto other industries such as construction and land reclamation. Laguna Spanish Mission church was known for its colorful interior. Probably their most famous member was Deb Haaland, U.S. representative for New Mexico's 1st Congressional District and former U.S. Secretary of the Interior.

Rachel sat down and pulled the old mini-cassette recorder from her bag.

"Okay if I set it here on your desk?" she inquired.

"Of course," Kanteena said. "There is a pull out writing surface on your side. Help yourself."

"Nice," Rachel said and readied her notebook. It was marked with a small stick note. The professor's name, address and phone were neatly written at the top. Six questions ready to go. Those questions didn't always get asked because Rachel was ready to go another direction should the opportunity arise. Interviews could be surprising in both good and bad ways.

"First, Professor Kanteena, I want you to know the other two interviews I have done on this story about the prison riot experienced unsettling events after I interviewed them."

"What happened?" she asked.

"One was frightened at her home by an intruder and the other shot in his backyard," Rachel explained. "They are apparently going to be okay. We want you to be aware and alert. And if you believe in protective stones, now would be a good time to carry obsidian."

"Are we talking about a witch?" she asked. "But what would that have to do with the prison riot that occurred more than 40 years ago?"

"We aren't sure, but we want you to know. Are you still willing to do the interview?"

Professor Kanteena opened her middle drawer and removed a leather medicine bag.

"I think I've got obsidian in here." She pushed the stones around on her palm. "Yes, here we are." She replaced the stone and dropped the bag onto her desk.

"Fire away," she said.

"Okay," Rachel answered. "Thank you."

"We know a lot about what went wrong at the prison. What we need to know now is what was done at the new prisons, and prisons in general, that can help prevent more bloodshed?"

"You may have already heard some of this," Dr. Kanteena began. "The prison, particularly the dorm, was overcrowded by more than double the number of inmates it was designed to house. During visiting hours, the prison allowed petty thieves and murderers to intermingle. Something as simple as metal flatware and trays in the cafeteria became weapons. Again the prison allowed the most treacherous criminals to eat meals at the same time as the least dangerous. Gangs would segregate themselves and nongang inmates were expected to find another space to eat. That didn't stop the fiercest from stealing their meals or attacking them. Tables in the eating area slowly disappeared so most inmates ate on the floor."

"Did the new prison meet new and safer standards?" Rachel asked.

"Have you read the *New York Times* story from 1981?" Kanteena asked. Rachel nodded.

"At that time, the prison system was kicking and screaming about following the recommendations the state Attorney General Jeff Bingaman made after an exhaustive six-month investigation of the riot. About the only improvement then was a pay raise for guards from $867 to $1200 a month.

"Of course, a new prison was built and the worst inmates shipped to other prisons, but even then violence continued. State Senator Charles Marquez, in 1981, reported that 70 percent of New Mexico prison guards had less than one year's experience and 32 percent left in less than a month's time while still in training. Because of that, training was not getting done."

"And forty some years later?" Rachel asked.

"Whether or not the Bingaman report was ignored or implemented depends on who you speak with.

"You're likely familiar with Mark Donatelli, an attorney who was a prisoner representative for at least 30 years. I'll read his quote so you have it exactly: *'There was an absolute and total failure by the Legislature,'* He was speaking of the prison's failure to respect the recommendations made in the Bingaman investigation. He concluded the state just built more prisons and didn't invest in halfway houses, education and job training that would have given prisoners a base for life outside prison walls.

"On the upside," Kanteena continued. "Guards must now complete eight weeks of training at the New Mexico Corrections Training Academy. In addition, prison staff learns defensive tactics and ways of communicating that quiets a situation instead of inflaming it. Despite this, inmate violence has reached its highest level during the past decade."

"What more could be done?" Rachel asked.

"You've heard the old axiom; idle hands are the devil's workshop? It's the same with inmates. There are too many who have nothing to do but get through another day. Education and job experience are necessary to both keep the prison population busy so they feel some growth and fulfillment while also learning skills for jobs post prison."

"Last question," Rachel said. "Do you think another riot is possible?"

"It happened in Clayton, New Mexico in 2017," Kanteena said. "All it takes are the right ingredients to come together and yes, it can happen again."

Rachel thanked the professor and left. She was relieved to see Chloe's car was still in its parking space, but she felt chilled by Dr. Kanteena's last answer. *It can happen again.*

As the professor readied for the drive home, she picked up her lesson plans, an application for an upcoming seminar, placed them with her laptop in her briefcase and headed for home. She overlooked the medicine bag with the protective amulets.

Chapter 22

M elinda Harris married at sixteen. She currently found herself in the trap of poverty: divorced with no support, no education and working at one of the hospitals as a nurse's aide. She was tired, physically and mentally. At work it was a constant merry-go-round of lifting, bedpans and helping patients shower. It was hard work but it wore on her emotionally too. Patients on post-surgery meds could be anything from hilarious to demanding. Sometimes they pulled out their IVs and she had to find a RN to replace them. And then, there were the days when most of the patients vomited from the meds received during surgery.

She pushed back her long red hair, a genetic gift from her birth mother. Melinda's adoptive mother's name was Monica Harris who married a Latino. There had been a big blowup in the family when her mother's parents disowned their daughter. Not much of that mattered when her mother, Monica, died giving birth to her brother. A few days after birth, the baby boy perished too. That's when her step-father decided enough was enough. He left to parts unknown. Grandfather Ozzy raised her with the best of intentions after his wife succumbed to an illness when Melinda was fourteen. Her boyfriend convinced her to marry him two years later. She wanted out of her grandfather's house.

He was always sick and his house was depressing especially when he awoke screaming at night.

Melinda dreamed of the Santa Fe lifestyle she read about in all the glossy brochures and magazines. She thought if she married this handsome white man her troubles would be over. That didn't happen. He was restless from the start, seemed to piss off every boss and couldn't hold onto a job. The bills piled up and one day he was gone. It seemed everyone left her, except Ozzy, but he hardly counted since he couldn't walk across a room without resting.

After one horrible year of wedded misery she took the only job she was qualified for as a nurse aide. She thought hotel cleaning would be a step up but none would even talk with her during the pandemic lockdown. Most of the hotels were laying off staff because of fewer visitors. But hospitals were open and business was booming with COVID-19 patients. The whole thing was an awful experience for her and most everyone employed at hospitals. So many people were dying she was no longer affected by death. It was just another body lying in a hospital bed, coughing, gasping for air and begging to see their family. For her, they became the enemy. She took extra measure to protect herself. The N95 mask she had to wear for a week at a time left indentations in her face for hours. The gloves, goggles and other PPE she often wore longer than advised. When she saw the orderlies rolling another body out the back into a hearse she felt relieved. Another widget processed.

Although post-pandemic, regulations had mostly reverted to what they had been before; she still had to wear a surgical mask when working. Glad that COVID seemed to have passed, she found her disdain for sick people had only amplified. That included her grandfather who was one big pain in the butt.

She turned her key in the lock of his front door and entered the gloom of illness. It smelled like the hospital. There was no place she could escape from the grasp of infirmity and death.

Ozzy was lying in his recliner asleep. That's all he had done since being released from the hospital. His oxygen mask was hanging from the chair arm. It should be on his face. But that barely registered. She'd deal with it later.

Melinda took her purse to her room and hung up her sweater. The bedroom was as pleasant as she could make it. It was green – not hospital green, but a mint color that made her happy. She bought the paint and did the work herself. She sat on the edge of her bed and flopped backwards enjoying the bounce. Once again, she daydreamed about when she would have all the bills paid and could get an apartment of her own. With a sigh, the young woman stood and stretched. The patient in 2352 had been on his call button all day. It felt good to move her body in a way that made her back feel better. She knew what would cheer her mood.

With care, she put on the jewelry the hospital wouldn't allow her to wear on duty. Most of it was costume but one necklace strand was turquoise and coral. She added rings and a cuff.

Dutifully, she returned to the living room to see what was up with the oxygen. Maybe he needed a refill. Upon a closer look, she could see her grandfather was dead: the staring eyes, colorless skin, mottled extremities and no pulse.

Instead of grief, she found herself feeling jubilant. It was over! She would never have to take care of him again. If she could sell the house, she might never have to see another sick person in her life.

"Tough luck Gramps," she said to his body.

CHAPTER 23

Because she worked in the medical field, Melinda knew it was the law to call the police concerning an unattended death. Looking out the front window, she watched the cruiser drive up. Quickly she pinched her cheeks hard to make it look like she was upset. She added some eye drops and let them run down her cheeks. It wasn't difficult for her to look downtrodden because that was her reality. She opened the door and waited.

Two officers came through the door and immediately saw her grandfather.

"I'm so sorry miss," one said. His badge read Officer Sandoval. "When did you find your ... is he your grandfather?"

"Yes," Melinda said. "It was a few minutes ago. I got home from work and found him. I work at a hospital so I know how to check a pulse. He had none and I called you."

"When was the last time you saw him alive?" Sandoval asked.

"This morning before I left for work," she said. "The TV was on and he was watching news. He does that every morning."

"You're sure he was alive then?"

"Yes, he told me to have a good day," she said. He actually said, "Don't be late," but why tell him that?

The other officer had been looking at her grandfather and motioned Sandoval over.

"This looks as if he struggled some," he said. "I think we need to get the lab out here.

"Miss did you move your grandfather?"

"No sir," she said. "I only felt for a pulse. Right arm."

"You didn't touch anything else?"

"No." She was getting annoyed. This was taking too long. "But I adjusted the oxygen last night and gave him his meds. So I have touched most everything."

"We're going to get the lab techs over here to have a look. Why don't you have a seat or if you prefer, you can go to another room. Just don't leave."

"I'll go into the kitchen. There are dishes to do."

When she left, the two officers exchanged a look.

"She's a bit cold," Sandoval said. "But you never know how people will be affected by death."

"Yeah, but this guy didn't just die," the officer replied. "Look how he's sprawled on the chair, like he was fighting for his life. The expression on his face is terror. The oxygen mask has been removed and is hanging off the chair. I don't think he'd take it off unless he ran out."

The EMT checked the oxygen level with his gloved hand.

"He's got plenty left. This man either died from a violent reaction like an allergy or he was killed."

CHAPTER 24

By the time Rachel returned to Santa Fe from her interview in Albuquerque, it was closing time at her office. She headed to Chloe's on Gonzales, managed to tickle the robot gate guy just right and gained entrance to Chloe's compound, at least that's the way she had come to think of her friend's house and grounds. Chloe's company Sun Dancing Realty remained successful despite the economic ups and downs and she had built a lovely house on several acres from the proceeds. Recently she had added see-through fencing so as not to block the spectacular views for her neighbors or herself.

Once inside Chloe's house, which required a second entry card, Rachel checked her office email from her computer. There was another Proton Mail message addressed to her. She hesitated to open it because that's how she received the petroglyph drawing warning her that "paths can be dangerous." She took a breath, or maybe it was a sigh, and opened it.

There was a rock art drawing of a person upside down with something flowing from his or her head. It was quite disconcerting especially when she read the text: "One down ... "

One down.

She picked up her cell and dialed Julian.

"Hey Rach, look who's using a cell phone," Julian said.

"Very funny. I didn't have a choice. Chloe has removed all her landlines.

"God forbid." Audible chuckle.

"Listen Jules," she continued. "I've received another rock art symbol." She went on to describe it.

"That seems fairly straight forward," Julian said. "I'll give my contact at the SFPD a call and see if anything has happened we need to know. Can you hang tight? I'll call back in a few minutes."

"Will do." Rachel poked at the green circle a couple of times until the call disconnected.

She busied herself getting cat food out of the small can while Chile Pod waited not so patiently, pacing back and forth, first curling around one of Rachel's legs, then the other. There were a few pathetic meows as she demonstrated how famished she was.

"Look, that poor, hungry, street urchin stuff doesn't work with me," Rachel admonished as the metal lid finally gave way making a scratching sound. She spooned some food into one of Chile Pod's bowls and re-plenished her water in the other. The tortie ate hungrily. Rachel knew she liked the food at Chloe's house better than what she got at home.

"Well, I guess Auntie Chloe's specialty food is good," she said sarcastically. "At the price she pays for it, it should be."

She left Chile Pod to gorge herself on some kind of pâté du jour, grabbed an expensive bottle of water from the fridge and settled on Chloe's comfy banco that wrapped around the kitchen table.

Chile Pod finished eating and hopped onto the banco with Rachel. She patted her leg to invite her feline friend to join her. The tortie daintily made two turns on her lap and curled up to lick the last of dinner off her face. Rachel rubbed the cat's head. She knew all the right places. Soon Chile Pod was purring contentedly.

Rachel found the remote behind a cheerful turquoise and pink throw pillow. She turned on the TV hanging over the nook. The local evening news was playing. Rachel muted the weather because the weather in Santa Fe was often sunny. The 10-day forecast looked familiar. The anchors returned and she unmuted the sound.

"Repeating the headline," the male anchor said. "A man has been found dead in his southwest Santa Fe home. Although he had been ill for some time, the SFPD is investigating. This is an evolving story and we will bring you updates as warranted."

Her cell rang. Rachel swiped it to answer taking some satisfaction that she could do it the first time.

"Rachel?" Julian asked.

"Who else? What did you learn?"

"Mr. Delgado was found dead earlier today," Julian said.

"He was the man they were talking about on the news?"

"It looks like it," Julian replied. "My contact said it did not look like a natural death. Since it was an unattended death, there will be an autopsy, but it will be more in depth as officers weren't comfortable calling it natural. Apparently, the body looked as if he had thrashed about. Now, that could have been a reaction to something or it could have been murder."

"That poor man," Rachel said. "He didn't deserve this after what he went through during the prison riot and the rest of his mostly miserable life.

"Do you think it was the bone fragments?" Rachel asked.

"We'll just have to wait for the results," Julian replied.

"What about his granddaughter?" Rachel asked.

"Oh, she was there, apparently found him. But I got the impression that if foul play was determined, she could be a person of interest."

"I'm going to call my ranger friend and see if he or his mother can enlighten me about this rock art symbol."

"Stella told me about it. I think that's a good idea," Julian said. "Take care. Maybe take someone with you. This is beginning to sound like one of *your* cases."

CHAPTER 25

Rachel had known that all along, although she was loath to admit it. Anytime there was a visitation, it became one of *her* cases. She sighed. It seemed to be a second occupation, one where she had to make it up as she treaded carefully. Rachel felt unqualified to take on such awe-inspiring mysteries in the spiritual world. Chloe said she'd been chosen. That was difficult for Rachel to accept. The *why* was a big question? For Rachel it was all on-the-job-training. She felt another course in mysticism coming.

She picked up her cell and called Dave Chee who answered promptly. After the niceties, she told him about the rock art symbol she received.

"That doesn't sound like well wishes," he said. "I think you better talk with my mother. She's visiting friends on the rez near Mexican Water, Arizona. I'll give her a call and get back to you."

As Rachel began watching the national news, she absently stroked Chile Pod who was peacefully napping. She wondered what this mystery would bring and how it connected to the riot of more than 40 years ago. What happened to poor Ozzy Delgado? Was there really a malevolent witch out there? She was startled from her thoughts by her phone.

"Hello Dave," she said.

"My mother is quite willing to help. Can you make the trip to Mexican Water? It's along Highway 160 about 60 miles west of Shiprock. You're invited to spend the night at the family hogan if you're up to a little roughing it."

"Yes," Rachel said. "That is generous of your mother and her family. Staying in a hogan is an honor as I understand it."

"Yes it is. Mom took a liking to you. Her family lives in a trailer a bit south of the highway. I'll text you the directions. Mother suggested you bring someone with you. It's a long drive. Maybe your friend Chloe?"

"Okay," Rachel said. "And Dave, thank you."

"You're welcome," he said. "One more thing. Try not to get caught on that highway after dark. The witches come out to play at dusk."

"Good to know," Rachel said, positive they could avoid traveling at night.

When Chloe arrived home, Rachel gave her some time to sort her mail, check her text messages and ooh and aah over Chile Pod. White wine in hand, Chloe sat down at the table.

"How would you like to go to the Navajo Nation with me tomorrow?" Rachel asked.

"Are you kidding? I didn't know you could just go?" she said.

"Got another Proton Mail delivery today," Rachel pushed the printed copy over to her. "I've talked with Dave and he invited me – and a friend to the rez where his mother currently is visiting family."

"Wow, Rachel, this is cool beyond words. Of course I'll go."

"Then it's settled. We leave at dawn – or maybe a little later."

"But where will we stay?" Chloe asked. "It will be an overnighter, right?"

"Oh yeah," Rachel said. "Much too far for a day trip. Dave's mother has offered us her family hogan to sleep in."

"So it's Dave now, is it?" Chloe teased.

"Well, Ranger Chee seems unnecessarily long."

"Uh-huh," Chloe said with a knowing look. It was a facial expression that annoyed Rachel. Chloe always used it when she thought she knew a secret.

"We'll take my partner's SUV," Chloe said, dialing her phone. "Could be rough terrain. I hope it's available."

The following morning after a paltry breakfast of yogurt and fruit – Rachel was mad for a plate of eggs and hash browns swimming in green chile – they packed the SUV with overnight bags, however Chloe's idea of what she needed for one night was about three times larger than Rachel's bag.

Chloe phoned Mari-Lynn to let her know Chile Pod was at her house and asked if she could feed her should they not return the following day.

One look at Chile Pod's food bowls confirmed she had enough food for a week should Martians march into Santa Fe. The cat would probably gain a pound or two overnight. Rachel checked the water bowl to find a large mixing bowl full next to her bowls. Rachel momentarily wondered why Chloe owned mixing bowls as she rarely cooked, preferring to cater most every meal, except breakfast obviously.

"I've got water containers in several places," Chloe said. "And there is more food in your bathroom."

"Thank you Chloe," Rachel said. "She will probably curl up on my bed."

"Shall I leave the remote out for her?" Chloe said not kidding.

"I'll move her monitor from the safe room to your bedroom," Chloe said.

"Just one thing." Chloe disappeared for a minute. When she returned there was a small cat bed in her hand that matched the rug on the far side of the bed.

"There," she said. "This is her TV viewing bed. Now, I've got a timer on the video. It comes on at ten in the morning and off at eleven at night. She's a late sleeper, right?" She stood back and took it all in with satisfaction. She turned on the screen. It came alive with birds and small mammals. Chile Pod settled in her *viewing* bed for the duration. *How did she know?*

"Are we ready now?" Rachel asked.

"Depends on how long it takes to say goodbye to Miss Pod." That proved to be about 15 minutes as Chloe fussed over the cat who was more interested in what she was watching.

"We'll be back," Rachel said as she gave Chile Pod one last smooch. The tortie was accustomed to such departures and took them in stride. It was actually more difficult for Rachel.

"Goodbye sweetie. We'll be back after one dark night." She held up one finger to illustrate.

Rachel thought the tortie blinked in acknowledgment. She fled before the tears that threatened began rolling down her face.

* * *

After a good four hours on the road, they came to Shiprock, that mammoth protrusion of a former volcanic neck. They had observed it for the last 40 or so miles. It became larger and larger. Even from afar, it was still a majestic vision. Because it was on Navajo land, they could no longer drive the dirt road to the base because people, the disrespectful type, had abused the privilege. Monuments are sacred to the Navajo, therefore only tribal members were allowed to visit the site. Rachel pulled off the highway and they got out. The pinnacle was closed to climbing in 1970 because of a fatal accident. Navajo believed that once someone had died the location must not be visited again for fear of disturbing the spirits.

"It's been a while since I visited here," Chloe said.

"Yes, me too," Rachel replied. "In the summer, it's RVs for as far as the eye can see. We're lucky to be here in the fall."

"This used to be completely buried," Chloe said. "I understand that a good 2,500 feet of dirt and rock used to cover it."

"Wind, rain and time," Rachel commented. "The Navajo call it *Tsé Bit'a'í* or 'rock with wings.' It was so named because the people believed their ancestors were brought here from the north by a great bird. However, later travelers to the area named it Shiprock because it resembles a clipper ship."

For a few minutes they stood in reverent silence. It was total. Not even the sound of a bird. The giant rock rose in solitude, nearly 1600 feet above the relative flat surroundings. Many people would call it desolate, but Rachel thought the expanse beautiful. The many colors that radiated from the land had called to artists for centuries. Shiprock itself jutted into the air with jagged rock formations pointing toward a cloudless sky. The dikes extending from the monument in several directions reminded Rachel of ripples along the surface of the ground. All in all, it was a study in what a volcano looked like below ground.

The ancientness of the Four Corners area drove home how we humans are nothing more than a footnote. Some 27 million years ago, this had been a volcano and in million more, its remnants would still stand, while generations of humans came and went, their problems made barely an addendum in this primitive place.

"Wow. Look at the time," Chloe broke the silence. "Should we get back on the road?"

"Yes. Much as I hate to," Rachel said.

As she turned back toward the car, she saw something nearby. A silhouette stood motionless in the near distance. She closed her eyes to refocus, but it was still there.

"Chloe, do you see that?" Rachel pointed.

"See what?"

"I was afraid that would be your answer."

Rachel continued to look at the shadow person. When it moved, she was certain they must leave and reach the relative safety of their destination.

"Let's go," Rachel said. "We've outstayed our welcome."

Chloe took the wheel as they continued on to Mexican Water.

"It is amazing how much we have become accustomed to noise," Rachel said trying not to think about what she had seen. "Have you ever heard anything so quiet?"

"No. I love these places in our state where there is a lot of nothing and yet there is life and history all around you," Chloe said. "We're lucky." She wiped at her eyes as she drove, clearly Shiprock had moved her in its everlasting splendor.

Shortly after, they crossed into Arizona, still on Navajo land. The bulk of the 25,000 square miles of the reservation is in Arizona but it also extends into New Mexico and Utah. While visitors could drive through it on the highways, they were expected to stop only at restaurants and other businesses. Usually official permission was required to go further off the highways. But tours were available by Native guides.

"Anything I should know about customs?" Chloe asked.

"Yes. No hugging or touching," Rachel said. "Navajos don't always feel comfortable with eye contact. Don't touch jewelry or ceremonial garb without asking and be prepared to be told no. My experience with the Navajo is they are reserved until they know you and warm and welcoming thereafter. Obviously, the way they have been treated over the centuries makes them cautious."

"Should we have left Shiprock earlier?" Chloe asked.

"Maybe a little," Rachel said trying not to sound too wary. "It is getting dark. Dave told me not to drive these highways at night."

A wolf's howl burst through the stillness getting Rachel's attention immediately. Its clarity was stronger and longer than usual. Rachel's body was rigid as all her senses sharpened.

"Something is up," she said. "I just heard Kiyiya."

"Could be an actual live wolf."

"I don't think so. That was the warning howl. We need to be very careful."

"Do we have protection?" Chloe asked.

"Yes, I have both the arrowhead and the corn pollen," Rachel replied. "I don't know how they protect, or if they protect everyone, or only Natives."

"That's reassuring," Chloe said skeptically. "We're only about 30 miles outside Mexican Water."

"Yes, but it is passing from dusk to dark," Rachel said. "I'm anxious." She checked that the car was locked.

"Oh god, don't tell me that. If you're jumpy that means I'm close to terrified."

"Just concentrate on driving and I'll keep watch."

"For what? What are you watching for?" Chloe's voice sounded edgy.

"Anything out of the ordinary, such as, has that light been following us long?" Rachel said while twisted about to see out the back.

Chloe glanced at the rearview mirror.

"That wasn't there even a few seconds ago," she replied. "And why one light? Is the other one out?"

Rachel turned to get a better look. The light was no longer there.

"I guess they turned off," she said.

"There wasn't a place to turn when we went past that spot," Chloe said.

"Okay, we're probably getting upset for no reason," Rachel said. But she didn't believe her own words. Everything in her was taut while she surveyed the area as much as possible in the dark. With the car lights on it was difficult to see anything but night beyond them.

"What was that?" Chloe pointed toward her side window.

"Where? What?"

"That!" Chloe pointed again.

"Oh no!" Rachel jerked back in her seat.

Chill bumps rose on her arms. The creature seemed to float outside their SUV. Without making any effort it stayed right next to them. Its face was grey and the eyes were red.

"Well, we're not even close to Paris or its famous cathedral," Chloe said trying to be funny. "I've read Hugo's book and have seen at least one of the movies and this seems much larger than the hunchback."

Rachel kept her eyes on the space beyond Chloe's window, and missed the creature now running along the car on her side.

"Rachel! Look out!" Chloe shouted, daring to take one arm off the steering wheel to point.

Rachel turned to see the thing peering into her window while seemingly floating along with the car. It was larger than any man she'd ever seen, hairy and it had a pronounced hump.

"Go faster," Rachel said.

"You obviously haven't noticed the speedometer. It's at 90 mph." Chloe gripped the wheel so hard she thought her fingers might break. Her breath came in short gasps. Driving at this speed was frightening. She feared she might lose control. But whatever was out there scared her even more.

It didn't bother the desert visitor who was staying with the car despite Chloe being well over the speed limit. Its skin was ashen. The orbital cavities were black and deeply sunken. Rachel saw the two glowing red eyes full of malice and glanced quickly away. The beast appeared to be a massive wolf running on two legs.

Rachel took another look. Its fangs streamed foam as the wind whipped it away. The witch hit the side of the SUV and bounced back unhurt. Rachel and Chloe strained at their shoulder harnesses as their bodies reacted to the terrifying impact. Chloe struggled to keep the SUV on the road, her fingers clenched the wheel. She watched in horror as it began changing shape.

"Bloody hell," Chloe said. "What are we going to do? Can it get inside the car?"

Rachel chanced another glance through her passenger window and saw Chloe's face. At first she thought it might be a reflection from all the glass.

"Chloe, why are you outside?" Rachel asked knowing it couldn't be true, but still seeing her friend's face.

"What do you mean?" Chloe asked. "I'm right here, driving like a bat out of hell."

"I saw your face looking at me through the window."

"It's messing with us," Chloe said. "How do we get to safety?"

"Dave told me to find a house or other structure as quickly as possible," Rachel replied. "Witches usually don't come in but can remain outdoors making noise and damaging the exterior."

"I'm going to try something," Rachel said.

"Anything," Chloe's voice was quivering.

With shaking hands, Rachel pulled out the obsidian arrowhead. The skinwalker continued to keep up with the SUV. It was almost as if it was hovering next to their vehicle. It showed no signs of tiring.

Without warning, it bashed against the SUV again, causing Chloe to struggle to keep the car on the road. Rachel tried to hold onto the door, but the wolf kept hitting the vehicle. One lunge was so powerful they began skidding across the left lane. Chloe screamed as the SUV plunged off the highway but held the wheel and furiously turned it to get them back on pavement. Gravel spun from the tires as she corrected their direction making a sharp right to try to dislodge the creature and regain purchase on the road.

"Hell Rachel. Where is the arrowhead?"

"It's on the floor. I'm trying to find it."

Unfortunately, the carpet was black as the obsidian. She grasped for it along the side of her seat.

"Hell, did it go under the seat?" She felt the knotted fibers of the carpet for the shape of the arrowhead.

The car swerved again as the wolf returned and crashed into the passenger side. Chloe fought for control against the relentless punches of the fiend intent on their demise.

Rachel found the arrowhead. Holding it tightly, she held it up much as an exorcist might hold a cross to dispel a demon, pressing it against the window.

There was a subtle change in the expression from malevolence to, could it be fear? In a second, the wolf disappeared as if consumed by the night.

"I think it's gone," Rachel let out a great breath. She thought her chest would explode her heart beat so fast.

"Holy shit," Chloe said braking the car to slow it.

"Oh god, Rachel. I've never been so frightened in my life." She slowed the SUV to a crawl. "But we've entered Mexican Water so maybe we're safe."

"I hope so," Rachel said doubtfully. But she feared being on the reservation might not protect them from this threat. It might make it more likely.

CHAPTER 26

The SUV turned into the drive of a trailer house about a half-mile off highway 160. Many on the reservation lived in mobile homes. Numerous tires covered the roofs. Rachel knew the tires weighted the metal roofs preventing the rumbling noise during wind. Some believed they cut down on lightning strikes

"Is this the right house?" Chloe asked.

"Yes, according to Dave's directions," Rachel said.

Chloe reached to open her door but Rachel stopped her.

"We should wait here in the car for a few minutes. When they're ready they will come to the door."

"Why?"

"It's Navajo etiquette. We sit here until someone invites us in."

"That's okay," Chloe said. "It will give me time to calm myself. Not sure I was this frightened in that cave where they were stealing water. I didn't think there was a chance in hell we'd come out of there."

Rachel and Chloe had been kidnapped while trying to stop the Dog Star from crashing into Earth. Evil men pilfered water from underground reservoirs in New Mexico. That activity had angered the ancients and Sirius had threatened the entire planet.

"That was real people," Rachel said. "Scary as they can be, the paranormal is more difficult because we don't know the rules. Besides, you did okay in that cave. Stood your ground. Told that guy in no uncertain terms to keep hands off!"

"How do we do this?" Chloe said. "Dealing with the paranormal, things most people don't even believe in."

"It's *we* now?" Rachel said.

"Oh, for heaven's sake, yes." Chloe replied. "It's us together. Pinky swear."

They locked their smallest fingers together. A look of determination and friendship passed between them.

"Together!" They both said.

Rachel broke the moment.

The light next to the front door came on and a woman stepped out.

"Dave's mother is at the door."

The petite woman wore a blue gathered skirt made in three tiers with some kind of printed fabric. It was topped with a simple white blouse. An open overcoat kept the wind at bay. Her hair was pulled back the same manner as when Rachel first met her in White Rock. She made her way down the steps.

Rachel and Chloe exited the SUV and waited politely by the front of the car. When Mrs. Chee reached them she said, "*Yá'át'ééh*," followed by placing her closed hand to her left chest, thumb touching her heart, then opening her hand as she waved it outward.

"That is hello in Diné and the movement she made with her arm is the same in sign language," Rachel explained. "It can also mean thank you from my heart."

"Hello again Mrs. Chee," Rachel said. "Thank you for allowing us to be here.

"This is my good friend Chloe," she added.

"It is my pleasure to welcome you to our home," Mrs. Chee replied. She looked closely at Rachel in the light from the porch.

"You have had a scare, no?"

"Yes, you're right," Rachel said.

"May I touch your hand?" she asked.

"Yes." Rachel held it out.

Mrs. Chee touched her fingers briefly. Her hand was light but Rachel could almost see the energy travel from her hand to Mrs. Chee's.

"You have already met the witch. Are you okay?"

"Yes," Rachel replied. "It was quite frightening, but we are okay."

"We will make sure you get an early start on your return so you do not have another encounter at night. It is a short distance to our hogan. You may leave the car here. Do you have bags? Get them and follow me."

She led them down a dirt path away from the trailer. It was perhaps 50 metres. Rachel could see a round structure ahead of them. There was a sliver of light that glowed at the edges of the door.

"Our hogan is far enough from the house so that the morning sun is not blocked," Mrs. Chee said.

"Hogan doors all face east," Rachel said to Chloe. "The first thing the Navajo see every morning is Father Sun."

"Most Navajo live in newer homes," Mrs. Chee said. "The hogan is reserved for ceremonies and to keep us balanced. We must remember where we came from to know where we're going. The hogan helps us to connect. Some have only a blanket covering the opening, but we have added a door for safety."

Mrs. Chee hurried to the stove in the center where a lantern glowed. She turned up the flame so they could clearly see the interior.

"This is a female hogan," Mrs. Chee said. "It has eight sides. The ceiling is shaped like a dome. The timbers are woven similar to a basket. We sealed the logs to give off a warm color making it feel welcoming. The floor remains packed earth much as earlier hogans."

"It's exquisite," Chloe said. "I've never seen the interior of a hogan before."

A wood-burning stove stood in the middle and was vented through the roof. In earlier days there would have been a hole in the ceiling to draw smoke from an open fire. There were no windows in the structure but moonlight shown through the glass surrounding the vent and pooled around the floor casting shadows along the walls.

A table sat a few feet from the stove with assorted dishes, glasses, cups and flatware arranged neatly in a dish drainer. Mrs. Chee picked up a kettle and set it on the cook top.

"You will want tea for good rest. This is our herbal tea. It looks like sticks," she chuckled. "Rachel can tell you it's good. If you prefer, the other is decaf English breakfast."

The sleeping area included two wool blankets on the ground, a small pillow on each.

"There is a camp toilet behind the curtain," Mrs. Chee pointed. "There is a pitcher of water and a wash basin on the table next to it. Bottled water on the shelf below the dishes."

There was a quiet knock and a woman entered the hogan carrying a tray. There were two bowls covered in foil and a small coffee pot. The woman placed the pot and bowls on the stove to keep them warm.

"This is my cousin Chenoa," Mrs. Chee said. "She made dinner for you."

"That is so kind of you Chenoa," Rachel said. She hadn't expected that, had planned to go back to the highway and eat at a restaurant, but this woman had made meals for two tired strangers although she had likely worked all day.

"Yes, thank you," Chloe added. "It smells delicious."

Chenoa smiled shyly and said: "You are welcome."

"Mrs. Chee," Rachel said. "This is wonderful. Thank you."

"Let us know if you need anything. And please, call me Doba." She left in a swirl of skirt.

"Wow," Chloe said. "This is beyond hospitable. I'm famished."

Chloe took off her coat. Rachel followed. It was quite comfortable in the hogan.

Chloe removed the foil from the stainless steel camping bowls.

"Oh, dear," she said. "What do you suppose it's made from?"

"It's likely mutton stew," she said. "Raising sheep is popular in this part of Arizona and it's frequently found in their dishes. That's fry bread on the tray. It looks luscious. And one is dusted with powdered sugar. Dessert!

"I know you prefer vegetarian, but this one time it will be okay," Rachel said. "It is kind of Doba's family to provide us with a meal."

Chloe took a small bite.

"Oh, that's wonderful," she said. "And it's mostly vegetables."

Chloe was correct, the stew was full of potatoes, carrots, onions, yellow corn and green chile. It was delicious. They ate hungrily while sitting in lawn chairs close to the stove.

Fascinated by the hogan's interior, Rachel took it all in and stopped at the weaving area.

An upright loom sat on one side of the room. It was a large loom, nearly Rachel's height. At the base was a sheep skin rug where the weaver would sit. A partially woven rug was stretched across the frame. Rolls of yarn, each a different color, were at ready stored in woven basket. Several weaving forks protruded from the basket. They were used to tap down the yarn and tighten the pattern. She could identify the pull shed, a round wooden tool that separated strands of yarn. A textile artist had once told her it created an opening in the yarn so the weaver could insert a batten. Battens or beaters were used to push the weft yarn into place after the stronger warp threads are set up. Weft threads fill in the design.

"That is stunning," Chloe said in a hushed voice as if she were in a house of faith.

"It is a sacred tradition," Rachel said. "The Diné were originally taught to weave by Spider Woman, one of their most important deities. She was instructed by the Holy People to weave the universe and teach beauty. While watching a spider weave a web she created her plan to weave the universe. That weaving knowledge is handed down from generation to generation. It is believed that Spider Woman, or Grandmother Spider, lived in Canyon de Chelly."

"That is one incredible place," Chloe said. "Remember when we went there together?"

"Of course," Rachel replied. "So much beauty in one place is hard to believe and you never forget it. I was particularly taken with Spider Rock, that massive 800-foot monolith in the canyon."

"This rug is the Burntwater pattern," Rachel explained. "Notice the brown background with geometric steps, spirals and triangles in rust and mustard flowing throughout the rug."

"How do you know so much about weaving?" Chloe asked.

"Interviewed several textile experts," Rachel said. "But I caution you, a little knowledge is a dangerous thing."

"I love those tiny accents of rose and blue," Chloe said. "They add interest and pull the eye inward from the borders. It would be a prized addition for anyone lucky enough to buy it."

"Native weaving began as more utilitarian like saddle blankets, winter wear and clothing," Rachel said. "During the late 19th century it transitioned more to rugs for trading and later for non-Native buyers."

"I'm lucky to have a few of those rugs," Chloe said.

"I wish," Rachel replied.

"I hate to bring it up," Chloe said. "But this camp toilet thing, how does it work?"

"Let's look," Rachel said pulling back the curtain.

"Looks sort of normal." Chloe eyed the white square toilet with suspicion.

"Oh, it's a campsite potty," Rachel said. "These are easy. Just lift the lid, do your thing and then flush."

"Flush what?" Chloe asked.

Rachel reached for the lever on the front.

"Pull this lever out on the front to allow *everything* to go into the holding vat," Rachel explained. "After you go, pull this up and then push down." She showed Chloe the round knob on one side. "And you're flushed." Green liquid whooshed down the toilet.

"What about odor?"

"You saw the green liquid?"

"Yes."

"That's an ecologically friendly odor preventer," Rachel said. "Much better than the blue kind. Yuck."

"Yuck was what I was thinking," Chloe said.

CHAPTER 27

"It's late," Rachel said as she finished washing her face and brushing her teeth. "Do you want to go to bed now?"

Having mastered the camping toilet, Chloe wasn't sure.

"Isn't sleeping on the floor going to be cold?" she asked. "Maybe I could doze sitting here in the yard chair."

"The metal chair?" Rachel asked. "Do what you want. I'm sacking out on the floor." She turned the lantern to low and went to check out the sleeping area. Rachel pulled the blanket back and saw a sheep skin beneath it.

"Look Chloe, it's has an insulation layer on the floor. I think it will be okay. People have slept on the ground for centuries. Think of it as being cradled by Mother Earth."

"You be cradled by Mother Earth. I'm fine," Chloe said.

Rachel removed her shoes, fluffed the pillow, rolled onto her back in her clothing and got comfortable. The ground provided excellent support and the wool kept her warm. Rachel had been sleeping only a few minutes when she heard her friend settling in next to her.

"Tired of the chair?" she said groggily.

"No way to get comfortable in that," Chloe grumbled. "Do I just crawl under the blanket and sleep on the wooly thing?"

"Uh-huh," Rachel muttered, her eyes already closed.

They'd been asleep a couple of hours when there was a thud on the roof.

"What was that?" Chloe sat up alarmed.

From the distance a wolf's howl reached Rachel's ears.

"Something's up," she said.

"I think there's something on the roof," Chloe said glancing upward.

A moment later that was confirmed. Another bang hit as though someone had landed topside.

* * *

In Tesuque, Mari-Lynn woke with a start. Her body was rigid. She pushed herself to a sitting position. Her friends were in danger. Closing her eyes, she waited and tried to relax. The visions came more easily that way. She felt foreboding sweep over her. What she saw made her fearful.

The vision showed her friends sleeping in a hogan made of timbers somewhere on the Navajo Nation. They were not alone. A tall, hairy creature with red eyes made no attempt to hide as it walked brazenly up to the hogan. Mari-Lynn pressed her temples with her fingers to see inside. They didn't yet know death crept outside.

As she sat cross-legged in bed, she felt her spiritual self rise out of bed and travel to the hogan where she continued to levitate. She could see a trailer nearby where their hosts slept. An SUV and a pickup were parked in front. The walkway to the hogan showed up in the moonlight. She could feel the cold as she hovered. Mari-Lynn also noticed another spiritual person in the trailer who was slowly waking to the knowledge that all was not right. She sent a message via telepathy to the woman sleeping fitfully inside the trailer. This mind-to-mind communication didn't always work, but Mari-Lynn could see the woman respond by throwing back the covers and sitting up.

She was about to send a similar message to Rachel when she noticed the creature stop and look straight at her. That had never happened before. If this monster was endowed with psychic abilities too how could she help her friends? This was indeed a fearsome beast. Evil looked into her soul. Mari-Lynn had always been the observer, never a participant.

When it howled its jaws unhinged like a snake. It looked like a super wolf, fangs dripping and red eyes flashing. Yet, it stood on two legs. Before Mari-Lynn could send Rachel a message she felt herself thrown back in bed trembling and drenched in sweat. Oh god, she thought, I've failed Rachel when she needed me most.

* * *

Inside, the high-pitched animal shriek did not go unnoticed by Rachel and Chloe.

"Good god, did we lock the door?" Rachel asked. "I'll check."

Rachel hurried across the large room finding her way by the remaining light from the lantern. When she reached the door it was apparent they had not locked the door. She lifted the wooden board and slid it into place. Somehow that didn't make her feel any safer. It was the footsteps she heard outside.

"Rachel, don't lock the door. It's me, Dad."

She was incredulous as she heard the words. Her mind told her it couldn't be but her heart wanted to open the door.

Chloe was beside her.

"Did you hear?"

"Yes, and you know it can't be your dad, right? Didn't Mario do the same thing once? Pretend to be your father?"

"Yes, he did," Rachel replied quietly. "But maybe my dad is trying to warn us or protect us?"

"No, Rachel. Listen to me. He could do that through the door. This thing – whatever it is – is trying to trick us into opening the door. If it's the skin-, er, witch, it will try anything to get us out of here. Remember, the witch likely won't come inside unless invited, but it can scare us half to death if we let it. And if we go outside, it will ki-kill us."

"Listen." Rachel pointed up. The stove pipe began to rattle as someone or something tried to pull the cap off.

"What the hell?" Chloe said. "What is it trying to do?"

"I imagine it wants to drop corpse powder down into the cabin. Since we won't open the door, it's trying something else. We can't allow this. That could kill us."

"What do we do?" Chloe asked. "Oh, the damper!"

They raced to the stove and quickly closed it. The fire had burned its last a couple of hours ago.

"Now, we call Doba." Rachel dialed her number.

Inside the nearby trailer, Doba Chee had awakened from a fitful dream that continued in a vision. In it, her two guests were awake in the hogan. Both women stood by the stove looking up. Doba could also see the outside. There was a large figure on the roof trying to pull the cap off the smoke pipe. Fortunately, it couldn't because screws had been added to prevent it being tugged free or blown off by the wind – unless it was quite strong. She believed this entity fulfilled the strength requirement. She must do something immediately to prevent it harming their guests.

The creature was on two legs wearing the skin of a wolf. Because it hadn't yet discovered how to remove the cap, it became enraged. The witch found a log down below next to the hogan and bounded to the roof again. It hammered the Plexiglass surrounding the pipe. Doba had to stop it before it broke through and poisoned the women.

She threw on a coat and boots, not bothering to dress. On her bedside table rested an obsidian arrowhead and a rawhide pouch containing corn pollen. She placed both in her coat pocket.

On the front stoop she was hit with a frigid wind. But it wasn't just cold, it carried supernatural magic: a *dark wind*. She knew because of the putrid odor that permeated the gusts. Evil witches reeked.

Doba answered her cell.

"I know. I'll be right there," Doba said. "Do not allow that witch into the hogan for any reason."

Rachel and Chloe huddled together inside. The only opening besides the door was the skylight surrounding the stove exhaust. They could see something moving around and striking the glass trying to break through.

"Doba is on her way," Rachel said. "But we need to be ready should she not get here in time."

Rachel raced to her purse and retrieved both the arrowhead and pouch of corn pollen.

"Hold the pollen please," Rachel said. "This worked in the car." Rachel held the arrowhead up toward the skylight. Immediately, the witch stopped pounding on the roof.

Doba raced down the path. When she reached the hogan, she held up her arrowhead. But the witch didn't leave. It stood defiantly.

Doba tried once again. She shouted.

"*Akóó níláahdi naních'įįdii!*" Diné for go away.

At first, the witch was indecisive. This was a powerful woman standing on the ground. She appeared fearless. The witch could feel the authority with which she spoke. It might win in a fight with her, but this wasn't the most important battle.

And then, something happened that changed the odds. A wolf appeared in spirit and stood next to Doba.

"There you are," Doba said in Diné. "My protector. Mother of many power animals."

That was enough for the witch. Dropping the log, it morphed into a hawk and flew from the roof.

Doba felt the witch's strength hit her chest like the *níyol* that blows in the worst winter storm. This one could be stronger than any she'd known. And somehow there was something foreign about it. It was her sense this one wasn't Navajo. The usual rules didn't apply. Doba approached the hogan door when she felt certain the danger had passed.

"It's Doba," a voice said loudly from the outside. "I'm pushing my arrowhead under the door. It is safe to open."

Rachel was relieved to see Dave's mother standing there.

"You two all right?" she asked.

"Yes, thanks to you and whoever added that cover to the ceiling," Chloe said.

"We have had trouble here before," Doba said. "We wanted to be prepared. But I have to tell you, whoever that is, it is strong. Usually, when I show the arrowhead to a witch, they disappear instantly. This one did not. I had to speak to it. Actually tell it to leave. You have been lucky twice today.

"Who is that beside you?" Rachel asked when she saw the wolf.

"This is Kaya," Doba touched the wolf's head softly. "She is the mother of yours."

"What are you two talking about?" Chloe said trying to see.

"You cannot see her," Doba said. "But this family of wolves is special. Each has been assigned by the Great Spirit to protect an individual with vision.

"The fact she is here tells me that you, Rachel, must tread your tomorrows carefully."

CHAPTER 28

The following morning, Rachel and Chloe set out in the SUV with Doba to a place she wanted to show them. After driving several miles, she pointed to a dry rutted road. Chloe slowed as the vehicle negotiated the rugged terrain.

"There is an area to the right where you can park," Doba said.

Chloe did her best to avoid the wicked cholla and shut off the car. Not only would it scratch the car but cholla could *jump* and impale tender human flesh.

Rachel leapt from the back seat to the ground and opened the front door for Doba. They followed Doba as she headed toward a hill. The hike would have been easy had it not been for the incline. The rise was not high but steadily upwards. The barely visible path worked its way around rocks, some quite large. It was more of a deer trail than anything. Doba led the way while Rachel and Chloe tried to follow in her footsteps. A short distance from the top, Doba stopped.

At the crest, a mound had obviously been constructed by humans, likely the Ancestral Puebloans. On top were large boulders huddled together as if to protect what they came to see. A path looped around the man-made structure of stones. Even more interesting, there were large stacked rocks that encircled the mound, almost in a Stonehenge fashion. They were set at equal intervals as if sentries protecting the revered site. Rachel felt her heart quicken with excitement.

"We must approach this sacred place with reverence," Doba said. "We must take a clock-wise approach. It is a sign of respect. We make one full circle around it and then enter."

Once they were near the monument the passageway looked to have been carved by man and time. It was sunken either by design or use much like one Rachel had seen in Bandelier. It must have been trod for centuries. Rachel could feel spirits all about her. The women were nearby cooking and tending children as the men built the mound. Their spiritual presence was welcomed by Rachel, their tribulations felt and their triumphs appreciated. She forgot all about the cold that seeped into every opening of her coat, how it hurt her ears and blew her hair.

"You see them too?" Doba asked Rachel.

"Yes. They are building this place where we stand."

As they finished the circle, Rachel could see why Doba had brought them. Carved by the hands of people a millennia ago were the images known as petroglyphs or rock art. She saw some of the symbols she found online. The spiral was the first she noticed.

"What does this mean?" she asked Doba.

"The spiral represents dimensional gates or portals," she said. "If we had a drone you could detect the outline of a spiral built into this mound. With these spirals we can travel inter-dimensionally if we know how. I have seen Star People enter and exit these spirals. You know them a UAPs or UFOs. When the Navajo people emerged into this dimension, we traveled through one of these portals. It is our story."

Rachel scanned the messages from another time looking for the one she had brought with her. There were many: some looked like humans possibly in costume, lines that Doba said might represent time and zigzag lines that resembled snakes.

In an elevated place on one boulder was a round opening. Rachel asked Doba what it did.

"Look through it," Doba replied. "It is in line with the horizon. This may have been carved to help the Ancestral Puebloans know the time of year. This is also a place where protection ceremonies may have been performed.

"This is what you're looking for?" Doba continued.

Rachel squinted at the upside down human carving. She took out the paper with the drawing on it and compared.

"This is it." It was identical to the warning she had received.

Doba looked at the page and the ancient glyph.

"I am sorry to say that is death. This line that is drawn from the head downward indicates blood coming from the mouth or head. And the message that accompanies it 'One down ...' means someone else will die. Has there already been a death?"

"Yes," Rachel replied. "A guard on duty the night of the Santa Fe Penitentiary riot has died. We don't yet know everything there is to know about it but we feel it is connected to the riot. He was a troubled man filled with guilt even though he was in no way responsible. Barely out of high school, they made him a guard and he happened to be on duty that night. Inexperienced, there was nothing he could do to stop it. He hid, terrified, as the massacre unfolded."

"That is sad," Doba said. "I'm afraid there will be someone else according to this message. Can you think of who it could be? They must be warned."

Rachel wondered about Professor Kanteena, but knew she was protected by the corn pollen and an obsidian arrowhead. But what about the mother of the man who committed suicide? He was a former inmate at the Santa Fe Penitentiary. Would she be next?

CHAPTER 29

Professor Olivia Kanteena thought taking a walk on the Paseo del Bosque trail along the Rio Grande would clear her head. Since the interview with Rachel Blackstone, she couldn't get the reporter's good-hearted warning about danger out of her mind. She parked off Montaño in Albuquerque, leaving her purse and briefcase in the trunk of her car but slipping her phone into a pocket. She set out for the jogging path.

The chainsaw art next to the parking lot had been carved by a fire-fighter after the 2003 Bosque fire. He had created an eagle rising from the flames, howling coyotes and other animals. One was a fireman standing on a dragon, "dragon" indicating a particularly bad fire. Usually she enjoyed looking at them.

Some of the stories about the Bosque trail were frightening – like the man who reported he'd been nailed to a tree. The homeless set up encampments and intimidated people who used the park. Fortunately, she hadn't had any such encounters. A stroll along the river usually calmed her. Still, Albuquerque's crime rate had made national head-lines so she tried to be alert to any threats.

After a few minutes, Olivia could tell her pulse had evened out and she was beginning to notice the birds and trees instead of her bothersome feelings. But something else concerned her. There was a fetid odor in this area. She dismissed it as a dead animal but it disturbed her enough that she dug in her coat pocket for her pollen and arrowhead. They weren't there! Hadn't she placed them in her pocket while talking with the reporter? When Blackstone had cautioned her others she had interviewed had died or been scared she remembered taking the bag out and showing her the contents. She checked the other pocket that held her fob and cell. Olivia could feel the panic rising in her throat, so she took out the phone. It made her more confident. Help was a phone call away.

She quickly turned. Behind her was nothing but an empty trail and the beginnings of another spectacular sunset. Ahead, a biker disappeared around a corner. The Rio Grande flowed to her left and there was no one exploring the banks or kayaking on the river. That left the treed area to her right. A few trees still held onto their autumn leaves, but most had turned brown and fallen to the ground. There was nothing apparent, but the feeling of trepidation would not go away. How could she have left her amulet and bag of pollen? And where did she leave them? It didn't matter now. The only thing that mattered: something was stalking her and she couldn't yet see it. She held her phone tightly.

A hawk flew overhead as she looked upward. The hawk didn't worry her. These birds of prey were only a threat to a small mammal, with the occasional insect or lizard for variety.

It circled languidly. This time, it swooped down at her as a bird parent might defend a fledgling against a passing cat. The intent was obvious: to bully her. It was working. Olivia wanted to go. She no longer wanted to be outside and felt vulnerable, was vulnerable. Retracing her steps to the parking lot, she heard a sound behind her.

She kept walking, hoping it would go away. But the fear in her chest was fierce. It was difficult to breathe. She tried to control the shivering and her pounding heart. Her options had run out. Olivia knew she was no longer in charge of the situation. She had to turn around and face whatever was there.

After casually glancing about to appear unafraid, she came face to face with an evil witch. Its eyes held her, and she couldn't look away. The elders always cautioned against staring directly at the eyes so the witch could not control thoughts. But it was too late. The red and glowing eyes allowed her to see only the beast.

It was sans clothing with fur covering its body and the neck heavy with jewelry. Its face and arms were grey. For a moment she thought it might be female, but never had she known of a female witch becoming malevolent. She knew this was imminent danger of the fatal kind. Without her arrowhead, she didn't know how to defend herself. It could run faster, jump higher and climb better than she could. Her chances of harming it were slim. The body of a skinwalker was tough, maybe impenetrable. With only the useless cell in her hand she stood silently, because who could she call to intervene?

Olivia waited, knowing these were her final moments. She crossed herself but couldn't force her eyes closed. By the time Olivia lowered her arm, paralysis had overcome her body.

The creature held a leather pouch. Powder poured from it into its palm. Before she realized what it was, the dust was blown into her face. She gasped. Particles of dust entered her mouth. In a few seconds, her tongue swelled. She couldn't know it was also turning black.

It ended quickly. She fell to the trail where her body convulsed. Olivia felt nothing; she had already sunk into darkness beginning her journey to her next life. When the biker returned, he found Olivia's body lying on the trail. He recoiled in horror.

CHAPTER 30

There was a joyful reunion with Chile Pod when Rachel and Chloe returned. Chloe got out special food for the tortie who scarfed it down and looked up hopefully for more.

Rachel's cell rang. She fumbled with her bag to extract it.

"Rachel, you back in town?" It was Julian.

"Yeah, we just got in," Rachel replied. "What's up?"

"We have some new developments. Can you come by the office? It's important."

"I'll be right there."

"Your little red car is getting a workout," Rachel said.

"That's okay," Chloe said. "Can't drive both of them at once. I'll stay here with the Pod. Would you like that Chile Pod?"

"Oh, she's going to like it," Rachel grumbled. "She knows treats are at hand."

"Are you suggesting I'd spoil her?"

"Yes. See you both later." After one last pat on the tortie's head Rachel left by way of the back door.

It took her about ten minutes to reach the office. Traffic had dispersed with the end of rush hour. Thanksgiving was next week and thousands would be incoming for their perfect Santa Fe holiday. Ugh! But she had to admit that without tourism, there wouldn't be much to the Santa Fe annual budget.

She parked in the lot at the High Desert Country offices. There was only one car there and it was Julian's. The front door of the office was unlocked and she raced upstairs.

"That you, Rachel?"

"Yes," she said a little short on breath.

"Come on in."

Julian set out a bottle of water from his small fridge and waited for her to open it and settle in his guest chair.

"How was the rez?" he asked.

"Interesting. But that's not why I'm here. What's up?"

"Ozzy Delgado died."

"I thought he was better and at home now?"

"He was, and that's where he died. My police source says they are investigating it as unnatural causes. The officers who responded to the 911 call said his body looked as if he'd tried to fight off someone. His granddaughter is a person of interest, although there hasn't been an arrest as yet."

"Geez," Rachel said. "I met his granddaughter briefly once and she seemed protective of him, overly so. In fact, she was kind of in my face."

"And there is something else," Julian continued.

"What?"

"The professor you interviewed at the UNM."

"Yeah, Olivia Kanteena. What's up with her?"

"I'm afraid she's dead too."

"What! But ... " Rachel couldn't comprehend so much loss in such little time.

"She was protected," Rachel said on the verge of breaking down. "I saw her arrowhead and pollen. She had them with her during the interview. I prefaced the interview by telling her about the intimidation of the people who had done interviews with us."

"I'm sorry Rachel, but she was found on the Bosque Trail, dead."

"Are you telling me she died while she was running? Like a heart attack?"

"They don't know," Julian said. "There were no apparent physical injuries like a knife or bullet wound. Autopsy pending."

"But how did you find out about her death?"

"The police found your card in her purse. When my source at APD learned of that, he called me. They did a search of her office. An arrowhead and pollen were found in a bag she left on her desk at the university."

"She didn't take it with her?" Rachel felt disheartened. "How could she not? I told her ... " Rachel thought she would hyperventilate.

"I'm sorry Rachel," Julian said.

"That leaves Mrs. Phillips in Española, the mother of the guard who committed suicide and Mr. Pacheco, the Hopi guide at the Old Main. Should I warn them? What about Mr. Delgado's granddaughter?"

"I think you should notify them, but I would pass on the granddaughter since she is a person of interest," Julian said. "But do so carefully. I trust Mr. Pacheco would be receptive to such a caution because he is Hopi and gave you the arrowhead. Mrs. Phillips might not be open to such advice. It's a careful line we must walk here, giving warning without setting ourselves up for a lawsuit. Our publishers' liability insurance is up to date, but I would prefer not to use it.

"On a different note," Julian continued. "There is a movie being filmed at Old Main and they would like some publicity. Would you care to cover that? We could run it as a sidebar. But they want you to come watch a scene they are filming tonight. You can take Chloe if you wish some company."

"Oh man, I both want to jump at that and am shaking in my boots already, but yes."

"Okay, here's the press release. They begin filming at eight this evening and you should ask for Russ Walker. He's the assistant director. A production assistant or PA will meet you out front and escort you into the filming area."

Rachel stopped by her office and called Mrs. Phillips and Ernesto Pacheco. Iris Phillips didn't answer. Rachel left a message telling her what had happened to two of the people she had interviewed and cautioned her to be watchful. She didn't mention shadow people or skinwalkers.

Ernesto answered his cell promptly.

"Hello Ms. Blackstone."

She quickly told him about the death. He assured her he was wearing his amulet around his neck and would not take it off.

"Ms. Blackstone."

"Please, Rachel.

"Rachel, you must wear your talisman too. It's not enough to carry it. Promise me you'll wear it."

"I will," Rachel promised. She made a mental note to take it by Mari-Lynn's to have her convert it to a necklace.

"This may have begun as a story for you, but it has turned into a deadly game," Ernesto said. "Walk with the Great Spirit." He was gone.

Before she left, Rachel tied a strand of black yarn around the arrowhead and then tied second knot so she could wear it as a necklace. She made prayer sticks when the occasion called for them, and always had four skeins of yarn on hand. It was a temporary fix, but at least she had it on. She took the pollen out of her bag and slid it into her pants pocket.

It was a short but solemn trek to her car, er, Chloe's car. But she knew Chloe would be all in for an evening at the prison film site. She hoped it would be a quiet one. But did she believe that?

CHAPTER 31

Old Main looked even more foreboding after dark. There was no electricity or water, hence, no power or working restrooms at the abandoned facility.

"Yuck," Chloe pointed to the two portable toilet rentals left in the parking lot. "You take me to all the elegant stuff."

"Making movies only looks elegant after it's completed," Rachel said. "I've covered enough TV and movie making to have learned that. Most of the actors and upper echelon use the trailers. But tonight for a shorter shoot, they've rented these deluxe portable re-strooms with showers. When they're finished with them, they push the stairs back underneath the unit and someone tows it off. They're already on a trailer so it's easy enough. Of course, these may be for the A-list actors and people such as the director and producer. The commoners may have to make use of the great outdoors while taking care to avoid the cholla."

"I thought they'd have trailers all over the parking lot." Chloe said.

"Well sure," Rachel replied. "If the movie has a lot of scenes to be filmed in one location, the trailers are brought in. They can rest and re-lieve themselves while studying lines, sitting for makeup or being coiffed. But for one scene it's not worth moving them so they use these. I understand this two-door model has facilities for men and women costs about $40,000 so it's not cheap."

A lone young woman approached them with a flashlight. Rachel assumed it was the PA. They left the car to go meet her.

"Hi," she said. "I'm Janis. You're the reporters to see Russ?"

"Yes, I'm Rachel Blackstone and this is Chloe Valdez. She's interning at the magazine." Rachel handed the PA her card.

"You look a little old to be an intern," Janis said to Chloe. Rachel stifled a giggle.

"I'll take you to Russ," Janis said. "No photos allowed on or near the set." She walked quickly away from them.

"So I'm a little old for an intern," Chloe said dripping sarcasm. "Next time, maybe I can be your assistant, or better yet, your boss."

Rachel ignored Chloe's comment but smiled in the darkness that protected her from Chloe's view. Rachel turned on her flash and followed the bobbing light ahead of them. Chloe carried a camp lantern.

Once inside, they caught up with Janis who was all but tapping her foot waiting on them.

"If you'll follow me, I'll take you to the video village."

"Video village?" Chloe whispered.

"You'll see."

They followed the PA through the prison to cellblock two. Inside were battery-powered lights in the absence of electrical power. It gave the prison cell an authentic look. As a set, it was way too authentic for Rachel. The film crew was setting up a scene. The bed had a mattress and a prison uniform hung from the open cell door. Two actors in prison garb rehearsed in the hallway.

Janis hurried on and turned into a dormitory room E, where the riot began.

"The video village is here," Jan told them. "There isn't space in the cellblock where we're filming. Wait here and I'll get Russ to talk with you."

Director's chairs formed a row in front of the "village." Monitors were spread out around the area. Cables taped in place littered the floor.

"What is all this?" Chloe asked.

"This is where they view what's happening in the scene," Rachel said. "All these people sitting in the chairs and standing around monitors are here for various reasons. Some are actors waiting for their scene. Others are here for continuity. There is usually one for costumes and hair. You've probably seen a movie where the actor's hair is styled one way and then later parted down the other side in the same scene. Continuity is important. How full was the wine glass at the beginning of the scene? Was the actor's collar standing up or flat? Movie audiences notice."

"There might be a scripty, or script supervisor here as well. That's the gaffer in the cell adjusting the lighting. Somewhere here is a director and an AD or assistant director. That must be my interview." Rachel motioned to Janis who was talking with a man at a monitor.

Janis returned to say: "Mr. Walker asked if you could wait until we reshoot this scene. The actors are ready to go so it shouldn't be too long. You may watch on this monitor."

Rachel and Chloe watched as two actors in prison garb slowly circled one another in the cell, fists ready to lash out.

"Looks like a rumble," Rachel said.

"That guy with the tats will win," Chloe replied. "The other man is simply outmatched."

"Quiet on the set. We're about to shoot," Russ yelled. "Action!"

The smaller actor swung at the other but missed his mark, the sign of a desperate man who knows he's going to get punched out. Behind the men were three cells carefully captured by the camera. Extras pretended to sleep while the fight continued. They had been there for hours.

Sound effects would be added later to make the blows sound realistic as no contact occurred in the mock fight scene. Rachel thought the actors were doing a good job of making it look real. One would swing and the other would turn his head quickly, mimicking being struck.

As the men worked to stay on their marks and act out the fight, something strange was developing. The two actors weren't aware, and no one watching a monitor seemed to notice either; they were so intent on getting the scene done correctly. Rachel noticed movement on her monitor. A cell door was moving.

"Do you see that?" she asked Chloe. "That door across the hall is moving. It is, isn't it?"

"Holy shit," she replied. "No one is pushing it. There's no electricity, yet that door is closing."

Everyone with a monitor seemed transfixed by the scene. Then, the door gained speed and slammed with a bang!

The whole crew went silent, stunned by what had happened.

"Cut. Cut!" Russ yelled. "What the actual fuck?"

The actors stopped play fighting, looked at the door in disbelief and ran out of the cell. In a few seconds, they joined the group at the video village.

"Was that special effects?" one of the actors asked.

"Not any we planned on," the director replied.

"That's a wrap for tonight," the director said unnecessarily. "Pack up. Everyone out! I've had enough of weird things on this set."

He was talking to a half-empty room. People grabbed their personal effects and fled. In their wake, chairs scattered on the floor. One monitor would likely never work again the rush to get out had been so urgent. Rachel wished she and Chloe were already outside, but she waited hoping for more information. Maybe she could write about what had happened and do a phoner with the producer.

"Those of you who are still here," the director said. "Please gather your personal belongings. We will come back and finish this during the day.

"Not me," one man said. "I'm outta here and I'm not coming back!

"Guess you're not getting this interview," Chloe's teeth chattered despite her effort to control it. Rachel felt her acute stress response kicking in and tried not to panic.

"Yeah, I'd say not," Rachel said. "I've read this kind of thing happens here frequently when filming takes place. Didn't think we'd witness it."

They scurried down the long dark hall.

"Should have left with the others," Rachel said.

"Do you remember the way out?" Chloe asked.

CHAPTER 32

"I think so," Rachel said. "I was here for the first interview. Of course, it was daylight."

"The people we were following disappeared and I couldn't tell if they turned a corner or just vaporized," Chloe said.

"We have to find the dining room and gym to get out," Rachel said.

"Sounds easy enough," Chloe said.

Before they took another step, a white object appeared from the gloom. With only seconds before impact, both women ducked. A huge shadow flew over them.

"What was that?" Chloe asked.

"Don't panic," Rachel said. "That's the owl who lives here."

"The owl?"

"Yes, it's totally a real owl."

"Okay," Chloe sounded doubtful.

Rachel began to pick up on an unpleasant odor as they neared the gym.

"Do you smell that?" she asked.

"Smell what?" Chloe said.

"You can't? It's so strong," Rachel said.

"Where are you going?" Chloe asked.

"I want to look in the gym."

But a few seconds later she regretted the impulse. There in the middle of the gym floor was a pile of burned bodies. The stench made Rachel gag. She bent over thinking she might lose her dinner. Chloe was right next to her unaffected. Rachel remembered that the gym floor fire was so hot it caused the metal beams of the roof to sag.

"You can't … see it?" Rachel said.

"See what?"

"Never mind. Let's go. I want as far away from here as possible."

Rachel followed the corridor to where she thought a right turn would take them to the front door.

"Turn here," Rachel said. "I think this is the way out."

"You think?"

They crept down the hall with Rachel swinging the torch back and forth much like a blind person would use a white cane.

They were presented with a confusing system of iron-barred doors. Originally it was meant to control access to and from the prison facility from the administration building by slowing the process in and out but tonight they only added to their dilemma.

"Which way?" Chloe asked. "It's like a maze."

"I think we need to keep turning right," Rachel replied.

"I'm about to panic," Chloe said. "This is awful. Why would anyone do something that would land them in prison?"

"You have to wonder," Rachel said.

After they had negotiated the doors, they emerged into a narrow hallway.

"This is the administration building," Rachel said.

"Did anything bad happen here?"

"The inmates broke into the main office and burned records. I don't think anyone was killed here."

"That makes it somewhat better."

Once the women exited the admin offices, they easily found the facility entrance. Standing in the prison parking lot Rachel could sense some of the rage and fear sloughing off her psyche.

"Let's get in the car," Rachel said.

"Try to stop me."

Inside the vehicle, Rachel thought they were not alone.

"I feel your presence," Rachel said.

"Of course you do; I'm right here," Chloe replied.

"Not you. There is someone else in the car."

"Oh shit, you don't mean?" Chloe looked at the back seat and saw nothing.

"Yes."

"I'm sorry for your plight, but you cannot leave with us," Rachel said. "You must stay here or move on, but you can't come with us."

She paused a few seconds.

Chloe turned on the overhead light. Rachel noticed a slight breeze as the spirit left them.

"It's gone," she said. "We can go now."

"Please do," Chloe said with relief. "My days of incarceration are over."

CHAPTER 33

S eeing the blue and purple doors at The Shed felt like coming home. The decorative lights around the door and restaurant façade were welcoming. Rachel felt the weight of the evening falling away as they entered their familiar haunt. Pun intended. They pulled up a stool at the bar and waited as Hector concocted the magic in a glass.

"We've been in a couple of terrifying incidents," Chloe began taking her first sip. "That was the spookiest. Geez, I saw that cell door close along with everyone else."

"But you didn't see the bodies burning?"

"No. Sorry. That's purely your dominion. Sometimes I wish I could see what you see and other times I'm happy to go right on without that kind of insight."

"I'm having that insight right now," Rachel said. "Look around casually Chloe. Tell me if anyone is taking more than a passing interest in us."

Chloe scanned the restaurant from her position at the bar without turning around. She saw no one in the large dining area paying any attention.

"I'm going to make a quick trip to ask the host something inane and check behind us."

In a few moments Chloe returned.

"Yep," she said. "There is a young woman in that small room adjacent to the patio. She has red hair and hasn't stopped looking at you since I saw her. She's alone."

"Okay," Rachel said. "I'll make a trip to the loo and check her out." She turned around to leave, but saw no one at that table.

"She's gone," Rachel said. "Do you think she saw you and got suspicious?"

"Not a chance. I was the epitome of stealth. Who do you think it was?"

"Was she wearing a lot of jewelry, long red hair, looked like she just got off the boat from Ireland?"

"Yes!"

"Sounds like Ozzy Delgado's granddaughter. I'm kind of surprised she isn't in police custody."

"Why?"

"She's a person of interest in her grandfather's death. I guess they don't have enough on her yet for an arrest."

"That's creepy."

"That's the least of it," Rachel said. "Just where do we stand with this mystery?"Rachel settled back onto her bar stool.

"We know two people with connections to the prison riot that occurred more than 40 years ago have been killed," Chloe said.

"While Ozzy Delgado had a direct connection to the prison as a former guard, why was Dr. Kanteena killed? She was only a student of prison reform as a sociology professor. She likely wasn't even born, or very young, when the riot occurred. There is no real tie to the riot."

"Didn't you say she was researching the consequences of incarceration?" Chloe took a sip of her pomegranate margarita and followed it with a chip heavy with salsa.

"Yes, she was," Rachel replied. "If anything she would have come down on the side of the inmates and their families. Why would someone who actually cares about the prison population be a target?"

"Do you have any of her papers?" Chloe asked. "That might give us some understanding."

"Only what was included in the press packet. That might warrant another look and I'll check out some of her published work."

"And maybe we check out her office at the university?" Chloe said conspiratorially.

"No breaking in," Rachel said.

"No, of course not, but we could probably get in during the day. Surely the police are done and they wouldn't have known what to look for."

"Do we know what to look for?" Rachel asked. "The police must have impounded her computer. We'd have to look for notes and research material."

"The third element of this mystery is the skinwalker, or evil witch, who is stalking not only us, but maybe Dave's mother and Iris Phillips," Rachel continued.

"Let's go to the UNM tomorrow and check out Dr. Kanteena's office."

Chloe immediately picked up her phone and texted her office to reschedule her appointments for the next day. She would not miss an opportunity for covert activities.

"You could let Julian and Stella know by texting them," Chloe said. "Maybe it could be viewed as extra research for your story."

"Here, you do it," Rachel said handing her cell to Chloe. "Would you like to watch me text them for future reference?"

"No, but I feel there might be a fourth part to that series, if it's not too bizarre for print."

They clinked their glasses and settled in for another round.

CHAPTER 34

Melinda Delgado Harris opened all the windows that hadn't been painted shut in her grandfather's house. She couldn't get the smell of death out of the air. Once done, she left by the back door and crossed the yard to the shed. It had been her grandfather's domain where he stored yard equipment and worked on home repairs. Since his illness, he hadn't even been able to walk let alone reach the shed.

She had slowly taken a couple of the tools at a time and either sold them or dumped them in trash bins. For her own gardening efforts she had kept a few of the hand implements. Later, she had moved her things out here, things she couldn't leave lying around the house. Melinda liked to think of herself as a practicing Wiccan.

The rug covered the pentagram perfectly. She originally used the pentacle, but decided that she might need protection from bad spirits and negative energies. The walls held other symbols: the Eye of Ra was a shield against evil, fire represented both a creative force and destroyer and the sun sign was her symbol of power. On her grandfather's work bench, she had created an altar. It contained candles, crystals, photos of her parents, Tarot cards and a spell book. Cushions occupied the floor. For inspiration, she included a red and white candle, a decorative pot containing black salt and two crystals: pyrite and tourmalinated quartz.

The shed had one window at the back. Melinda shoved the tall table there and added a planter with the pentacle symbol on the side. In it, she planted wolfsbane. By spring it could be transplanted to her small garden next to the shed. She kept wolfsbane seeds wrapped in lizard skin in a drawer in her bedroom and another in the shed. If she required invisibility this would keep her safe from view.

A blackthorn tree grew next to the shed. Its thorns could be processed into cyanide if drastic measures were required. Her grandfather appreciated her work to make the yard look nicer. He never suspected the real purpose. She'd even hand dug a small flower garden to plant her herbs for spells among the flowers.

Melinda was aware the police suspected her of killing Ozzy. She also knew that an unattended death automatically necessitated an autopsy. That meant she had stay on the down-low until the police finished their investigation and the damn reporter her article. Her rotating hospital schedule made it easy for Melinda to follow Rachel. Ever since her grandfather's interview she had been obsessed with the journalist. She'd read her award-winning story on the looting of natural resources and how she went undercover, was kidnapped and escaped with her life. The woman could research and investigate. Melinda was certain Rachel could discover her secret and put her inheritance at risk.

Sitting on a bar stool, she lit a black candle and a ginger incense stick to perform a "return to sender" spell. It was too early for black magic but she was willing to use it if necessary. There were several lemons in a bowl, she took one and cut it in half. Reputed to absorb negative energies she released its powers into the air. Taking a handful of cloves, she pressed three into each half.

With her eyes closed she chanted: "You can come after me, but you cannot find me. I am invisible. Justice wins."

Blowing out the candle and incense, she took the lemons and shut the door. There was no reason to lock it. To anyone looking, it was a shed like any other storage structure.

She returned to the house. In her bedroom she placed the lemons under her bed. It would cleanse her and the cloves would guard her while she slept.

Melinda showered and climbed into bed. Tomorrow she would begin getting rid of everything that was her grandfather's including all the crappy furniture. She didn't care if she sat on the floor as long as every trace of him was gone. When she inherited whatever bit of estate he had left her, she would renovate or move. Maybe she would dream the best path.

She had slept for mere minutes when awakened by a sound on the roof. Melinda quietly pushed the covers back and trying hard to prevent the ancient mattress from squeaking, padded across her room and locked the door. Sagging to the floor she strained to hear anything. The footsteps on the roof stopped.

For a few minutes there was no sound. Whoever was up there was leaving. She heard the lattice break on the side of the house. The aging trellis supported an old clematis vine her grandfather had planted decades ago. A portion of it had succumbed to someone's weight.

Melinda crawled to her bedroom window and looked out at the backyard. Someone quite large was running behind her shed and disappeared into the gloom.

CHAPTER 35

The next morning, Rachel and Chloe set out for Albuquerque and the University of New Mexico.

"If we're not going to break in, how are we going to do this?" Chloe asked.

"Opportunity," Rachel said. "We'll hang around and wait for any chance to get inside the professor's office."

"Maybe we should have worn disguises," Chloe said. "I've got this great new outfit for nighttime adventures."

"The receptionist hasn't seen you," Rachel said. "Why would you need a disguise?"

"I guess I wouldn't." Disappointed.

Chloe did love a good B and E. Even if it meant being uncomfortable in her high-heeled boots. Rachel chuckled.

"What are you laughing about?"

"Nothing, just something Chile Pod did last night. She is really groovin' in that high-tech kitty bed.

"Here we are," Rachel continued hoping Chloe wouldn't ask. "Traffic on the '25' gets worse every day. But we're on the campus now." She parked and laid her media parking pass on the dash.

"Okay." Chloe said. "Now what?"

"We check out the professor's office and see if anyone is there."

"Is this the building?" Chloe asked.

"Yup, that's it."

"Don't they have a school of architecture here?"

"Yes they do."

"Guess they went with the neoclassical adobe style. Ugh!" Chloe said in disgust.

"It's even better inside," Rachel said. "Kind of post functional."

"So bare bones and no character?"

"See for yourself," Rachel opened the door.

"Her office is on the first floor." Rachel led the way to the last office at the end of the hall."

Chloe looked around the empty space.

"We have this open area here with the windows," Chloe said. "Where's her office?"

"Across from the restrooms," Rachel pointed.

"The hinterland."

"She didn't have a lot of tenure."

"I noticed the windows open but they are awning style and not large enough for a human to crawl through."

"True," Rachel said. "That's why we have to use cunning."

"Do we have that between us?"

"Oh sure," Rachel said lacking confidence. "Here's my plan."

"You have a plan?"

"Yup. I'm going to sit on this bench and I'll signal you when the receptionist comes out. She has already seen me so you will have to sneak in when she leaves the office. I will get her attention while you move in."

"Where am I while you are on the nice hard bench distracting her?"

"In front of the loo door. When I scratch my head, you walk away from the toilet and slip through her office door before it closes. I'm sure it locks behind her so you'll have to be fast."

"So I don't actually go into the crapper?"

"Correct."

"Sounds like a plan that won't work, but I can't come up with anything else so what the hell."

"Thank you for your confidence," Rachel said bowing slightly. "I was up most of the night looking at photos of this building. Remote surveillance."

"Never heard of that."

"Ye of little faith," Rachel said. "Places please. It's nearly lunch. Surely she will leave soon."

"Oh, now we're going Hollywood," Chloe grumbled as she took her position down the hall.

They waited twenty minutes and no one left the office. Rachel walked over to the door and tried the knob. It opened.

"Oh excuse me," she said. "Wrong office."

"No worries," the young woman said. "I'm going to lunch now."

"Say, would you meet me around the corner and point the way to the humanities building?" Rachel asked.

"Sure, I'll be right with you." She picked up her backpack.

Rachel signaled Chloe and kept walking.

Chloe stepped away from the restroom door as the student receptionist hurried to lunch. In a couple of seconds Chloe reached the door and glided inside where she waited in the reception area for Rachel to return.

After the girl gave her directions, Rachel made as to leave. When the student was out of sight, she returned to where Chloe waited.

"I thought you left me," Chloe whined and opened the door.

"I had to make it look like I was headed to the humanities department," Rachel said with phony reproach.

"Okay, okay," Chloe said. "Now what?"

"In there."

Rachel pointed the way to the professor's office. They stepped inside the Kanteena's private office down a short hall.

"It looks like the police were pretty thorough," Rachel said visually checking the desk devoid of any work related papers and closed file drawers. "I'm sure any devices were confiscated and the files, some of which had been left sticking out of drawers, have had a toss."

"Then, what are we looking for?" Chloe asked.

"Anything related to the prison riot," Rachel said. "Research papers, books, notes, that sort of thing."

"I'll check the desk," Chloe began opening drawers and looking at every piece of paper and notebook she found.

Rachel pulled the top drawer of the file cabinet open. She carefully read the tabs which indicated lesson plans for each semester she taught. Nothing related directly to the prison riot but rather on prison administration, planning and employee responsibilities and training. There was a folder on consequences of incarceration. The second drawer down was quite neat so she guessed the police weren't really interested in student conferences. Rachel looked for any student who might have had issues such as violent tendencies or was disruptive in class. She found no red flags. In the bottom drawer were test copies and research papers. None seemed to ring any alarm bells.

"Well, I've come up with nothing," Chloe said. "How long do you suppose she'll be gone for lunch?"

"I'd say we have about 15 minutes left and I've come up with nothing too, but there are the bookshelves to look through. I'll start from this end and we'll meet in the middle."

"What's this?" Chloe said. "Here are two books on the prison riot. One is *The Hate Factory* and the other's called *The Devil's Butcher Shop*." A newspaper clipping fell from the first book.

Rachel picked it up. It was a yellowed obit.

"Geez Chloe," Rachel said. "I think you've found the clue we needed."

Chapter 36

"This looks like it might be a family member of Professor Kanteena's," Rachel said. "Who died in the riot?"

"That might explain why she went into this profession," Chloe said. "But with her death, it may be unresolved."

"True. Time to make our departure," Rachel said.

"It may be too late," Chloe whispered. "I think I heard the key in the door."

"Oh no," Rachel whispered. "Quick, back in reception and sit down."

"What?"

"We don't have a choice. No escaping by window. No other door. Let's move."

When the student intern entered the office, she was surprised to see the two women waiting for her but didn't seem alarmed.

"I thought the door was locked," she said.

"No, we walked right in," Rachel said. "Didn't mean to frighten you. Maybe you remember me from the other day. I was here to interview Professor Kanteena. I had a quick follow up question and thought I'd drop in. This is my intern Chloe."

"Oh yeah," the student said. "But maybe you haven't heard; she died."

"What?" Rachel feigned. "I'm so sorry. You must be devastated."

"It's awful, but I didn't know her very well."

Ah, the indifference of youth. Death seemed so far away it didn't register how final it was.

"Sorry to intrude," Rachel said. "We'll be on our way."

"Oh, that's okay. No big deal."

When they were safely in the car Chloe said, "Lucky she's such a shallow person or we could have been in trouble."

"Yes, she definitely has some things to learn you don't get from books."

"Back to Santa Fe," Rachel added. "Can't wait to get away from here."

Rachel dropped Chloe off at her real estate business and then returned to the High Desert Country offices.

"Hi Stella," Rachel said as she entered the office. Stella was watching her tiny TV as she typed something into her computer. She listened through earplugs so as not to bother the reporters around her. If only most of them were so considerate. Some used earplugs to transcribe and others didn't. At least the noisy clatter of early day newsrooms didn't apply anymore. Computers had solved that, and probably saved the hearing of many a reporter.

"Hi yourself," Stella said. "Julian has some news for you regarding that never ending story you're working on. I hear it's going to four parts."

"Yes. That's what I hear as well."

"Okay then," Rachel said. "He's my first stop."

When she reached Julian's office she stood quietly outside as he finished a phone call. He then waved her in.

"Sit," Jules offered.

"What's up?"

"The autopsy results are in on Mr. Delgado."

"It appears he died from an undetermined poisoning. That could explain the contortions his body went through. It could have caused seizures. He may have fought to breathe as his heart and respiratory system shut down."

"That's dreadful and not at all what I would have thought," Rachel said.

"There's one more thing," Jules said. "The autopsy found a small piece of bone in his shoulder. They think the emergency room must have missed it that night they removed the shot."

"Was it?"

"Yes, it was human," Jules added.

"Geez," Rachel said. "After the experience Chloe and I had on the Navajo Reservation it is not a revelation."

"What experience was that?" Jules asked.

"We were attacked by a skinwalker while driving toward Mexican Water where we stayed," Rachel explained. "It then returned after we had gone to sleep and tried to break in through the roof, we assume to drop corpse powder into the hogan. But the Chee family had covered the roof opening to prevent it. Corpse powder and bone fragments are both tools of the trade for a skinwalker.

"Jules, at one point it sounded exactly like my dad. I almost opened the door. If Chloe hadn't stopped me, I don't know what would have happened."

"That would have sufficed as an invitation, right?" Jules asked.

"Yes. I'm afraid so. If it hadn't been for the mother of a friend who was also staying there, I'm not sure Chloe and I would have survived."

"Who is this friend?"

"His name is Dave Chee; he's a ranger at Bandelier."

"Ah yes, I remember," Jules said. "From the story you did earlier." Jules had a steal trap for a mind. He never forgot her contacts or anyone else's. "And his mother?"

"Her name is Doba Chee. She's lives on both the Navajo reservation and in White Rock. She has, uh, similar abilities to mine only much stronger and refined. She invited us to the reservation to spend the night in the family hogan. I took the rock art drawing with me and she told me it meant death." Rachel took a copy of the email from her jacket pocket and gave it to Jules.

"I can see how that could easily be interpreted as death. It came by the same means as the first one?"

"Stella found it in the main office email."

"She mentioned you received another one. Anything more?" he asked.

"I've got another piece of the puzzle for you, if you can make it fit," Jules said. "The Española police sent the fireplace sample from Mrs. Phillips house to the Albuquerque lab. It has tested positive for human remains. I'm assuming corpse power?"

"I'd bet on it," Rachel replied.

"You feel this is all connected with the prison riot you're covering?"

"Yes," Rachel replied. "My first sighting of the shadow people was at the prison on the original tour. Since then, it's compounded with further sightings and ever growing threats."

"What about the UNM professor? Any word on what caused her death?"

"So far, without conclusive results," Jules said. "It looks like a perfectly healthy late thirties woman just died while taking a walk in the Bosque. We'll know soon what the ME comes up with."

"I'm betting on respiratory failure," Rachel said.

"I'm assuming Mrs. Phillips knows about what they found in her fireplace?" Rachel said. "Or should I call her again?"

"It's a police matter now," Jules said. "But that still leaves your Mr. Pacheco and Mr. Delgado's granddaughter. Again, the police are keeping track of her. So no official contact with her."

"How about an unofficial contact to warn her?" Rachel asked.

"Totally on your own time," Jules said. "Can't stop you. And she may need a heads up." He winked.

"Thanks for the update," Jules said. "And be careful as you wrap up this story. Too many people have died already. Proceed with extreme caution. You have that cell phone charged and turned on?"

"Yes," Rachel said reluctantly. "As ordered."

"Requested," Jules said with fatherly concern.

"I'll be careful," Rachel said. "No more interviews. I won't put anyone else at risk now that we know this is all connected. The people in charge of the prison at the time of the riot are either deceased or not talking anyway. So I'll add some of my research with the interview done with the professor."

But once outside in the parking lot, she felt an urgency to speak with Melinda Delgado. Things didn't feel right.

It was a short trip to the Delgado residence. Rachel took Agua Fria. It was only a few blocks from the street that was home to the magazine office. It's a mix of older domiciles and newly built modern condos with no historical elements. She pulled into the drive and turned off the car. The quiet consumed her. The house appeared unoccupied as she observed it from the walk. The drapes were closed and there was no car in the drive.

With no answer at the door, Rachel went around the side of the house to look in the backyard. It wasn't difficult because the privacy fence offered no privacy at all. The gate hung open from one hinge. There were so many broken pickets that not even a dog could be kept in. But then again, she didn't see a dog or any bowls.

Stepping through the open gate, there was a large cottonwood tree with a chaise longue and lawn chair beneath it. A table had toppled over onto the ground. In the far corner stood a shed. A much younger tree, a species she didn't know, grew next to it. Among the dried up mums that grew next to the shed, Rachel recognized lavender and rosemary. There were several other plants that had succumbed to November freezes. Crumpled sage leaves lay on the ground among spent yarrow blossoms. She didn't suspect their purpose.

Rachel knocked on the shed door. It seemed the courteous thing to do, but no response. She looked back at the house. It appeared achingly vacant. If she didn't know Melinda lived there she would think it abandoned. Knowing she shouldn't, Rachel opened the door a smidgeon. It was not at all what she expected. Instead of tools and clutter, it was decked out as a witchcraft workshop. She saw symbols, tarot cards and black and white candles on the workbench.

She stepped inside while chastising herself for breaking and entering once again. Of course, she hadn't really broken into it, the door was unlocked.

The interior was lovingly done as though a refuge from illness and decay. Rachel could appreciate the time and effort Melinda must have put into making this a comforting place for herself. Just outside the edge of the rug, black electrical tape had been applied to the floor. Curious, Rachel lifted the rug and gasped as the pentagram came into view. What was going on here? Why was Melinda practicing witchcraft? The hair on her neck prickled and a chill came over her. Rachel regretted coming by. Her suspicions that Melinda was up to no good might be playing out in real time. In the corner next to the door was a baseball bat that Rachel assumed was for self-defense.

There was a jingle outside she couldn't place, but she was no longer alone and there was no place to go.

"What are you doing here?" Melinda stood in the doorway and she was not happy.

CHAPTER 37

"Hi," Rachel said. "I came by to caution you about ... "

"Caution me!" Melinda nearly roared. "What the hell are you doing in here?"

"Fair enough question," Rachel said. "I came here to warn you. Two of my interviews regarding the prison riot have died, including your grandfather. We are concerned about your welfare."

"Aren't you thoughtful," Melinda's voice oozed sarcasm. She even mimicked a southern accent. "Thinking of little ol' me."

"Despite what you think, that is why I'm here," Rachel said. "It appears your grandfather and the death of a professor at the UNM may be related to the story we have published. We don't want anyone else in jeopardy."

"Get out!" Melinda shouted. "You have no right here."

"I agree with you." Rachel kept an eye on Melinda's rapidly growing anger. "You've done a lovely job in here."

"Out!"

Rachel slipped in front of her realizing the jingle she heard was from all the necklaces Melinda was wearing, but she couldn't remember why that was significant.

"And don't come back!"

Rachel made a quick retreat. She was afraid Melinda would pick up that baseball bat and swing at her. However uncomfortable, Rachel felt she'd learned Melinda could be violent if she wanted, both physically and through black magic. She would exercise extreme caution when it came to this young woman. There was no telling how far this disturbed person might go.

Rachel didn't see Melinda light the black candle as she left by way of the broken fence.

"I'll show her," Melinda muttered to herself. The flame burned tall and steady. "She doesn't know who she's messing with. I banish you, Rachel Blackstone, from my life. And may you experience misfortune."

As she stood appreciating the perfect flame a hissing sound floated around the shed interior.

Melinda smiled. "The spirits are nearby."

CHAPTER 38

Ernesto Pacheco arrived at Old Main to conduct a tour. This was not his usual tour, but one he had been asked to do for students of criminology. They were studying the emotional effects of incarceration and how prison riots evolve. He dreaded it because Cellblock 4 would need to be included.

His group was young but eager to learn. Most were men, but there were two women. They asked appropriate questions as he led them through. He pointed out the administration offices where records were burned, took them to Dormitory E where the riot began.

In his description he included how overcrowding works on people's minds and mixing of harden criminals with nonviolent offenders can turn into the nightmare that became reality at the Santa Fe Penitentiary. Some in the group took notes and a couple of students recorded his words.

They followed Pacheco to the gym where he described the heat of the fire that buckled steel support beams in the ceiling.

In the dining area he reiterated that inmates should not be mixed because of the gang behavior that resulted in fear and intimidation.

He showed them the control room.

"It took rioting inmates about three to five minutes to break into the control center," he said.

A student asked, "Weren't the panes bulletproof?"

"Although the windows were considered bulletproof, a fire extinguisher took out the glass in three strikes," Pacheco replied. "Anarchy prevailed."

Pacheco made his way to Cellblock Four. He turned to face his group.

"We know there is a kind of dark tourism present in some of the people who come visit here. We must not lose sight of the fact this is where 16 of the 33 human beings were slaughtered. Yes, they were serving sentences, but their sentence was not the death penalty," Pacheco said. "Most of those killed here were in protective custody. All those who were murdered were under the age of 40; one was nineteen. Those who killed them essentially got away with it.

"Now, no photos are allowed in this cellblock. Those of you with cell phones – likely all of you – are prohibited from taking any photos. Understood?"

Everyone nodded.

As he approached the cellblock, Pacheco felt the fury and horror he always sensed in this area of the prison. He tried to push it away and continue the tour.

"These marks you see here," he pointed to the floor. "It is generally accepted that a man was decapitated here."

There was a shared gasp from the students. Several involuntarily placed their hands across their mouths in shock.

"This portion of the floor with burns is that of an inmate who was immolated," Pacheco continued trying not to dwell too long on the information.

"Geez," said one of the women in horror.

A male student fled from the tour overwhelmed by something he couldn't understand.

"Imagine you are in custody for forgery or embezzlement," Pacheco said. "Yes, they are crimes, but they're white collar and no one was physically hurt or killed. Now, you're in the safest place in the prison where the most trusted inmates are allowed some privileges and your fellow cellmates are not likely to hurt you.

Pacheco evaluated the weight of his words on his students. These *kids* probably wanted to go into criminology to help the victims and punish the bad guys. But this was another level.

"Some of these inmates were child molesters in protective custody," Pacheco said. "That's truly evil, but many were not. Others were snitches, helping the police and going to testify in court. The inmates watched in horror as the rioters used blowtorches to cut the bars. Imagine how they must have felt knowing what their fate would be in only minutes.

"Your job will be a lot bigger than you may know," Pacheco continued. "There is more to incarceration than locking up and throwing away the key. I know some of the professors at UNM who teach your classes. This tour was important to them because it reinforces the lectures and textbook studies. Not everything you learn is found in a classroom. Riots are a reality in prisons. It only takes a few seconds of inattentiveness and things go wrong fast. It almost happened again in Grants in 2020.

"This cellblock was a nightmare when lawmen finally entered. It was a mess of ripped mattresses, scattered belongings, water from broken toilets, blood and bodies. This is sacred ground."

The students had become very quiet as the reality of a prison gone wrong settled into their consciousness.

Pacheco invited them to step inside the cellblock, but he didn't want to. Most of the students entered and seemed completely unaware of all the commotion he was seeing. Vast numbers of shadow people filled the confinement area. Occasionally, one of the students would rub their neck as if someone had touched them, but no one seemed truly aware of what caused it. The shadows swarmed back and forth even uttering tortured screams. He wanted to cover his ears but knew he would look ridiculous and no one would understand. So he stood back and hoped the students got their fill quickly.

Pacheco felt sick. It was time to go.

For a moment he stepped inside to let them know the tour was ending.

"Come on folks," he said. "Time to move on."

He felt his feet slip beneath him and he landed on the floor his hands barely caught him. It was as if a rope had been tied to his legs and yanked.

Two students rushed to help him up.

"Hey man, are you okay?" A tall thin man in his twenties asked.

"We have to leave," Pacheco fairly croaked the words out once he was standing. His voice sounded hoarse, foreign.

Before he could step out of the cellblock into the hall, he was impacted again. It felt like he'd been hit by a linebacker. This time he was thrown flat onto the floor, his breath blasted from his lungs.

"Drag me into the hall," he asked the two men.

Once he was in relative safety, he stood with assistance and instructed the group to go down the hall and out of the building.

"I have to lock up," he lied. He needed them gone because he knew the witch was still there. And it was close, practically breathing down his neck. He could smell the putrid odor. It was so strong he couldn't believe the students hadn't detected it. They likely thought he was an old fool who couldn't stay upright. He watched the group file down the hallway and turn to leave Old Main. When the last one was out of sight, he took a breath, pulled out his arrowhead and turned to face the ogre.

CHAPTER 39

It was enormous, towering over Pacheco by several feet. Devoid of clothing it stood on two legs with wolf fur covering its body. Heavy jewelry hung around the neck. His experience with evil witches included running alongside his vehicle taunting him, but he'd always been able to get to safety. This time, someone in spirit had invited it into Cellblock Four. There would be no getting away and Pacheco was mortally threatened by this witch.

He avoided looking at the eyes which would be difficult anyway given how tall the creature was. Backing away a few steps he could see the ashen coloring of the skin. The wolf's lifeless head rested on top of the witch's head, mouth open, and fangs at ready. He'd heard these witches carried a stench. There was no mistaking the odor of the body it wore. But there was something else, a faint sweet odor, almost like fragrance. He couldn't discern aftershave from perfume and maybe he was wrong. It surprised him that such insignificant thoughts intruded into the unfolding horror. He held the arrowhead and hoped it would save his life.

The witch walked backward awkwardly as if it was unused to using only two feet. Its knees were bent like a child with rickets. All its joints seemed swollen and misshapen. The arms were too long, the legs too short. The claws looked lethal. But the dead wolf's front legs hung limply – useless.

"I will not kill you today," it said.

Pacheco staggered back. He was wary. He did not trust the words. The voice was otherworldly, as if being distorted technically.

"Tell your journo friend she must stop or you will both pay for it with your lives."

"Stop what?" he asked wanting to be sure.

"Stop investigating the prison riot," it said. "There are things best left undiscovered. Retribution will follow if the dead are resurrected or disturbed. I will not tolerate it further."

Despite the altered voice, the witch was well-spoken. Pacheco wondered if that was noteworthy.

"Have I made myself clear?" It reminded him of something his mother had said to him as a boy. In fact, it was his mother's voice he was hearing.

"Yes," Pacheco said. He had to fight with himself not to call out to his mother. It was not her, but a witch's incantation.

It drew close and leaned its full body over him. He closed his eyes and mentally crossed himself as he was unable to move. The snarling fangs hovered near his head, dripping saliva with anticipation. Pacheco had never been so frightened, certain the promise not to kill him was a ruse.

"You *will* convey that message?" It was a command, not really a question.

Pacheco nodded.

"If you do not, I will know. You should have your advance directive in order."

"Yes. I will tell the reporter."

It was gone. The hallway at the prison was vacant of people and spirits. Message received.

He stopped by the main office where he had a locker. His jacket and a medicine bag containing several protective crystals and two arrowheads were inside. He quickly scrawled a note stating he must return to the rez for a family issue and wouldn't be returning. He added a thank you for the volunteer opportunity they had given him and left it behind the front desk.

Pacheco fled the prison. When he was safely inside his car he said loudly: "Go away!"

They did not leave. Spirits swooped inside his car until it was packed with them.

Pacheco tried not to panic, but he couldn't allow the shadow people to follow him. He fumbled around in his glove compartment and found the sage bundle he was looking for, lit it and cleansed the interior of the car. Once satisfied they were gone, he backed out of the space.

As he pulled out of the parking lot he was aware of them watching him leave.

CHAPTER 40

Rachel was surprised the next morning when Stella buzzed her. She had planned on writing quietly in her office where she had gathered her research and transcribed the professor's interview.

"Ms. Blackstone, Mr. Pacheco is here to see you," Stella said in her best professional voice, smooth as honey.

"I'll be right down."

"Mr. Pacheco," Rachel reached out a hand. "Would you like to come into our conference room?"

He hesitated. "This might be a conversation better had in the outdoors."

"Okay," Rachel said. He looked so serious a knot formed in her stomach.

"Before you go," Stella said. "You might want Mr. Pacheco to have a look at this. I just printed it off of our main email."

"Another Proton email?"

"I'm afraid so."

"Thanks Stella."

Rachel took the sheet of paper dreading to look at it.

She grabbed her coat off the hook in reception and opened the front door. He insisted she go first, ever the gentlemen.

"We have a bench outside," Rachel said. "Our publisher made this a nice area to relax in but we almost never have a chance to utilize it.

"What has brought you here today?" she asked.

"Let's take a look at what you received first," he said.

The pictograph was of two stick-like people, knees bent, brandishing swords and shields. The caption read: "Are you ready?"

"That's the symbol for combat," Pacheco said.

"Combat?" Rachel said. "As in battle? Why would there be fighting?"

"It could be a metaphor," he said. "You should take this seriously. Sadly, there is more.

"I was doing another tour at Old Main. This was a student group studying criminology and wanting to learn how to avoid riots. Of course, they wanted to see Cellblock 4 so I was told to accommodate them."

"What happened?" Rachel asked. "You look shaken."

"When we reached Cellblock 4 I could feel, practically breathe the rage and fear. I stepped inside to tell them it was time to leave. I was literally knocked off my feet in front of these people who had no idea what was going on. They looked at me like I was crazy. Someone helped me up. As soon as I steadied myself, I was attacked, thrown on the floor. I couldn't hide my fear.

"There were shadow people all over. The horror those inmates suffered permeated my soul. I felt each of them all at once. Their cries for their mothers, pleading for their lives and the shocking realization they would not survive. Members of the tour drug me into the hallway. I told them to leave the prison.

"And then, the witch appeared. This is where you come in," he said.

"Me?" Rachel could see the alarm on his face. His breath came in short spurts. His eyes darted about as if fearing it would appear again.

"The witch told me in no uncertain terms that you are to stop the investigation of the prison riot and to go no further in telling the story," he whispered as if someone was eavesdropping. "Rachel, it will kill us if we have anything further to do with this."

"Good god," Rachel said.

"The spirits inside those walls followed me outside. I had to sage my car before I could even leave the parking lot. No way were they going home with me.

"I'm here to warn you," he continued. "You must stop exploring this massacre and let it go for your own safety and those you care about. This witch has so much power accumulated over 43 years. That's a lot of years to build strength and plan revenge."

"Did you notice an odor?" Rachel asked.

"Yes. Putrid with a hint of something sweet. I suppose it could be aftershave.

"One thing I'm certain of, this person wanted this badly or they couldn't have become a witch. Imagine what it had to do to become this ogre: killing a family member, killing and skinning the animal and preparing corpse powder from the body of their former loved one. It's gruesome. But this individual did it. That's a lot of motivation.

"One more thing," Pacheco said. "This entity is well-spoken. Maybe educated. Maybe a long-time reader."

"I don't know what to say," Rachel replied. "We've only have one more installment of this four-part story. I don't think my publisher will back down."

"He has to," Pacheco said. "No story is worth dying. And I believe it will come for your boss, other people who work here, your friends. It will not stop. There is something it wants to hide; someone it wants to protect or perhaps it's all about revenge.

"Are you wearing the arrowhead?" Pacheco continued.

"Yes." Rachel pulled it out of her shirt to show him.

"Good," he said. "I'm going back to the reservation for awhile. My people believe these things are real. I won't be an outcast by speaking about my fear or knowing they exist."

"Please take care of yourself," Rachel reached for his hand and held it a moment. "Thank you for coming here and telling me."

"It's not just information I'm imparting," he said. "It is a dire warning. Don't write another word about this story. It could kill us both."

He squeezed her hand quickly and left.

CHAPTER 41

Rachel felt numb as she slowly walked back to her office. This had suddenly become very personal. She kept walking until she came to Julian's office.

"Hey," he said. "Come. Sit."

She told him about her conversation with Ernesto.

"Jesus," Jules rubbed at this beard. "I've never backed down from a story. You do that once and it never stops. That's not how good journalism works.

"But there are lives at stake," he added."

"When this began I had a visit from Skeleton Man," Rachel said.

"Whoa. Remind me who that is," Jules said. "I can keep up with your human contacts but the spiritual ones are more challenging."

"I'm beginning to get used to talking about spiritual entities," Rachel said. "I must be going over the edge.

"To answer your question, Skeleton Man is also known as Másaw, the Hopi Lord of the Dead. He told me I must see this journey to its end. He also told me to 'Beware the *wùuti.*' I looked it up on my phone – yes, I can do that," she said hoping to add a speck of levity to a frightening situation.

"I said nothing." He held up both hands, fingers spread.

"*Wùuti* means woman in Hopi," she said. "Mr. Pacheco told me he picked up a fragrance from the witch when he confronted it at Old Main. But he couldn't be sure. They are so odiferous it's difficult to sort odors and identify them."

"There weren't any women inside the prison the night of the riot if I remember correctly," Jules said. "Not until the National Guard sent in a MASH unit."

"My research supports that too," Rachel said. "That leaves us in the dark. I've no idea which *wùuti* Skeleton Man was referring to."

"Are you staying with Chloe?" Jules asked.

"Yes, Chile Pod and I have been there since this came up."

"Good, continue. I feel better if you're there. From what you've told me, the place is a fortress and should protect you from most anything."

"With the exception of those who do not walk the earthly plane," Rachel said. "I don't always know with whom I'm speaking. They could be from the astral plane. Even weirder, they could someone who has passed or is yet to be born. Thus far, I've only known the deceased souls."

"That's creepy enough," Jules said. "I can't intellectualize either way. But I saw some of what happened at Tent Rocks that night to have some idea of what you're up against."

Jules referred to the night Rachel rescued her brother from Mario, the evil spirit she had accidently returned. She had taken control of a storm with the Hopi shaman's help and saved her brother, Jules and herself.

"You're also driving Chloe's car?"

"Yes."

"Ask her if you can continue. Leave that gas-guzzler in the garage for the time being. People know that car. The one you're driving now isn't associated with you."

"I take it we're completing the story?" Rachel asked. "And the Merc is waiting on parts at Juan's Auto Casa."

"Head down," Jules said. "Work on the last piece at Chloe's. Move all manuscripts and research you have onto another computer – I'll give you one out of supplies. Keep all other assignments on your normal work computer. We'll wait this out. Your assignments will be on other stories for the moment. For all intents and purposes it will appear as if we've moved on. And then, we see what happens."

"What about Ernesto Pacheco? It threatened to kill him too."

"Two good things: he's on the Hopi reservation in the safety of his people and he is aware of what is needed to stay safe. He has a talisman I assume?"

"Yes."

"Can you procure arrowheads for the rest of us? I want one for everyone who works here. And you should have one for Chloe. I'd leave one in both houses as well."

"We've gridded both my house and Chloe's with protective stones in each corner. I've also done my office here."

"That's good. Okay, as soon as we have the stones, we can proceed."

"I'll stop by Mari-Lynn Alo's shop on the way home," Rachel said.

When she walked into Chrysalis, she seemed to be expected. Mari-Lynn looked up without surprise as Rachel entered the shop and waved her over to the glass counter. As usual Mari-Lynn was swaddled in gauze fabric that appeared animated with her every move. Today, it was pale yellow accented with sage green. Rachel didn't know if Mari-Lynn draped the fabric herself or if the dresses were made that way. But she was always stunning with minimal makeup and flowing silver hair. An obsidian arrowhead with embedded turquoise hung from a gold chain around her neck. The chain was wrapped and crossed the arrowhead in the shape of a triangle perfectly encasing the polished round turquoise piece. The color of the stone picked up the green from her dress but Rachel thought it was not there as a fashion accoutrement.

"That's a handsome amulet," Rachel said.

"I heard there was an evil witch about and I always want to be prepared," Mari-Lynn replied.

"Then I'm guessing you know why I'm here?" Rachel asked.

"I had a bit of a vision," Mari-Lynn said. "It prompted me to overnight obsidian arrowheads and protective stones. Was I right?"

"Yes," Rachel said. "I trust your insights more than my own. What was your vision?"

"I was at home yesterday putting up Christmas decorations, yes I know, a bit early. As I reached up to place a string of lights I felt the lights drop away and I was holding a sword. Mind you, I nearly fell off the ladder. Once safely on the ground I noticed my other hand was gripping a shield. These were of an early origin, maybe as ancient as the Ancestral Puebloans."

"Geez, Mari-Lynn, what happened?"

"I experienced a rerun of sorts; a vision I had earlier. There was fabric or something floating all around me. It was white and red. There were rods in the vision. They streaked in front of me. This symbol was new. I'm sorry, I couldn't tell what it was, but the dread that accompanied it was palpable. My feeling is something truly horrific is going to happen."

"Any idea what?" Rachel asked.

"If only we knew," Mari-Lynn said.

"I appreciate the heads-up and for listening to your intuition telling you we would need these." Rachel pointed to the amulets.

"I hope I have the correct number of arrowheads."

Rachel counted each staff member from the office, added one each for Chloe.

"Perfect," she said. "Why is this one different?"

"This is for your baby, Chile Pod. I used my buffing tools and rounded all the edges so she can't hurt herself. You can tie it onto a harness or collar and she will be protected too. Both of our cats are sporting them currently. And I got one of these for Celeste too." Mari-Lynn pointed to her necklace.

"Thank you Mari-Lynn for thinking of my Pod girl. And yes, I have a harness for her and she will be wearing it with the arrowhead this evening.

"Get this," Rachel said conspiratorially. "This is an office expense. Jules decked me out with the office credit card." Rachel slapped in on the counter.

"Well," Mari-Lynn said slyly. "Has the big guy come around?" She referred to Julian.

"Indeed, it would appear so," Rachel said.

Mari-Lynn ran the sale and came around the counter with one of her elegant bags. A monarch flew in bright orange and yellow across the recycled paper. Rachel gave her a hug and took the amulets.

She returned to the office and dropped off the bag of arrowheads and stones. Stella was composed as usual. It was difficult to bewilder her.

"I'll leave it to Julian to inform the troops," Stella said with a wink.

"I'd like to be here," Rachel said. "But I've got two houses to protect."

Before returning to Chloe's, Rachel stopped by her house. Since most of her visitors first made their appearance outside her kitchen window, she placed the arrowhead on her dining table. Then, she made sure her house was still gridded with protective stones. Everything in place, she left for Chloe's.

When she parked the car in the garage, Chloe met her.

"You're home early?" she said. "And you have that look of trepidation. What's up?"

"We need to check your protective grid is in place. But first, we need to get you and Chile Pod decked out with these arrowheads."

Chile Pod strolled into the kitchen, having heard her person mention her name.

"Hey little girl," Rachel said. "We need a wardrobe update."

Chloe handed her the tortie's harness, having pulled it out of the kitchen cabinet where she kept the cat food and treats.

Rachel affixed the charm onto the back strap and buckled the harness onto the cat.

"There. Protected from whatever lurks around," Rachel said.

Chile Pod shook her body as if she had taken a dip in the sink, but could not dislodge the amulet. With a shrug, she began eating the canned food offering Rachel gave her.

"I have an arrowhead for you too," Rachel said. "You must wear it on your person at all times. If you don't have a chain, I used yarn for mine." She pulled it from inside her shirt to show Chloe.

"Things have gotten that serious?" Chloe said. "I'm in danger too?"

Rachel told her friend about the encounter Ernesto had at Old Main with the criminology class. She listened while she fitted her arrowhead with a length of black yarn.

"Fragrance?" Chloe asked. "Could it be female?"

"Skeleton Man hinted at that when we spoke, and Ernesto seems to have confirmed it."

"And you have a new computer?" Chloe nodded to the laptop Rachel had placed on the kitchen counter.

"Jules wants me to use this one for writing the prison story. He wants to make to appear I'm working on other things."

"That sounds like a good plan," Chloe said. "But you are going to finish the fourth installment?"

"Yes, but pub date to be determined."

"Who do you suspect to be the skinwalker?" Chloe asked.

"There are only three women involved in the story and one is already dead. That leaves the pharmacist in Española whose son killed himself and the granddaughter of Ozzy Delgado. Ozzy died under suspicious circumstances.

"I went snooping the other day and found a witch's haven in her backyard. There was a pentagram on the floor and black candles."

"That could mean she might deal in black magic?" Chloe asked.

"Yes, I think so."

"And therefore, she might also participate in evil witchery?"

"Possibly."

"What about the other woman, the pharmacist?"

"Iris Phillips does wear an ample amount of jewelry, like Melinda Harris Delgado.

"Is that a thing? The jewelry?" Chloe asked.

"Yes, skinwalkers tend to wear many strands of necklaces.

"According to Jules, powdered human remains or corpse powder was found in her fireplace after a night visitor stamped about on her roof," Rachel continued. "She reported the incident to the Española police. They took a sample of the fine particles from her fireplace and had it tested at the Santa Fe police lab."

"How disturbing," Chloe said.

"What about the professor?" Chloe asked.

"No cause of death yet," Rachel said. "But I'd bet on the wild thing."

There's something else." Rachel unfolded the email with the rock art. "We received this at the office today." She spread it out on the counter.

"Looks like two guys fighting," Chloe said.

"Yes. Ernesto said it means combat."

"Who would be fighting?" Chloe asked.

"I expect it will become apparent," Rachel said.

Chapter 42

"I have a confession of sorts," Rachel said while she and Chloe were having a bit of port after dinner."

"A confession? I'm all ears." Chloe leaned forward across the table. "This is a new experience."

"I can't get the bed flat. I've been sleeping on the floor. There I've said it." Rachel was truly annoyed to admit it, but the bed app had totally bamboozled her.

"Why didn't you just ask for help?" Chloe said suppressing a giggle.

"Because it was so kind of you to get us that space-age bed and well ... "

"Come on girls," Chloe said. "Let's go wrangle that bed."

Chile Pod trotted down the hall in front of them and jumped up on the bed. She snuggled into her yurt as if to say, "See, I don't have any trouble with it."

"Traitor," Rachel grumbled.

"You've been sleeping on the floor since you began staying here?"

"I'm afraid so." Rachel shook her head.

"Okay, give me your phone." Chloe pointed the phone at the bed, pushed buttons until it was flat, turned off the color therapy and the vibration.

"Would you like the TV off too?" Chloe burst out laughing but tried to cover with her hand. It was no good. Her body shook.

"That would be nice." Rachel was humbled. She could fight off evil entities but couldn't control a techie bed. Ouch.

"I can't believe you have slept in here with all … this! Wait here. I'll be right back."

In a few minutes Chloe reappeared with her joint box.

"Let's adjourn to your *portal*," she said.

Each of Chloe's bedrooms, Rachel thought there were four but had never been certain, were equipped with their own bath and *portal* or porch. A pony wall made of adobe bricks, stuccoed and painted one of the Santa Fe approved colors of brown surrounded the outdoor space and made for a great footrest. When they had relaxed into thick cushioned chairs and put up their feet, Chloe said: "I think this calls for a medium-sized joint. Do you agree?"

"Yeah, I do." Rachel felt defeated, and in front of her friend.

Chloe lit the joint, took a hit and handed it to Rachel.

"This is the good stuff," Chloe said reverting to her hippy lingo. "Celeste at New Harvest has the best. We shouldn't have to face our problems head-on. We need a little help from our friends now and then."

"Thanks for fixing the bed," Rachel said.

"Anytime girlfriend." Chloe reached across and hooked her pinky in Rachel's for a few seconds. "Friends forever."

"As long as there is no blood-letting." Rachel took another draw.

* * *

Rachel woke to Chile Pod repeatedly tapping her nose with her paw.

"What's up sweetie?" She could just make out the tiny tortie standing on her chest urging her awake. Chile Pod looked up toward the ceiling. Rachel followed with her eyes. A few seconds later, Rachel heard what the Pod girl heard: Someone was on the roof!

"Holy Shit," Rachel muttered. "What now?"

"Chile. Hide." The cat knew the word and scampered across the room to burrow into the pile of pillows Rachel had tossed on the floor. Once under them, she peeked out to get approval.

"Good girl," Rachel said. "Stay until I get back." Chile's colorful face disappeared into the pillows.

Rachel walked down the hallway to Chloe's room and knocked on her door.

"Come in," Chloe said sleepily.

"Sorry to wake you," Rachel said. "We have company."

"Oh shit. You mean ... "

"Yes, someone is on the roof. I'm glad we checked your house grid. But did we close all the dampers in the fireplaces?"

"No, we used the one in the kitchen last evening!"

Rachel began running down the dark hall, through the dining room knocking over a chair and leaving it lie. Chloe closed in behind her. In the kitchen, they scrambled past the counter losing one wine glass to the floor. Next to the *banco* surrounding the table was the *kiva* fireplace.

"I hear something," Chloe said. "Is it banging on the chimney?"

"At the very least," Rachel replied. "I suspect it wants us to hear."

Chloe yanked off the screen and Rachel reached for the damper pull. It resisted at first and then gave way.

"Now it can't toss anything into the fire box," Rachel said.

"What's it doing now?" Chloe whispered as scratching sounds filtered down the chimney."

"I think trying to take off the chimney cap."

"What should we do?" Chloe asked. "Call the police?"

"Oh, I can just hear this emergency call," Rachel whispered. "Mr. Policeman, there is an evil witch on our roof. Please help."

"Okay, okay," Chloe said.

"I want to say, stay inside where it's safe. If it's the skinwalker, they can't come in unless you invite them. But I'd like to see who is up there: male, female or monster?"

"Oh no Rachel! You really don't mean to go out there?"

"I have my protective amulet; I should be okay."

"My gun is in my room," Chloe said. "Do you want it?"

"You have a gun?" Rachel was incredulous. Chloe had always been anti-gun, even marching in the Plaza to protest.

"Only recently," Chloe said. "It's not an AR-15, just a small revolver, not even automatic."

"I'll pass," Rachel said. "I'm going out the front door and around."

"How can I help?"

"Stay inside," Rachel said. "I'm not going to introduce myself, just see if I can identify it."

"Rachel, if you've never been careful before, this is the time to do so."

"I'll be right back."

Chloe checked the viewer and let Rachel soundlessly out the door. The front *portal* was larger than the others. It looked welcoming with comfy chairs and large flower pots full of pansies. There was a rain barrel at both ends of the porch to catch the precious liquid from the roof.

Rachel took the path for a few strides. Once off the path, she stood on gravel. Chloe's property was xeriscaped meaning much of the yard sported various colors of gravel with native plants sandwiched in. Especially charming in the summer when the lavender bloomed and the bees buzzed it all day. Although good for the environment, xeriscaping was quite noisy to walk on. Every step meant stone grinding against stone.

"This was stupid," she mumbled to herself and turned to go back. The door looked like safety. She wanted to run for the house because the shadow on the roof had noticed her. It seemed to have given up on the chimney cap and was looking directly at her standing exposed in the moonlight. Rachel started for the house, but stopped in her tracks when she heard the plaintive meow.

"What is she doing outside? Oh my god," Rachel whimpered.

"Chile, where are you?"

Rachel heard another distressed meow. Where was she?

"Chile Pod, come to me." Rachel cried loudly, no longer caring about the witch.

"Rachel," Chloe called from the door. "What's going on?"

"Chile is outside," Rachel croaked as she fought back tears. "I've got to find her. How did she get out?"

"Come back," Chloe yelled. "I'll go look for Chile. There's no way she is outside." Chloe disappeared inside the house.

Rachel struggled to reach the door, finding she could barely move, but determined to get back inside. Each step was a struggle. Her legs were heavy and didn't want to cooperate. She realized it must be the skinwalker pulling her strings. With effort, she pulled the arrowhead from inside her shirt. Each inch was a triumph as she held it up in front of her face in the direction of the roof. The creature stood on four feet on the roof, but when it felt the power of the arrowhead it cowered.

"Go!" she screamed but it came out garbled. It was enough. The witch changed form from a four-legged wolf-like creature into a hawk. It screeched as it flew away, taunting her.

"Rachel!" It was Chloe. "I have Chile. See, she's in my arms. She's okay."

Rachel raced to the door and lifted Chile Pod from Chloe's arms to hers where she cradled the furry bundle like she was as valuable as the Hope Diamond.

"It was the skinwalker again, wasn't it?" Chloe asked.

"Yes, and I fell for it again."

CHAPTER 43

It was a sunny morning in November. Mari-Lynn was working in her garden. She planted her crops much like the Ancestral Puebloans growing the Three Sisters: corn, beans and squash. It was late for her to be putting her garden to bed. She had pulled the dead corn stalks and the vines of the other crops, chopped them and laid them on the ground. Today she was turning them into the earth where their decaying matter would replenish her soil for spring planting.

She raised her head at the sound. It reminded her of growling dogs. Sometimes feral dogs ran in packs and could kill other animals and on occasion, people. She scanned her property but there was no one around. Mari-Lynn returned to her shovel.

This time the growling was more urgent. Her head pounded. She dropped the shovel and fled to her porch. Winded from the short sprint she sat down heavily on the upper step. A vision had never been this painful before. She braced herself for what was coming.

The air swirled around her, the constant growling became wind. Momentarily, she thought it was simply the vision, but then she saw the chamisa waving as if a high mountain windstorm had moved in. Her hair lost its ribbon and tumbled on the ground. She swept her hair back from her face to see more clearly. The white and red bits were back churning all around her. This time the rods were accompanied by round objects. They were so real; she ducked several times to avoid being hit, but they passed right through her.

As she watched, the rods assembled into bars that formed cages. At first they were empty, but one by one they filled with animals. Unrecognizable. The animals or perhaps humans appeared distorted and vaguely outlined without color or substance.

It wasn't just the things seen; she felt fear – fear for her life. She recoiled at a repulsive scent in the air. It was rancid, not quite that of decay, but a sickening odor she couldn't identify.

There were so many emotions coming at her, she couldn't sort them. Mari-Lynn fought them off with her hands, pushing them away: fear, disgust, confusion, surprise.

Before Mari-Lynn could see more, it all swam into a vortex and drained from her sight. She shook from what she'd seen – or hadn't seen. This was the most vivid of the evolving vision and the most frightening.

When it ended, she stood on shaky legs. Once inside she called Rachel.

Her message was short: "It is closing in. We must talk. Bring Chloe."

* * *

Two hours later Rachel and Chloe met with Mari-Lynn at Cathedral Park next to the Cathedral Basilica of St. Francis of Assisi in downtown Santa Fe. They sat on concrete flower barriers around the Settlers Monument. It marked the 400th anniversary of Europeans establishing the first permanent settlement.

Not everyone agreed this was a good thing especially since Don Juan de Oñate was their leader and first governor. His legacy was fraught with controversy. In a city with three dominant cultures, history can be painful and dividing as well as rich and significant.

The sculpture was a complicated assemblage with five representations: Franciscan monks, settlers, soldiers and Mary La Conquistadora. She hovered above the others. At the base of the sculpture were animals sacrificed to bring them to Santa Fe and then later to provide sustenance. Some provided food while others pulled wagons up the perilous *La Bajada* (The Descent) long before I-25 made it easy. A few died trying to haul their cargo up the 1,300 foot climb. Later, the *road* was improved with 23 hair-pin turns. It would be the late 1950s before the construction of the interstate a few miles away.

The cold had infiltrated the ground so the women tucked their coats beneath them.

"Why here?" Chloe asked Mari-Lynn.

"I wanted somewhere outside so as not to contaminate a place, but somewhere spiritual to protect us."

"That's ominous," Rachel said.

"I've told Rachel about this vision but now I've had it several times and in each instance it adds another element," Mari-Lynn said. "There are white and red bits, for want of a better word, and they float around me. I can't tell what they are, but the sensation I pick up is alarm. Later the vision added rods, you know, like the kind ufologists talk about."

Rachel and Chloe exchanged looks of confusion not knowing how to define what Mari-Lynn had seen and yet knowing it had to be relevant.

"The most recent revelation included sound: either the howl of a wolf or dog or perhaps wind. And then, the strangest thing happened; the rods aligned. They became what looked like cages. Before I could comprehend that, vague images appeared inside them which might have been animals or people. At that point, the wind ceased and the shapes disappeared.

"Does this resonate with anything you are working on Rachel?" Mari-Lynn asked.

"Tell her what you've been writing," Chloe prompted.

"You may have read in High Desert Country the three-part story on the prison riot of 1980."

Mari-Lynn nodded. "Yes, I've been reading them."

"It was supposed to be a four-part story," Chloe said. "Julian has taken her off the story because of threats to harm her and others working at the magazine."

"Good god," Mari-Lynn said. "That's awful, but why?"

"We don't know," Rachel said. "Two of my interviewees have been killed. The man, Oswaldo Delgado who I interviewed for part one and the professor I interviewed for the most recent article."

"What about the woman from Española, I think her name was Phillips?" Mari-Lynn asked having read the story.

"As far as we know she is fine. She called the police one night because she heard someone on her roof. The officer, who knows about such things, took a sample of ash from her fireplace, that when tested, proved to be human remains, or corpse powder as it's known to Native Nations in the area."

"Corpse powder?" Mari-Lynn said. "Do I want to know?"

"It's the skin of a deceased person, usually fingerprints or other identifying body parts. Once dried and pulverized it becomes corpse powder. It is done when someone kills a close family member and uses the powder to cause illness or death in perceived enemies. The evil witch you spoke of in your shop."

"And has this woman become ill?" Mari-Lynn asked.

"Not to our knowledge," Rachel replied. "I wanted to call her, but Julian said it's a police matter now and I'm no longer working on the story because of the threats."

"What about the man you interviewed for the first story?" Mari-Lynn asked. "The tour guide at the prison?"

"He has returned to the Hopi reservation for protection," Rachel said. "And I don't blame him. He is similar to us in that he sees and senses things that others simply don't know are there. He thinks there is a skinwalker involved in this. When he showed me Cellblock 4 we both knew there were shadow people in there, but he also believes that a skinwalker has emerged. That's why he originally gave me the arrowhead."

"The night the two of you stayed on the rez, I was there," Mari-Lynn said. "I woke and knew you were in trouble. I visited your location and levitated above the hogan. At first, the entity did not see me. I observed it, but it quickly tracked me. Before it sent me straight back to my bed, I saw a woman sleeping restlessly inside the trailer house. I nudged her awake telepathically because I could sense she had intuitive awareness."

"That's why she came out and confronted the skinwalker?" Chloe asked.

"Yes, although I think she would have awakened soon without my help," Mari-Lynn said. "I thought you needed assistance immediately.

"I must caution you both," Mari-Lynn continued. "Whatever this thing is, it is powerful. I've never been shunted off like that before. It knocked the breath out of me. Normally, I can levitate and observe without detection and certainly without peril. I can also tell you the woman living in the trailer is potent."

"What about me?" Rachel asked. "Can I prevail against this monster?"

Mari-Lynn considered a moment. Her eyes shifted as she took in the quiet park.

"I don't know," she said finally. "It's strong. I don't know if anyone can triumph but there are three of us."

"But you two are the only ones with psychic abilities," Chloe said. "I'm not endowed that way."

"You have always come through," Rachel said. "Never doubt your resourcefulness, tenacity and courage. Remember you faced down a Drac in the gallery and helped me ring that bell to stop the end of the Fourth World of the Hopi. You have game, shall we say."

"Do you feel it?" Mari-Lynn continued looking at Palace Avenue. "There is something close by but I can't see it."

Rachel looked around her. There was a cloudless azure sky and a light breeze. You couldn't ask for a more perfect Santa Fe day. Across the street a few tourists milled about. Although she couldn't see them she knew the vendors at the Palace of the Governors had their bright blankets spread along the long portal heavy with handmade jewelry, pottery and sand paintings. Visitors would be strolling looking at the goods and enjoying the day. Everything seemed typical, but it didn't feel right.

Despite the normalcy of the moment, Rachel sensed a presence. Anxiety rippled through her body and her consciousness. She remembered the latest petroglyph drawing she had received, two people with swords drawn and shields raised.

"Yes, I feel it," Rachel answered finally.

"There are hostilities coming," Mari-Lynn said. "It will be dangerous. I can warn you Rachel, but you will be the one to end this. Prepare anyway you can."

Rachel chucked her coat, suddenly feeling too warm.

"What season is this?" she asked. "One moment it's winter and the next early fall. It's too soon for hot flashes."

"I'll tell you what season it is," Mari-Lynn said. "It's the season of the witch."

CHAPTER 44

Since they were downtown, Rachel and Chloe elected to stop at The Shed for a bite and libation.

"I don't mean to make light of this frightening situation," Chloe said. "But I'm famished. Fear seems to do that to me."

"You ladies look a bit fretful today," Hector slid his hand along the bar as he wiped it down for them. "The usual?"

"Yes thank you, Hector. It's been a rough day." Chloe batted her false eyelashes at him. It was the best she could do today. It was as coquettish as she could muster.

"Are you always here?" Rachel asked. "You must be the hardest working bartender in Santa Fe."

"That I am," Hector said. "I've got a cot in the back." He winked at her and Rachel tried to smile like Chloe but it ended up being more of a goofy grin than a flirty smile.

"Rachel, I swear," Chloe said. "You're a total failure as a femme fatale. That response was reminiscent of your reaction to meeting Logan Masters. You'll never live that down."

Logan Masters was an actor who frequented the Santa Fe area to film his TV series and movies. He'd been a favorite of Rachel's until she met him. Calling the introduction a total failure was not an exaggeration. But later she had interviewed him – a situation she where she felt in control – and they'd hit it off. In fact, without his encouragement she wouldn't have adopted Chile Pod and that would be a true loss.

"You just had to bring up Logan," Rachel said. "You know, if he hadn't been married I might have dated him."

"Hmm," Chloe said. "Well he was, but there is that handsome park ranger."

"Dave is a friend," Rachel said. "His mother helped us."

"Yes. But if you didn't have your park ranger pal, you wouldn't have met her."

"Hey, I would swear that woman is watching us. Take a slow look to your right. She's at a table."

Rachel turned slightly to pick up a salt shaker and recognized Mrs. Phillips sitting alone at a table for four.

"That's the woman from Española I did the interview with," Rachel whispered. "The one whose fireplace contained corpse powder."

"She looks healthy to me," Chloe said.

"I'm going to speak with her." Rachel got up.

"Hello Mrs. Phillips. I'm Rachel Blackstone. You were gracious to do an interview with me for High Desert Country. How are you?"

"I'm well, thanks."

"It's funny how we don't notice people in places we frequent until after we meet them," Rachel said. "Do you come in often from Española?"

"When I have an appointment." She pushed away her drink, partially eaten food, threw down some cash and made to leave."

"It was nice to see you again," Rachel said.

"Uh-huh." Mrs. Phillips marched from the dining room.

"Was that as strange as it looked from here?" Chloe asked.

"Brush off, but not all interviews want to run into the reporter who interviewed them. They feel embarrassed or maybe they said more than they planned. It's like you had a relationship, however temporary, and it's gone."

"Well, not to worry," Chloe said. "Hector is here with our drinks. Delivered with a smile." Hector beamed at Chloe. She had her flirt back in gear. Margaritas are potent elixirs.

"What do you think about Mari-Lynn's visions?" Chloe asked taking a bite of her green chile vegetarian tamale.

"I don't know what it means or how to prepare."

"You, we, have always had to play this by ear," Chloe said. "I don't know about you, but this one has me more than a little worried. The fact that a 40-some year ago prison riot is involved is concerning. I remember reading an interview with a woman who was a member of the MASH unit sent to treat the wounded. She was horrified by the causes of death and the injuries of the living. The MASH unit had been in Viet Nam and she said nothing they saw in combat compared to what they experienced at the prison; the brutality of the injuries and the methods of murder were beyond comprehension."

"That was in my research," Rachel said trying not to pull up the details. "If it is, in fact, a skinwalker seeking revenge, I don't really blame whoever it is. But two wrongs have never made a right."

CHAPTER 45

Rachel couldn't sleep as scenario after scenario played across her mind. It was 2:00 a.m. Not even Chloe's sleep enhancing bed could quiet her brain waves. She decided not to fight it and threw back the covers.

She sat at her desk in the suite at Chloe's house tapping a pen while she turned on the new laptop. In the dimness of the bedroom, the glow from the computer lit Rachel's face as it booted up and showed her the photo of the day. There would be no rest tonight even with her blue light-blocking glasses. She opened a new reporter's notebook to take notes as she browsed.

After a few moments, the Bureau of Vital Statistics appeared on her screen. Iris Phillips had changed her name when she moved to New Mexico some 55 years ago: Originally Iris Blumenschein. Maybe she didn't want to be identified as German living so close to the Atomic City. Some communities still shunned Germans even after V-E Day ended WWII. It raised a red flag for Rachel.

She input Melinda Harris' name. Nothing. Rachel checked births, marriages or divorces and still found zip. Of course, she could have been born in another state. Rachel tried the DMV and produced more zip. Surely she had a driver's license, but maybe in another state? Or, was she driving without a license? Melinda was devoid of social media accounts, at least under her real name. A young woman with no social media presence was odd to say the least. Another red flag.

Rachel rested her chin in hand, index finger across her lips as if keeping secrets. It was Melinda's secrets she wanted to know.

Social Security might be able to help her but without the SS number it was unlikely they would talk, which Rachel thought a good thing. And it would be difficult to get information from her employer. Employers generally didn't give out personal information about employees, not even if the reference was poor, too many lawsuits. Legally, they would need a warrant and that wasn't Rachel's jurisdiction.

Exasperated, she tried voter registration knowing it would likely be unfruitful. Voting had always been a private affair in New Mexico until July 2022 when New Mexico voter registration became public. A poor idea in that many people don't want their private information made public. Some may have stalking issues or stolen identity or just don't want other people knowing their personal business. But VoteRef.com had sued and won. And then, a stay was granted. March 2023, Gov. Lujan Grisham signed the New Mexico Voting Rights Act which "prohibits the transfer or publication of voter data online." It also provided provisions that make it easier for Native Americans to register and vote.

Rachel recognized a dead end when she saw it. If Melinda Harris Delgado had changed her name, she might have done so in another state. That left only 49 to go.

About an hour later she hit some gold using Melinda's grandfather's name. Under Oswaldo Delgado she found a marriage announcement in a Colorado newspaper. It listed Delgado's son, José Delgado as the husband-to-be and Monica Harris as the bride. Near the lower page there was a photo of the two of them with Monica holding a young girl on her lap. The child had red hair. Rachel wondered where Melinda inherited the red hair as her mother was a brunette. Another thing puzzled Rachel: no one looked happy.

She printed off the announcement.

Buried at the bottom was the phrase, " … along with adopted daughter, Melinda, they will make their home in Santa Fe, New Mexico." Melinda had taken the maiden name of her mother. Did that mean her step-father was out of the picture? Maybe he never adopted her.

Back to Vital Statistics. There were correlations between journalism and police investigations. One could follow a lead to no resolution or find themselves back at the starting gate. But Rachel did get one answer. She found where Melinda's mother had died. She would have to file a request with the Bureau to get the cause of death. That takes time. However, she was buried in a Santa Fe cemetery. An excursion was needed.

The loss of sleep hadn't been completely in vain, but she still didn't understand everything. Rachel knew Melinda wasn't a bio relative of her grandfather. How that factoid might shape Melinda's inheritance now that Ozzy was dead she could only guess. She kicked off her scuffs and crawled into bed. Chile Pod nuzzled her person and went back to sleep. All was well in her world.

Rachel grabbed her phone and opened the dreaded bed app. Maybe she could do just one thing. She looked for brown noise. It was supposed to quiet racing thoughts. She was certain it was grasping at straws, but she'd give it a try. After a couple of pages, she found it and touched "brown noise."

It was pleasant, similar to flowing water and wind mixed together. Without pushing another icon, the canopy covered her in brown light. She stroked Chile Pod's little body. Her fur was silky and soft. The cat began to purr and Rachel fell asleep petting her. She would never, ever admit to using the brown sound. It was the purring that lulled her into dreamland.

CHAPTER 46

The following morning Rachel approached Chloe about an outing to the cemetery to see Melinda's mother's plot. Maybe the stone would give up some clues.

"You want me to go to a cemetery?" Chloe asked. "You know I hate those places." She shook her shoulders in an attempt to resemble a shiver. "They always give me the creeps."

"It's just this once, but I need to find the grave of Melinda Harris' mother."

"Why?" Chloe was suspicious and raised an eyebrow.

"I need to know how she died and getting that information from vital statistics can take time."

"Oh, okay." Chloe reluctantly agreed.

An hour later, Rachel drove through the gates of Rosario Cemetery. It was a Catholic place of rest. Sisters and priests who came to New Mexico to live and serve were buried here. Established in 1868, the Rosario Cemetery was adjacent to the Santa Fe National Cemetery where military veterans were buried.

"Would you mind looking up Melinda Harris?" Rachel asked Chloe who quickly input Monica Harris' vitals into the cemetery's "Find a Grave" site.

"That way," Chloe pointed using her GPS to give Rachel directions.

When they reached the grave, they found a flat headstone with engraving: "Beloved daughter and mother lost in childbirth." She had been 18, barely starting her life.

Next to her grave was another headstone which read: "Son of Monica Harris Delgado. Together in death." He had been two weeks old when he died.

"That's terribly sad," Chloe said.

"It sure is," Rachel answered. "But it gave me the answer I needed. She died giving birth to Melinda's brother."

"How does that help?" Chloe asked.

"Ozzy Delgado raised his son's step-child after her mother died," Rachel said. "That makes him a first-rate person."

"It also means if his son can be found, his granddaughter may not inherit," Chloe said.

"Exactly and how does that play out in this mystery?" Rachel asked. "Did Melinda kill him? Could she be the skinwalker?

"I think she warrants a closer look," Rachel said. "Maybe a little snooping would be appropriate."

"Let's go back to my place," Chloe said. "I'll change into my cat suit."

Rachel checked at the hospital and found Melinda Harris was on duty until 11:00 p.m.

"Unless it's an emergency, you'll have to call her after that," the charge nurse told her.

"Okay, thanks." Rachel turned to Chloe. "We're good until eleven."

"I'm ready," Chloe said. She was wearing a black leather jumpsuit and looked rad in it.

"Mrs. Peel," Rachel said. "Are we needed?"

"Very funny. I admit I got the idea from seeing all *The Avengers* episodes you made me watch. Diana Rigg looked so cool in hers. Where did you come by all those DVDs?"

"They were part of my inheritance from Dad. He was a fan. After I saw Rigg, I totally understood why. Dad once told me all the boys wanted to date her and all the girls wanted to *be her*. It was a 'sixties TV show. What can I say; I'm a sucker for retro."

"I think your car says that loud and clear," Chloe said drolly.

"Hate to admit it, but I'm getting quite attached to your car," Rachel said. "And I'm beginning to wonder if I'll ever get the Merc back."

"The Auto Casa being slow?" Chloe asked. "I read it's difficult to get parts on those discontinued cars."

"Thank you for your input.

"Say, I thought you were vegetarian?" Rachel continued.

"This is not leather," Chloe said, pretending offense. "It just looks like it." She smoothed the faux leather of her outfit.

"Sorry," Rachel said. "But it looks authentic."

About a quarter hour later, Rachel parked a few houses from Melinda's grandfather's home. It was dusk but not yet dark.

"Let's walk slowly by the place first. Like were taking an afternoon walk – in a cat suit." Rachel said with playful disgust.

"I heard that tone," Chloe laughed.

"What tone was that?"

"That expression of chagrin that indicates I've committed a crime-solving social blunder, but you are going to live with it."

"You read a lot into my cat suit comment."

"I admit in this neighborhood, it probably wasn't the best choice of attire," Chloe acknowledged. "But where would I wear it?"

"Halloween?"

Before Chloe could reply they came to the Delgado house. They slowed their pace.

Rachel squatted to act as if she was tying her shoe. She glanced at the house. It looked empty; only one light burned in a bathroom.

As they rounded the corner, Rachel said: "There is an alleyway behind their house; let's take that and try the back door."

Reaching the Delgado property they eased in the back gate behind the shed.

"There's barely a tool left in there," Rachel said. "Melinda has taken it from tool shed to witch's covenstead. She's added a lock to the door since she caught me in there."

Rachel pointed to the shiny new padlock on the door.

"Let's try the house," Rachel said. "First, gloves." She pulled four gloves from her bag.

"We've graduated to gloves, have we?" Chloe said, eagerly pulling them on with a snap.

The two women walked, first along the side fence and then to the back of the house. Rachel cautiously pulled on the handle of the slider. It gave.

"She locks her witchy shed, but not her house?" Chloe asked.

"I think the lock is broken. Aim your cell light down here," Rachel said. "See when I slide it into place, it doesn't lock. It doesn't even catch."

"That's one for our side," Chloe said. "Shall we?"

Rachel stepped inside and called out: "Hello? Anyone home?"

When there was no response, Chloe followed her into the small, dingy family room using her phone flashlight. The house had a musty smell that hinted of dust and perhaps a mouse or two. The furniture was simple: a recliner and ancient sofa with areas of stuffing protruding from the worn upholstery. It was in even more disrepair than the front room where Rachel had interviewed Mr. Delgado. A small box TV sat on a table attached to an antenna that hung on the wall adjacent the sliding doors.

"Wow," Chloe said. "This is sad."

In the breakfast nook a table was stacked with papers and envelopes. Upon closer inspection, they appeared to be financial.

"Look." Rachel picked up a document. "This is Ozzy Delgado's will."

"See who gets the inheritance."

Rachel turned several pages until she reached the beneficiary page.

"José Delgado. His son. Not the granddaughter. Melinda's out of luck."

"Oh, that really opens a can of worms," Chloe said.

"This is the deed to this house. And it's owned by Oswaldo and son José Delgado."

Below the deed was a piece of notebook paper with Oswaldo Delgado written in cursive over and over.

"Someone is trying to replicate Mr. Delgado's signature," Rachel said.

"I guess we don't have to wonder who that might be."

"Nope. My bet's on Melinda."

"We need to locate Melinda's room. See if it holds any secrets."

The hall to the two bedrooms was short. One room looked as if it hadn't been used in years. The layer of dust seemed to support that theory.

"This must be it," Chloe whispered.

Melinda's room was girly green with a few ruffles on the bedspread. There were four mannequin's hands on the old-fashioned dresser where an abundance of necklaces and bracelets hung. Stacks of rings clung to each finger.

"That's disturbing," Chloe said.

"How much jewelry she owns or the way she stores it?"

"The hands!" Chloe shuddered. "They are very lifelike."

"What's this?" Rachel said, opening the lower drawer of the dresser. She carefully lifted something that looked like dried skin. It had been shaped to hold seeds.

"Lizard?" Chloe was repulsed.

Rachel almost dropped it, but instead gently placed it back.

"What are the seeds?"

They resembled raisins but with spiny projections.

"Don't touch them," Chloe said. "According to my gardener, that would be wolfsbane, also called monkshood. It's beautiful but deadly. In the olden days they would make a paste and spread it on arrowheads and spears to kill their enemies. Aconitine mainly affects the heart but also the nervous system. It only takes 2 mg. to kill, even less to make one sick. It's called wolfsbane because Europeans used to poison wolves with it. Wolves seem to draw ire from many people who don't understand how important they are to the ecosystem."

"And you think you've no talent to help with these missions," Rachel said kindly. "How do you learn so much about plants when your gardener does all the work?"

"I listen," Chloe said. "It's something I'm good at. All day I listen to people tell me what they want in a house. It spilled over into backyard agriculture."

"Say, do you smell lemon?" Chloe sniffed and walked in the direction of the bed.

"Check under the bed."

"You do it," Rachel replied. "Things kept under beds are similar to basements and attics. You don't want to go there."

"Okay scaredy cat. I'll look."

Chloe got on hands and knees. Rachel wasn't sure how as her clothing fit snugly, but Chloe made it look easy. She carefully lifted the dust ruffle.

"Ah, here we are." She pulled a bowl holding two lemon halves riddled by cloves. "I'm assuming some kind of spell?" Chloe replaced it exactly as she found it.

In Melinda's bedside table was a spiral pad lying open to a list. One might dismiss it as a shopping list, but this wasn't anything so innocent. It consisted of places around Santa Fe: The Shed, Cathedral Park, the magazine office, Mari-Lynn's Chrysalis Metaphysical shop and Chloe and Rachel's home addresses.

The two women stared at one another.

"What the hell?" Rachel said.

"Yeah," Chloe said. "All places we've frequented recently."

"Let's get out of here," Rachel said.

* * *

On the Hopi reservation, Ernesto Pacheco was repairing the corral fence that surrounded the barn on his family's small farm. His nephew was herding the goats today and would soon return them back for feeding. Ernesto had been closing up holes in the battered enclosure. He stopped with hammer raised to drive a nail when a vehicle turned onto the drive. Because of the ongoing drought, the truck kicked up quite a bit of dust. It slid to a stop while the brown cloud continued. Ernesto didn't recognize the pickup.

A woman got out of the driver's side. She was casting a dark aura as Ernesto watched her stop, hands on hips, looking for someone. Surely she was lost, but he didn't like that she emitted a sinister light. With reluctance, he walked across the corral and let himself out through the gate by the water trough. The nearer he came to the woman the more uneasy he felt. Normally, he would have gotten closer to talk with someone, but he stopped several yards away.

"Trying to find someone?" he asked.

She didn't speak at first, just continued to look around at the farm.

"You Ernesto Pacheco?"

How could she possibly know him, here on the Hopi reservation? He was alone. His aunt had taken her weaving to sell. Her hand-made rugs would fetch a nice profit. The money would buy food for the family.

"This is the Pacheco farm," he said.

Her appearance changed subtly. For a moment Ernesto saw her as a witch with hair covering her body and a wolf's head atop her own. And then, the image was gone.

"You'll need to get in the truck," she said. "We have a date with destiny."

"I'm needed here on the farm," Pacheco said. "What's this about?"

"I'm afraid I have to insist," she said.

That's when Ernesto saw her pouring something into her hand from a canvas bag. It was a light-colored powder. She pulled the string on the bag and replaced it in her jacket pocket. Ernesto watched calmly as she walked around the truck and approached him.

He still didn't know who she was, but he knew what she was. That had to be corpse powder in her hand.

"You have no way to stop me blowing this into your face." She seemed to evaluate something and he soon knew what. "You're not wearing the arrowhead."

She was correct. Thinking he was safe here, nowhere near Santa Fe, he had removed the protective amulet. He cursed himself for his carelessness.

"Now, get in the truck," she ordered.

CHAPTER 47

Chile Pod finished leftovers from Chloe's refrigerator, a succulent liver pâté. She inhaled it and looked around for more. This was much better than Rachel ever had in her fridge. She was lucky if hers contained a couple of beers and a past its sell-by date taco. Chloe's fridge held recyclable containers filled with delectable but healthy food from the best caterer in Santa Fe. Rachel felt fortunate to find no blueberries or yogurt which was the usual breakfast fare at Chloe's. When at home, she frequently grabbed a green chile cheese burrito on the way to work.

"You're supposed to savor it," Rachel said. Chile Pod gazed at her with adoration wondering if she needed to know what her person said. Rachel had rescued the little tortie when she bought her house in the South Capital area. The cat came with the property. Rachel hadn't really been a cat person before meeting Chile Pod, but quickly became one. She couldn't imagine life without her now. The cat was sociable, having never met a stranger, but more psychic than Rachel when it came to unwanted guests. She was lovely to curl up with at night and great company during the day.

Her phone rang. Rachel was off the clock and wanted to ignore it, but the universe, or something, nudged her.

"Hello?"

"Is this Rachel?"

"Yeah, who's this?"

"Ernesto."

"I'm sorry. I didn't recognize your voice," Rachel said. "I thought you went back to the reservation?"

She couldn't understand why she hadn't recognized his voice. There was an uncharacteristic tone in it.

"You must come to the prison," he said.

"What?"

"The prison. You must come."

"But why? Are you there?"

"I can't go on," he said.

She couldn't remember specifics, but something he said rang a bell in her cerebral cortex.

"Why?"

"Come to the prison, Cellblock Four." He disconnected.

The last place Rachel ever wanted to go again was the prison. She certainly wanted to avoid it at night and the sun was sinking fast behind the Jemez. As she looked southward through the window toward Albuquerque, she heard Chloe coming in by way of the garage door.

"Hey Rach. You look like you've seen a ghost, although I suppose apparitions are not all that upsetting to you anymore."

"We have to go to the prison," Rachel said.

"What are you talking about?" Chloe replied. "Why would we go there, at night no less?"

"I received a call from Ernesto Pacheco."

"The guide you interviewed at the prison?"

"He told me he was returning to the rez where he would be safe and others would believe him. I didn't think he would ever go back to that prison.

"He didn't sound like himself," Rachel continued. "His voice sounded peculiar or maybe it was what he said ... "

"What?" Chloe asked.

"That's it. I can't put my finger on it.

"Chloe," Rachel continued. "I didn't think I'd ever ask you to get your gun, but get it. I don't know what to expect, except it's going to be bad. Remember what Mari-Lynn said. 'There will be hostilities. Prepare anyway you can.' "

"Okay," Chloe said cautiously.

"Before you load it, we must dip each bullet in ash. I hope fireplace ash will work."

"Rachel, you're scaring me. What do you think we're walking into?"

"I don't know, but Ernesto didn't sound himself. I don't believe he would return to the prison unless there was a compelling reason to do so.

"Are you still wearing your arrowhead?" Rachel asked.

Chloe lifted it slowly from inside her clothing, not just to show Rachel but to remind herself it was there.

"I'll get the gun."

When Chloe returned Rachel had removed the fireplace screen.

"What type of wood have you been burning?" Rachel asked.

"White ash."

"How did you know to burn that? And how did you get it? My understanding is that it grows in the eastern U.S. We mostly burn piñon."

"I thought it might come to this so I did some research. And then, I ordered the white ash, burned it and left the ashes in the fireplace, you know, just in case."

They squatted before the kitchen kiva, each dipping a bullet in the ash. But no sooner had a bullet been dipped than the ash fell back onto the hearth.

"This isn't working," Rachel said. "The ash falls off. How are we supposed to keep the ash on the bullets?"

"I don't know much about guns except I took a course on gun safety," Chloe said. "I do have some wax. Would that hold the ash on the bullet?"

"Let's try it."

Chloe hurried to her bathroom and returned with a small plastic box with several short lengths of wax.

"How did you come by that?" Rachel asked.

"I still use my retainer from time to time."

"Oh. How did I not know that about you?" Rachel asked. "Never mind, another time.

"This might work," Rachel continued.

"Where do I put it?" Chloe asked

"I'm guessing right on the tip of the bullet so it doesn't clog the chamber and we'll add the ash."

Painstakingly, Chloe rubbed a thin coating of wax to each bullet while Rachel dipped them in the fireplace ash. Chloe then loaded the chamber.

"There," Chloe said with finality. "We're loaded for bear, or skin-walker."

"Remember," Rachel said. "You must hit the skinwalker in the neck while in animal form. Any other body location and the bullet will pass through without harm."

"Are we ready for this?" Chloe asked.

"Would anybody be ready for this?" Rachel said.

She poured out plenty of cat food for Chile Pod, hugged her. Chloe kissed the top of her head and Rachel gently place her on the floor.

"We'll be back," she said to Chile Pod. "I mean it. We'll be back."

But there was no way to be certain. This was unknown territory.

CHAPTER 48

Doba Chee sat on the patio of her family's property in northern Arizona. She watched as the end of the day slipped behind the mountains to the west. She was restless. Usually, Doba could settle in a watch the sunset in peace. Today she was antsy; a vision was imminent.

Doba had seen this monster before. It was the night Rachel and her friend Chloe visited the reservation. It had red eyes. She immediately averted her gaze because she knew they held most of the power.

In a heartbeat, the entity shape-shifted into a woman. Doba closed her eyes to better see what the individual was doing. She saw her take human skin from a dehydrator: the fingerprints of a corpse. She was using a mortar and pestle to grind it. The common kitchen appliance also contained what looked like jerky. Once the woman had inspected the skin, satisfied the thin slices of dermis were dry enough, she pulverized them.

The landscape changed again. This time it was a dark place with bars. There were moving shapes and cries of anguish. Two women were approaching the chaos. It was Rachel and her friend.

After the vision, she tried Rachel's cell. No answer. What she dreamed was coming to pass. Rachel needed to know what she knew. Doba called her son and asked him to go check on Rachel.

Dave Chee quickly dialed Rachel's number to be sure she was un-reachable. He flinched as her voicemail picked up.

"Rachel, this is Dave. My mother asked me to check you. It's impor-tant. She says it's happening tonight: the *dark wind*. She has seen the witch make corpse powder. It appeared to be a female. She said to go with the Great Spirit. And this is odd but I'm sure relevant: you have to close your eyes that you might see.

"I assume you're going to the prison again. I'm on my way," he added. "Please be careful."

CHAPTER 49

As Chloe backed out of her garage there came a howl across the valley. Rachel lowered her window to listen. It echoed as it bounced off the Sangre de Cristos.

"Is that? ... " Chloe asked.

"Yes, Kiyiya," Rachel said. "He's warning us. I haven't heard that cry before. His alarms are usually a plain wolf's howl. This is almost screaming – obviously urgent."

Rachel named the wolf Kiyiya meaning "howling wolf" in the Yakima Native American language. They first met on a lonely highway in eastern New Mexico. Originally, Rachel was afraid of him, but came to realize he had been assigned to protect her. By whom, she had no idea. Maybe the spirits Doba talked about.

Chloe parked her car in the lot at the prison.

"Are you sure he said to meet him here?" she asked.

"Yes, he was quite clear," Rachel said.

"Why isn't there light in any of the windows?"

"Cellblock 4 is at the back," Rachel explained. "And there would only be a flashlight."

"Oh yeah, I forgot," Chloe said. "But I haven't forgotten how scary it is."

Only a dilapidated pickup was parked in the lot.

"Does Mr. Pacheco drive a pickup?" Chloe asked.

"I don't know what he drives," Rachel said. "But there is something familiar about this vehicle so maybe it's his."

"Well that's nice," Chloe picked out a torn bumper sticker with her torch. Rachel turned on her lantern for additional light. "Part of it is missing, but I remember what it said: *If It's Tourist Season Why Can't We Shoot Them?* Not kind." What was left of the sticker read: "If It's ... oot Them?" The remainder had been torn off.

"Some people drove around the Sunport so arriving tourists could see their bumper sticker," Rachel added.

"Was that your phone chiming?" Chloe asked.

"I guess. Not a good time for a message."

"Maybe you should check."

"Okay." Rachel pulled the cell from her back pocket.

"It's from Mrs. Chee by way of Dave. She says it is happening tonight and the witch is a woman! Go with the Great Spirit. And this is odd: I may have to close my eyes that I might see."

"Very strange," Chloe said. "I hope it becomes apparent what she meant."

"Just a moment," Rachel said. "I have to get something from the car."

"I'll go with you. Not standing in the dark by myself. Thank you very much."

Rachel retrieved two masks and eye protection from the glove box.

"If there is corpse powder, all the skinwalker has to do is blow some in our faces and we're dead. These are N-95 masks I've carried since the pandemic. I put them in your glove box in case we ever needed them."

"Holy shit," Chloe said. "Now I'm really scared." She placed the mask over her face and adjusted. "Not comfortable," she said. "But better than dead."

"Let's see if we have to break in," Rachel said.

"That's odd," Chloe said as she pulled on the door. "It's unlocked."

They went inside. The reception area was eerily dark.

"Something menacing about this whole thing," Rachel said. "Can you feel it?"

"Yes," Chloe said.

"Cellblock 4 is this way," Rachel said and stopped. "We need to stay together, if that means holding hands, we have too." They interlocked arms, holding lights with their free hands.

They negotiated the labyrinth of barred doors and emerged into the hall past the hospital and the psychological unit to the end of the prison.

About halfway, Rachel stopped and listened. The silence was insidious.

"How can silence be so sinister?" Chloe whispered.

"It's too quiet," Rachel said. "No reappearance of that owl. No rats scuttling about."

"Do you want to go back?" Chloe asked.

"It would only put off whatever is going on," Rachel said. "It began here, makes sense it has to end here."

"Is that what you think, this is the ending?" Chloe whispered.

"Yes, I think tonight resolves this thing one way or another."

"You know I won't be able to see everything you do. What can I do to help?"

"Chloe, you can see the witch, have seen it. We may need to kill it. You have the gun."

"Oh my god," Chloe said. "You want me to kill it?"

"Don't know. We'll have to respond in whatever way gets us out alive."

The wolf's howl echoed down the main prison hallway. It was difficult to tell what direction the cry had come from yet Rachel felt some relief.

"Kiyiya is here," Rachel said. "That's comforting."

"I don't see him," Chloe said.

"Me either, but he's here."

Rachel could see the shadow people with her lantern. They had indistinct edges and were darker in the center. Some had legs only while others were only torsos or heads. Those with heads had red eyes. They came through the prison wall and then disappeared the way they had come. The spectres seemed to be everywhere flitting in front of her, touching her and Chloe. She slapped away one who kept tapping her shoulder. The creepers among them slithered along the ceiling in ways no human could.

Taunting her, the jeering was followed by hysterical laughter.

"Do you see them?" Rachel whispered.

"What?" Chloe asked.

"Shadow people. Everywhere. They probably won't hurt us."

"Probably?"

"Scare us? Freak us out? Yes."

"Are they ... touching me?" Chloe asked. "Because I thought I felt something touch my neck."

"No," Rachel lied. "Just your imagination." She needed Chloe to hold it together.

When the two women reached the end of the hallway they waited. It wasn't their party. In the gloom, Rachel's lantern revealed the cell door standing open.

"That's Cellblock Four." Rachel pointed. "That's where the massacre occurred."

"Do we have to go in there?" Chloe asked.

"I do, you don't."

"No way, I'm not leaving you to do this by yourself." Chloe was defiant.

"Whatever you do, don't close the door behind us," Rachel said. "There are no keys to unlock these doors."

"No problem," Chloe retorted.

Both women jumped when a cell door slammed shut behind them.

"How can that happen?"

"Remember the night we visited the movie set," Rachel said. "It has happened before. They're trying to unnerve us."

"It's working," Chloe said. "How can you be so matter-of-fact about all this?"

"I'm not," Rachel said. "I'm scared, but the only way out of this is through it."

They stood before the open door of Cellblock 4 hesitating.

"We don't know if we can get out," Rachel said. "That door we heard bang could have been someone locking us in. Getting out may be impossible."

"Rachel, I hate being in here. It's so claustrophobic. What if our lights go out? Did we check the batteries? Oh my god!"

"Chloe, don't let them get to you. Even though you can't see the shadow people they are casting a spell of sorts. Fight it."

Chloe unlocked her arm, grabbed Rachel's hand and squeezed.

"Riding shotgun with a handgun," Chloe tried for a laugh.

"There's the Chloe I know. You ready?"

"Yes *amie*." Rachel smiled. She had never appreciated Chloe more.

"One hand on your flash, the other on the gun," Rachel said.

CHAPTER 50

The prison was hushed, but Rachel could sense the fury and hostility that skulked in the walls. As they approached, the screaming she'd heard before began again. Young men called out for their mothers, begged for their lives and prayed for deliverance that wouldn't come.

Next, Rachel was assaulted by the odor of blood. When her feet felt wet, she looked down at the floor. She walked through a slush of water, sewage and blood. Pieces of paper, clothing and torn mattresses floated around her. She shuffled her feet trying to get out of the putrid sea. Instead, she thrashed against the cold concrete wall unable to extradite herself from the horrendous vision.

"What is it?" Chloe asked. "What's wrong?"

"I'm hearing the inmates plead for their lives and seeing what it looked like after the massacre. It's horrible. My feet are in several inches of refuse and blood."

"I don't see anything but a floor," Chloe said.

"Like what you see?" said a woman's voice.

"Who's there?" Rachel demanded, trying to sound authoritative.

"You know me," Iris Phillips stepped into the lantern light.

"Mrs. Phillips, what on earth are you doing here? I was expecting

Mr. Pacheco." Rachel tried to sound innocent but at that moment was fully aware that Phillips must be the skinwalker.

"Go inside the cellblock and I'll tell you," Phillips said.

"No," Rachel said. "I won't do this inside where all those young men were murdered. It wouldn't be respectful. I can sense their agony and I don't want to disturb them further. Either we resolve this here in the hall or we're leaving."

"Do you see her?" Rachel asked Chloe.

"Oh yeah," Chloe whispered.

"Her son witnessed what happened that night and killed himself," Rachel quickly explained. "Except that's not what happened, is it Mrs. Phillips? He didn't take his own life, did he?"

It was a shot in the dark, but Rachel was certain she was right.

"What are you talking about?" Chloe asked.

"Mrs. Phillips is our skinwalker, are you not? Which would mean you killed your son and made corpse powder and bone pellets from his body. You've been killing the people I interviewed. I thought it was strange you didn't become a casualty.

"Why?" Rachel continued.

"He pleaded with me to put him out of his misery. It wasn't the first time. He told me what he saw in war wasn't as bad as the prison riot. He didn't want to be a burden anymore cycling in and out of addiction and jail.

"Why did you become a skinwalker and why involve me? I wasn't an inmate nor did I work here at the prison."

"You dredged up all the pain."

"But you willingly did the interview with me." Rachel tried to get Phillips to reason. "You realize I have an editor and he assigns stories for me to write. I didn't come up with the story of the riot on my own."

"You created the conduit here," she said, her voice beginning to change into something much lower. Rachel would swear she was growling. "I have unfinished business in this god forsaken place. Can you see them too?"

At that moment Kiyiya howled.

"Did you hear it?" Rachel asked Chloe.

"Yes."

"Stay alert. Shit is about to hit the fan."

As they watched in horror, Phillips stripped off her clothing and replaced it with the skin of a wolf. The sightless wolf's head stared blankly. Its skin hung over Phillips' backside, the wolf's legs and tail lifeless. Her 80-year-old skin rippled as she changed shape and became more muscular. When the transition was complete she had grown much taller, a figure much more wolf than human. Hair covered Phillips' face and then spread across to her torso. At first, it seemed awkward but in a few seconds it seemed to become one with her. With the transformation complete the wolf body was supple and healthy.

Chloe gasped next to her. "What's that smell?"

"It's Phillips. Skinwalkers have a fetid odor. I can smell it too. It may be a distraction. She is capable of many things: all bad."

"Is it just me or are the walls moving closer together?" Chloe asked.

Rachel had been watching Phillips so closely she hadn't noticed, but with every second the walls did seem to be on a path to join as one.

"So if you can't get those responsible, you'll go after anyone?" Rachel tried to keep her attention focused on her questions.

In a heartbeat Phillips morphed back into a human.

"What's going on?" Chloe asked.

"She can't talk while she is in witch form," Rachel whispered. "Her power would cease."

"I tried to get prison officials to talk with me," Phillips said. "But there are few left and those that are wouldn't speak to me.

"The rioters got away with it," Phillips added.

"Yes, most of them did," Rachel agreed. "After all was said and done, there was little justice."

"Bring him out!" Phillips commanded.

From the darkness emerged two shadow people shoving Ernesto Pacheco. These shadow people were wholly formed. Rachel glanced away from their eyes and kept her attention on Ernesto.

"What have you done?" Rachel shouted.

"Are you okay Ernesto?"

"She kidnapped me from the reservation and brought me here," he said of Phillips. "Caught me out alone."

Rachel held up her light and saw Ernesto's face had been beaten. There was bruising and red marks. A trickle of blood had dried on his lower lip.

"Who kidnapped you?" Rachel asked.

"The witch," he said. "Thought she was lost, but it was a trick."

"Come with me Ernesto, we're leaving."

Rachel crossed the hall to assist Ernesto. Her feet sloshed through the cesspit of the dead. She wondered if Ernesto could see it too.

"Let go of him," she demanded of the shadow people. Intimidated, they surrendered him.

"No one is going anywhere!" Phillips said.

"We are!" Rachel said. "This is insane. No one here hurt you."

"Someone has to pay!" she said. "I didn't kill my own son for nothing. I already have his blood on my hands, what does it matter?"

"You've killed Ozzy Delgado and Professor Kanteena who did nothing to you. Ozzy endured the same trauma as your son and Kanteena was trying to make conditions better at prisons. What is the point?"

"I do not have to justify my actions to you or anyone."

With that another door down the hall swung shut like an exclamation point. They were now trapped with one of the most feared creatures in the Native world. Something Rachel fully believed in since their night spent at the Navajo Nation. She glanced at Chloe who had her gun in hand pointed squarely at the witch.

"Do you think that scares me?" the monster asked. "It does not. No gun can bring me down."

Rachel thought it was all over but the shouting. And then something quite bright caught her eye. She turned to look. Kiyiya appeared in all his brilliance. He stood behind the bars down the hall observing. In an instant, he walked through the barrier as if it wasn't there. Rachel saw it and while she found it difficult to believe she had become accustom to it. Kiyiya was simply astonishing.

The ruff of his neck was standing up and he snarled so convincingly that Rachel hoped she had never inadvertently offended him. His white coat and inner brightness lit up the prison hallway. His ears laid back, saliva dripping from his fangs, he was full-fight ready. The cavalry had arrived.

CHAPTER 51

North of Santa Fe, Mari-Lynn woke with a start. Her breath came in gasps as she tried to inhale normally. Her heart pounded so hard she could hear it in her ears. It was happening, the battle she had dreamed. Of that, she was certain. Sliding her feet into scuffs she walked to the kitchen and put the kettle on. She sent a quick prayer to the Great Spirit asking for her friends' safety and lit two candles. There would be no more sleeping until she knew Rachel and Chloe had slain the dragon.

Celeste followed her into the kitchen and touched her arm.

"What's wrong?" she asked.

"I can't shake the feeling catastrophe is about to occur."

"I hope you're not about to have another vision," Celeste said. "I worry sometimes and this is one of those times. The night you were blown back in bed was terrifying."

"I didn't realize that you could tell when I was having one of those," Mari-Lynn said.

"The signs are there," Celeste said. "It's like you leave your body here. It lies so still and you're unresponsive. There have been times I actually took your pulse to make sure you hadn't died. When you return, your body convulses. That night you traveled to the rez, when you returned, the bed shuddered. It was a violent return. I told myself I'd wait three minutes. I counted. And then, you woke and were so frightened."

"I'm sorry I scared you," Mari-Lynn said. "The skinwalker saw me. That's never happened before. This creature is potent. I'm concerned Rachel and Chloe may be in over their heads."

"They stopped the demise of the Fourth World of the Hopi, they can do this," Celeste said. "But fate does seem to send them more difficult assignments each time.

"I'm going back to bed," Celeste said feeling defeated. "There is nothing I can do."

"You go ahead," Mari-Lynn said. "When I know they're safe, I'll join you." She sipped her tea while looking out the window to the south. Although she could not see it, Old Main was there in all its anguish. She sat down at their table, her trembling hands holding her cooling tea cup. Waiting.

* * *

In Los Alamos, Dave Chee slammed the door of his house, neglecting to stop long enough to lock it. He swung himself into his SUV. When he reached the end of his block, the car careened around the corner. As Dave turned onto New Mexico 502 he checked his watch. It was a forty-minute drive to Santa Fe. He was going to try and make it thirty.

CHAPTER 52

Rachel supported Ernesto's arm until they were both standing next to Chloe, whose hands trembled as she held the gun.

"Rachel," she said. "I can't shoot anyone, not even a monster. You'll have to do it. Besides, it's too difficult to aim looking through these glasses."

Rachel could identify. Despite the time of year and lack of heat in the prison, sweat was seeping into her glasses and under her mask. But she dare not remove them.

"Has she blown corpse powder at you?" Rachel asked Ernesto.

"No, although I don't know why she held back. She's angry about the prison tours. Said this is sacred ground, yet she's throwing this macabre bash here."

Rachel pulled off her scarf and covered Ernesto's mouth and nose with it, being careful not to further injure his mouth. She tied it in a knot behind his head. It wasn't an N-95 but she hoped it would stop the worst of the powder should Phillips try to poison him.

"Chloe, we need to get Ernesto out of here. He needs medical attention."

The three of them backed slowly away, trying not to be conspicuous. If they could reach the bars Kiyiya had passed through, they might be able to escape.

Phillips must have been paying more attention to them than Rachel thought.

"You will find that door locked," Phillips said. "Your sneaking about will get you nowhere."

Chloe tried the door, shook it – the one they came through when they arrived. It was locked.

"There are no keys other than the front door," Ernesto said. "We never close the interior doors."

Even as Chloe jerked and kicked the bars in vain, the mêlée behind them seemed to heat up.

They stood at the gates of hell and felt impotent. Who won the battle would determine their future. All they could do was hope Kiyiya would prevail.

"Chloe, give me the gun. I think I could use it to help Kiyiya."

"Gladly."

Rachel slipped the gun into her back waistband.

Phillips had fully transformed back into a skinwalker. Now on all fours, she snarled at Kiyiya. The skinwalker wolf was black and Kiyiya was glistening white. The two wolves slowly circled, heads down ready to strike. Phillips took a swing at Kiyiya with her paw. It was a wild swing that missed him.

"The witch hasn't fought before," Pacheco whispered. "She is powerful, but inexperienced. Did you notice that swing? More like a cat, not a wolf. I wonder what else she doesn't know. Your power animal has fought before. If she learns quickly from him it could be a bloodbath."

Kiyiya ran at the black wolf knocking Phillips off her feet with a body blow. While she was out of balance, he bit a hind leg. With 400 pounds of pressure per square inch it was badly damaged and bloody. It infuriated Phillips even more. She passed a front paw over her leg and it immediately healed.

The witch took an angry swipe at Kiyiya's throat. He jumped back but she nicked him. White hair and red drops of blood floated through the air as if in slow motion. They multiplied as she tore at him once more. Tufts of white fur drifted into the slurry at Rachel's feet.

"Oh god," Chloe gasped. "He's hurt."

Rachel had never seen Kiyiya fight before. He always seemed to out-smart the opponent. This time he had to exchange blows.

"Ernesto," Rachel said. "Is there any way I can help Kiyiya?"

"Call on his family," Ernesto said.

"How?" Rachel asked feeling panicked.

"You must close your eyes so you may see them," he said. "Call upon your guides for assistance."

Dave Chee's words echoed within her: *you have to close your eyes that you might see.*

"My guides?"

"Do you not know a shaman from the other side who can help you?" Ernesto spoke haltingly.

"How do you know that?" Rachel asked. He was referring to Joseph, the Hopi shaman who helped her before. Mrs. Chee had spoken of him. Joseph had been with Rachel from the beginning of this journey. He helped her return the evil spirit. Although Mario killed Joseph the shaman continued to help Rachel from the spirit world.

"I know the good shaman Joseph too," Ernesto said.

"Go ahead," Ernesto urged. "Close your eyes and call upon him."

Rachel did as Ernesto said and sent a silent message to Joseph. She visualized his kind face. Now he was an elder in the Hopi Land of the Dead. During her visit to Skeleton Man she spoke with him again, seek-ing advice in stopping Sirius as it threatened to crash into the Earth. When he appeared to her there it was as a large light-filled orb.

Help me defeat this ogre.

In a few seconds: *Help is nearby.*

Almost in movie form, Rachel saw an open field surrounded by tall pines and aspen. A family of wolves rested in the moonlight. Two young wolves and one adult slept. A carcass lay between them. They had fed well. The female awoke. Rachel could see her ears move about like radar checking for threats. In an instant, the wolf was on its feet scanning the area. The wolf awakened her family. She howled long and loud. It resonated to the far reaches of the canyon. Her mate and growing pups joined her.

One moment the wolf family was there and the next they were not. The clearing was empty. Only the moonbeam remained.

"Your liberators have arrived," Ernesto pointed to a wall.

The wolf family she had visualized entered through the concrete wall. Other wolves in spirit followed. All emerged into the corridor as though the wall didn't exist. First their head and front paws, followed by their filmy bodies. The wall seemed to part for them as they easily passed through the partition.

"That is your wolf's mother and family," Ernesto said.

* * *

Dave Chee reached Pojoaque. From there it was a straight shot to Santa Fe. It usually took about 20 minutes. Maybe he could do it in twelve. He wondered if Rachel and her friend were okay. His mother had been passionately urgent when she called. So much so, he brought his gun. He'd never used it except on the shooting range and he hoped tonight wouldn't be an exception. The highway this time of night was practically all his. His foot weighed heavily on the accelerator. All he could see was the white of the SUV's headlights. Nothing else mattered.

* * *

"That is your wolf's parents and two siblings," Ernesto explained.

Rachel recognized the mother wolf. She had appeared in a vision Rachel experienced during a labyrinth walk and again that night outside the hogan. In her vision, Kaya told her son Kiyiya he was destined for greatness in the spiritual world. He would become a fierce protector. On the day of his death from a rifle blast, he fell into darkness and landed on his feet. He shook off the disorientation and saw a woman on a highway. She was standing outside her car; a lesser spirit was intimidating her. He stepped forward. The spirit fled. Somehow he knew this woman – who was frightened of him in that moment – was to be protected by him. He'd shadowed her since. Her name, he came to know, was Rachel.

The family of wolves slowly fanned out and circled the skinwalker. Each step was calculated: wolf packs first tire their prey and then surround it before killing.

"What's happening?" Chloe asked.

"Kiyiya's family has joined the fight," Rachel said. "And a whole host of other wolves I don't know."

"Oh no," Rachel gasped. Shadow people were falling in behind the evil witch. Their alliance was clear. Some filtered through the walls while others slithered along the floor and ceiling. As they arrived, each produced a shield and took rods from the cell bars to be used as weapons, just as Mari-Lynn had predicted.

"She called in reinforcements," Ernesto said. "These shadow people are malevolent."

"What do you mean about the shadow people?" Chloe asked. "Remember, I can't see them. Are they hurting Kiyiya?"

"No, at least not yet," Rachel explained. "But the shadow people are arriving with weapons to help the skinwalker."

"What are we going to do?" Chloe asked. "We can't let them hurt Kiyiya."

"I wish I knew," Rachel said. It took all she had to refrain from rushing into the middle of what was shaping up to be another massacre, this time in mystical form.

"Look Rachel," Chloe said. "The walls are getting closer."

They did seem to be closing in on them, but the movement was slow.

"Black magic," Ernesto said. "The walls are not moving. They only appear to be. Ignore the illusions and concentrate on the real threat. The witch has command of most of what is going on."

It was difficult to tell the skinwalker from Iris Phillips. Phillips seemed to move effortlessly from one form to another speaking only when human.

* * *

The lights of Santa Fe came into view. Dave Chee needed the exit for the 599 bypass, also known as the Santa Fe Corridor. It led directly to Hwy 14 and the penitentiary. The road had been constructed to move nuclear materials from Los Alamos National Laboratory to the Waste Isolation Pilot Plant (WIPP) underground disposal site near Carlsbad. WIPP had its share of protests as it made New Mexico the radioactive waste capital of the country but there were communities that greatly benefitted from the facility and they welcomed it. The bypass also provided an alternative to the traffic on St. Francis and Cerrillos Road, two crowded commercial corridors.

Chee turned and headed south on the bypass. His anxiety heightened with every moment.

CHAPTER 53

With her army of shadow people, Phillips felt safe enough to change back into a human. She approached Rachel and her friends. She was naked except for the jewelry hanging from her neck. Being naked didn't seem to bother her. If you could get past the horrendous odor that lingered around her, there was a hint of cloying fragrance.

Phillips laughed at them. Her mirth was heavily tinged with acidic sarcasm.

"Three tiny humans all wanting out of the ghost-filled prison. Pathetic." Phillips said. "I thought you would be a more formidable opponent."

Rachel reached for the gun behind her back. She had no idea if this gun had a safety. She thought most revolvers did not. Her father had taught her to shoot as a teen. He thought it a skill everyone should have, like being able to swim, but she had never owned a gun. Her thumb rested on the hammer. She pulled it back. Phillips turned and walked away. Rachel released the hammer slowly but kept it on Phillips.

Phillips quickly donned the wolf skin. The witch looked at Rachel, but it was her father's face Rachel saw.

"Surely, you wouldn't shoot your own father," it said.

All the love she had for him made her lower the gun. Tears welled in her eyes making it even more difficult to see through the safety glasses.

"Dad?" she said.

"Rachel," Chloe shook her. "What are you seeing? It's not your father. Don't let her fool you."

She shape-shifted again. Rachel took aim, but dropped her arms in defeat.

"I can't," Rachel said. "I just can't."

"Give me the gun," Ernesto said.

Relieved, Rachel handed it to him.

The skinwalker cast her furious gaze at the Hopi elder. The man leaned against Chloe who was supporting his arm. He took aim and fired. Although he missed her throat, which was vital to kill, he hit her shoulder. The wound oozed a yellow liquid. With a wave of her paw over the gunshot wound, it too healed.

The witch turned her wrath on them. Her growl transformed into a roar that filled the hallway of the prison and echoed back to them. The three of them moved farther down the dark hallway. There was no place to hide. Rachel felt desperate.

Phillips took to four legs to continue her battle with Kiyiya. He and his family fought off shadow people, but Kiyiya sensed the witch was back.

"Somehow we have to help Kiyiya," Rachel said.

"The three of us have to put our fear aside," Ernesto said. "Shadow people feed on fear."

"Good luck with that." Chloe said.

"We walk side-by-side right up to them and stare them down. No fear."

Rachel, Chloe and Ernesto interlocked their arms and moved as one toward the battle. The wolves held their position; but the shadow people kept multiplying. The friends stood quietly hoping to form a fearless faction.

"We stand here, close our eyes to the chaos and think calmly," Ernesto said. "If you meditate, go there. If you don't, think of something you love outside this prison."

Rachel knew Chloe would excel at this because she meditated regularly, but she wasn't particularly good at it so her mind turned to Chile Pod waiting for her back at Chloe's. She thought of Dave Chee and his mother, two new friends she was happy to know.

After a few minutes Ernesto told them to open their eyes. To Rachel's amazement, most of the shadow people were gone except several strong individuals who ran at them. Chloe, who could not see them watched as Rachel and Ernesto fought off something, their arms flailing in front of them.

Only Phillips embodied as a wolf and Kiyiya remained in the corridor. Kiyiya glowed in white, his neck injuries no longer visible. He could self-heal too.

Kiyiya ran at Phillips while her attention was focused on the disappearance of her supernatural army. He plowed into her side knocking her down.

"We have to find a way out," Chloe said.

"You're right," Rachel said. "But the door is locked."

Hold fast to mother wolf and pass through the bars. Joseph's words appeared in her mind.

When Rachel turned, Kaya was standing before them in her normal size, also radiating light.

"Everyone grab onto some of Kaya's fur," Rachel said. "Joseph told me she can get us out. We must trust she can take us beyond the bars."

Rachel walked to one side; grasped the ruff of Kaya's neck. Ernesto helped Chloe because she couldn't see the wolf. Rachel had experienced this kind of magic previously when she and Chloe held Kiyiya's fur so they could cross a field invisibly.

They approached the bars blocking their escape. Rachel wondered what passing through them would feel like or would there be no sensation? It was frightening as the partition drew closer, she braced. This was another leap of faith for her and Chloe. She thought Ernesto must have participated in something similar previously. He looked peaceful and had closed his eyes. Rachel followed his lead.

As they continued, Rachel felt a gentle tug. She imagined the bars going through them but not stopping or harming them. In a moment she was on the other side. She would never be able to describe what had happened because it made no sense to a fact-driven reporter new to this inexplicable world she lived in. When they cleared the bars Rachel turned to thank Kaya, but her body seemed to evaporate.

Rachel noticed the bloody mess she had been walking through was gone. The lantern showed her shoes were clean. There was no indication of what she had taken place on the other side.

Ernesto was drained. The passage through the bars had taken every reserve he had. His body sagged despite dragging his feet forward. Most of his steps were misplaced. Rachel removed her scarf from his face so he could breathe better. They were, after all, nearly out of the prison.

* * *

Dave Chee turned into the prison lot and parked his SUV. Old Main was dark. An old pickup and Chloe's car were parked outside. How to gain entry? What would he face once inside? Convinced something not of this world would be waiting. He'd read the stories about the old prison, the riot and the supernatural sightings. Because his mother had second sight, Dave believed it when she explained her visions. Flashlight in hand, gun in the other, he made his way to the gate house.

Dave halted when lights appeared from inside the prison. He could see them bobbing as someone – it looked like two people because there were two lights. Crouched behind the gate house, he waited to identify them.

"Rachel, we may have to carry him," he could hear Chloe saying.

"Ernesto," Rachel said. "Please let us carry you."

"No, I'm okay."

"Can I help?" Dave left the shadows. "Is everyone all right?"

Startled, they stopped talking and waited.

"Who's there?" Chloe asked. "Show yourself!"

"Dave Chee," he said. "Thought you might need some assistance, but it looks as if you have everything in hand." He was surprised at how comforted he was to see Rachel – and of course, her friends.

"We need to get Mr. Pacheco to a hospital," Rachel said as she removed the mask and safety glasses.

"I can help with that," Dave said. "Come Mr. Pacheco. I'll run with the siren to get you there quicker."

Before they could escort Ernesto to Dave's SUV a voice above them called out.

"Not so fast!" The words were spoken with such authority for a moment Rachel thought it might be a higher power. But this voice sounded impious. It did not have the loving voice she had always associated with the Great Spirit or any other pure presence people have worshiped.

Ernesto raised his head and looked upward.

"There," he pointed. "Shine the light toward the guard tower."

There was Phillips on the tower walk. She was smiling as if she held all the cards. Maybe she did. Their ordeal wasn't over.

The relief Rachel felt as they left the front door of the prison was quickly extinguished.

"I am not done with you. You must all die. That includes your friend who was stupid enough to follow you," Iris Phillips said.

"*La chienne est de retour!*" Chloe said.

"What?" Rachel asked.

"The bitch is back!" Chloe translated from French.

"She is very potent," Ernesto said. "The older the human is when it becomes a skinwalker, the more supernatural powers it can exert. Without a shaman, I'm not sure we can defeat her."

"She is around eighty," Rachel whispered to Ernesto.

"Then we are in much trouble," he said.

"Listen to him," Phillips said. "Let's be done with this."

Rachel thought for a moment trying to remember something she had read about skinwalkers.

"We need a lock of her hair or article of clothing, maybe her jewelry," she said.

"A 'turning around' rite," Ernesto said. "But how?"

"I'll go inside the tower and try to get something from her," Rachel offered.

"Take the gun," Chloe said.

"No, put it away," Rachel replied. "Dave has one and I'm sure he's a better shot. I don't think bullets are the answer."

"Rachel," Dave said taking her elbow. "Are you sure you want to do this?"

"That seems to be my job now," she said. "I have the arrowhead. That will give me some protection."

"Be careful," Chloe said hugging her. "I need my friend and Chile Pod needs you."

"You would take care of her if I don't make it?" Rachel asked.

"With everything in my being." Chloe gave her a hug.

Rachel considered curling up with her cat and a cup of tea. Sounded like heaven.

"Chloe," Rachel said. "I may need a distraction. Be ready if that moment comes."

"You know I will," Chloe said. If it had been daylight, they would each have seen the tears in the other's eyes.

The intrepid reporter walked through the darkness to the door of the watch tower finding her way with the flashlight off. It would be needed once she was inside. The door creaked as she pulled it open. Rachel began climbing the steps to the lookout. She turned on the torch holding the beam downward. There was stuff everywhere left over from a time when it was needed. Rachel didn't expect to surprise Phillips. Rachel knew if Phillips was in skinwalker form she could read minds and would be one step ahead of her.

"Rachel Blackstone, ace reporter and newbie medium," Iris Phillips said.

Rachel directed her light at Phillips and was taken aback to see she was human.

"I keep growing younger," Phillips boasted. "Wish I'd known earlier and I wouldn't have had to use anti-aging products and prescriptions for human growth hormones. Don't know how many injections of HGH I stole for myself," confessed the former pharmacist.

"But this, this skinwalking thing is amazing. I have more energy than when I was young and my skin and muscle tone are Olympic quality, don't you think?" She did a half-turn each way to show off her body, totally without shame or embarrassment. The only thing she wore were the many necklaces Rachel had noticed earlier.

Rachel passed on a response. She expected a frightening evil witch not this self-aggrandizing half-human gushing about her youthful vigor.

"You need to go," Rachel said. "Leave or we will be forced to kill you."

"How do you propose to do that?" Phillips laughed. "The gang that can't shoot straight. I can jam guns and stop bullets in mid-air."

Rachel knew that, but there was something she couldn't retrieve.

Something she needed to remember. A quick inventory of the turret, showed the way through. It too, was scattered with junk that had once been useful: chairs, portable electric heaters, equipment that worked the lights and sirens. An old white dial phone sat on a window ledge. Oddly, a flush toilet stood right in the middle. A large mirror showed the staircase behind her. Years of grime had left splotches on the windows.

Rachel watched as Phillips went through the door back onto the outside platform. Prison guards once used it to observe inmates. Here they carried their weapons while walking back and forth looking for escapes or altercations. It was one of three watchtowers. Each was high enough they could see every inch of the enclosure around the prison.

While she kept the flashlight on Phillips she changed into the formidable skinwalker. If she rushed her on the platform maybe Phillips would fall or perhaps she could grab one of the necklaces.

Before she could run at her, Phillips held up her hand reaching for something. A silver cord appeared in Phillips hand. The witch swung out over the shadowy emptiness.

"Can you see her?" she yelled to her friends below. Chloe held up the lantern and Dave his flashlight searching for Phillips.

"She's on the gatehouse," Dave shouted.

Rachel waved her flash around wildly trying to see Phillips. When she caught movement, she confirmed Dave's sighting.

Without thinking, Rachel grabbed the silver cord that returned after Phillips let go. She wasn't good with heights, especially those that didn't have adequate protection from things like falling. The dark helped because depth perception wasn't as good at night, making it less intimidating. Taking it with both hands, she tugged to see if it would hold and took to the air toward the building where the skinwalker awaited. She flew through space with no wings. It felt more like a bungee cord attached to nothing. And yet, she did not fall to earth.

When her feet impacted the roof it jarred her teeth and Rachel thought her knees would never be the same the shock was so intense. She floundered around trying to gain purchase somewhere, anywhere. Her feet slipped on the old roofing.

Chloe, Ernesto and Dave winced as they saw Rachel crash onto the roof.

"I'm coming up there," Dave shouted.

"No, don't," Rachel said. "Don't want anyone else getting hurt."

"I'm a park ranger," Dave said already on his way. "I climb things every day."

By the time he reached the tower room and was standing on the platform, the line had disappeared.

"Rachel," he yelled. "Are you okay?"

Having finally steadied herself on the roof, her gaze turned to Phillips. Rachel wouldn't allow herself to look at her face. She saw the cord the skinwalker held, effectively denying access to Dave. Phillips threw it to the ground. In horror, Rachel watched by the light of Chloe's lantern as the rope coiled around her and Ernesto making it impossible for them to escape.

"Rachel," Chloe screamed while desperately trying to remove the rope. "Look behind you!"

Phillips was walking on two legs. The roof gave her no problems and she unafraid of falling. With a sweep of her arm, the wind picked up. She held a crystal of some kind in her hand. A light emanated from it. It morphed into a powdery substance that Phillips threw toward the watchtower with the help of the breeze. As it reached the tower the particles exploded into flame. Dave dove back into the protection of the turret.

Picking himself off the floor, he heard his cell chime. In the dark he opened his text app. A message from his mother read: "R must get witch to speak in witch form!" How could he tell her without the skinwalker also hearing?

He forwarded the text to Rachel.

"Are you kidding me?" Rachel was horrified her phone was chiming. It was probably spam anyway.

CHAPTER 54

Rachel wrestled with several things at once: keeping an eye on Phillips without looking her in the eye, staying on the roof and struggling to get her phone out. She felt like a clown juggling at the circus with too many balls in the air.

When the cell was finally in her hand, she looked for the dot over the icon. She thought it a text. It was from Dave. Rachel looked in his direction as if to ask why but of course, he couldn't possibly see her, only her lighted phone. She opened the text, a forward from Dave's mother. She read it and quickly pushed it back in her pocket.

"Mrs. Phillips," Rachel said addressing the human. "I don't get it. You became a pharmacist in order to help people. I don't believe you earned that degree just to make money. Didn't you do it to help others?"

There was no reaction.

"I understand why you're here," Rachel tried again. "Everyone who was in this prison on the night of the riot carries the trauma with them. You and your son suffered greatly. So much so, you took your own son's life and became this ... this monster."

She had no idea if Phillips was hearing her. She didn't speak. From what she knew about skinwalkers, there was no repentance or regrets.

The acts that one commits to become evil are atrocities in themselves, breaking social, even sacred taboos.

The skinwalker kept coming closer. Rachel felt the panic. She took out her arrowhead and held it in front of Phillips, who stopped advancing, but didn't step back. Before Rachel could think of anything further to force her to talk, the prison yard began filling with light. Rachel risked a look and saw Kiyiya's family moving through the prison walls and assembling much like an army battalion. One wolf trotted across the yard where it broke the binding holding Chloe and Ernesto with powerful jaws. Chloe moved Ernesto to a more protective spot behind the watchtower.

The bodies of the wolves were glowing and Phillips was exposed for what she had become. It was her turn to be afraid. Her fangs oozed saliva. She took her eyes off Rachel and watched the wolves. The skinwalker made another step toward Rachel. She wasn't done yet.

Rachel wasn't done either. She had to get the skinwalker off the roof so the wolves could finish her.

Rachel steadied herself. She needed to make a decision but the witch would know what she thought, was reading her mind even now.

"Now Chloe!" Rachel shouted.

Free of the cord, Chloe sprang into action.

"Hey bitch!"

The witch instinctively looked at Chloe waving her hands wildly much like a seeker in Sedona dancing around a bonfire during the Harmonic Convergence. All that yoga was paying off in these few seconds. Rachel couldn't believe her friend's gyrations were so frenetic.

While the skinwalker was distracted for a few moments, Rachel moved quickly and shoved her with everything she had. Phillips was caught by surprise. The next thing she knew, the monster was on the ground surrounded by wolves.

"You can't do this!" Phillips screamed in rage while in skinwalker form. The instant she spoke, Phillips returned to her human body, her power gone. Her nakedness seemed to bother her now. In a second, she lost her height and weight advantage. Her muscles shrank and withered. She wrapped her arms around her to hide her body and ran, painfully, in her 80-year-old woman's body. Decades of neglect were apparent with every step. Her back was hunched over with osteoporosis and her arthritic knees throbbed with each stride.

The wolves approached Phillips. She was harmless now and they parted to let her go. Phillips entered the prison and disappeared into the ghostly building.

The *dark wind* followed her and calm returned to the prison yard.

Except for Kiyiya and Kaya, the wolves faded away, their mission consummately done. Dave rushed down the steps of the watchtower to the gate house.

"Rachel, I'm right beneath you. Slide down and I'll catch you."

Clumsily, Rachel scooted across the roof until the toe of her foot found the edge.

Dave laid the flashlight on the ground.

"Okay, let go."

She tried to relax by exhaling, instead found she was holding her breath. With another leap of faith, Rachel slid off the roof. Dave caught her, but because of the lack of light it wasn't pretty. He staggered and they fell to the ground with a thud. Dave bounded to his feet to help Rachel to hers.

"You all right?" Dave asked.

"All things considered," Rachel said. "Yes."

"I think someone stayed around to say goodbye," Dave said pointing to Kiyiya and Kaya, their glow lighting up the yard.

Rachel walked unsteadily. Dave stopped in front of the two wolves in spirit. He stepped back to give Rachel her moment. A moment she didn't realize was coming.

"Thank you Kiyiya and Kaya. You saved our lives," Rachel said.

Kiyiya ducked his head shyly as if to say it was just another day at the office. Kaya turned to look at her son. Rachel felt the pride of his mother. Both wolves gave her a small graceful bow and then faded away.

Rachel, overwhelmed, wiped tears from her eyes. In the distance, the two wolves howled the all clear. Their voices echoed from one mountain range to another.

"Oh my god," Rachel turned to Dave. "Did you see that?"

"Yes I did."

"What were they doing?" Rachel asked.

"The wolf is the pathfinder," Dave said. "They were making tribute to you finding your path."

CHAPTER 55

"We'll meet you at the hospital," Rachel said.

Dave supported Ernesto with one strong arm and helped him into the passenger seat. He left the parking lot with siren blaring.

Rachel and Chloe stood outside Old Main. The only illumination came from the lights they carried.

"That was one frightening evening," Chloe said. "I feel like we should help her, but maybe she prefers being left alone for now."

"I don't know if she wants help," Rachel said. "I think we're done here. We need to follow Dave and check on Ernesto."

The women scrambled into Chloe's car and left the horrendous crimes of the prison behind them unaware the pickup started a few moments later and left the parking lot traveling in the opposite direction.

At the hospital the three friends waited for news as a team worked on Ernesto. After about an hour, a doctor came out of the treatment area.

"Hello, I'm Dr. Abeita," he said. "Are you Mr. Pacheco's friends?"

"I'm Dave Chee with the State Parks Division and these are Mr. Pacheco's friends, Rachel and Chloe. They rescued him."

"He is going to be okay," he said. "We're keeping him overnight as he has a concussion. The rest of his injuries are contusions. He'll be sore for a few days. He's given us his family contacts and we're trying to reach them now."

"Thank you doctor," Dave said.

Abeita nodded and returned to the ER.

"Okay," Dave said. "I need to go home and get some sleep. Are you both all right?"

"Yes," they said in unison.

"Rachel, please contact my mother. She will be staying up until she hears from you. You know," he paused and ever so slightly smirked. "Mother texts." He gently mocked Rachel's lack of tech skills. "You could let her know all is well. All is well – right?"

"Yes," Rachel said. "All is well. Thank you for coming." And she was surprised by how heartfelt her words were.

After Dave left, the two women sunk into the comfy seats in Chloe's car.

"First, I'll text Mari-Lynn and let her know we're all right," Rachel said.

"You want help?"

"I think I can handle this," Rachel replied.

Next, Rachel typed a message for Dave's mother telling her everyone was okay and her son was on the way home.

"I'm wired," Chloe said once Rachel's text went through. "The Shed for a late dinner? I'll buy the margaritas."

* * *

After the encounter at the prison, Rachel felt it was safe to return to her house in the South Capital area. It would be nice to sleep in a bed that didn't do tricks. She pulled the car into the garage, took Chile Pod and went inside. Before she could feed Chile Pod the cat's ears perked up and she leapt to the counter and surveyed the courtyard. Rachel followed her gaze. Although she saw nothing, that familiar feeling told her she was about to have a visitor from another plane.

"Okay," she said to her psychic tortie. "You stay here and I'll go check it out."

She mumbled to herself as she approached the center of her yard.

"Geez, you'd think I could get a break."

The now familiar odors and rattles commenced while she waited for whatever or whoever was to come. Rachel glanced at the kitchen window and saw Chile Pod watching her. She wasn't hiding so that seemed a good sign.

In a few minutes two figures materialized. One was Másaw, and the other Joseph, the Hopi shaman.

Dread gripped her body as she waited for them to speak.

"Rachel," Joseph began. "We have come to warn you."

"Warn me about what?" Her stomach was tying itself into a knot.

"First, we wish you to know you've exceeded our expectations," Joseph continued.

"Uh," Rachel croaked out. "Uh, thank you, how so?"

"Your presence and abilities were made known to us before you realized them," Joseph explained.

"What?" Rachel surprised. "I don't understand."

"For a long time we have needed a human – you might call it a liaison or negotiator."

"I'm nothing like that. I just kind of dabble in, in this." She protested not finding a word that would adequately describe what she did.

Joseph smiled faintly, amused at her discomfiture.

"Because of this, we have come to tell you evil will beset you again," Joseph said.

"It will not be immediate," he assured her. "You must be aware."

"Másaw," she asked. "Why did you accompany Joseph?"

"To impress upon you," he said in Hopi, but it appeared in her mind in English. "You must be wary. Another *dark wind* is fomenting. This one will be far worse."

"Másaw is correct," Joseph said. "You must be prepared."

"For what?" she pleaded.

"Not all monsters hide in the shadows," Joseph said. "Some conduct their evil in the light of day."

Másaw held out his skeletal hand to her.

"Please take," he said.

Rachel extended her palm. She felt the bony fingers scrape gently across her skin as he deposited something. It was all she could do not to yank her hand away, the feeling of death was so intense. Thinking that Másaw had dropped a hint she glanced at what he left her. In her palm lay five kernels of dried yellow corn, Másaw's signature. He had never handed them directly to her. When she looked up for an explanation, they were gone.

"What fresh hell is this?" Rachel muttered. There was no one to hear her. At least, she didn't think so.

CHAPTER 56

A few days later, Rachel wrote in her breakfast nook where she had created her "office corner." Most people would have chosen the spare bedroom to set up an office. She liked the nook. While a tight fit, she didn't care. The view was better, no fence. A snapshot of the courtyard where her many visits occurred.

Chile Pod snoozed on her lap as she wrote her latest assignment, an arts story.

Juan's Auto Casa finished the repairs on her aging Mercury Marquis. Chloe's car had spoiled her and she planned to save for another car. She felt the Merc's days were numbered even with the blessing done by Lloyd Loretto, the shaman mechanic.

Ernesto went home to the Hopi reservation to be with his family. Rachel spoke with him before he was released from the hospital. He would no longer be working at Old Main as a guide. She was happy about his recovery. This was a man she wanted to stay friends with. When reporting, journalists usually have about 20 to 30 minutes to do an interview. In that time, Rachel could decide if this person was someone she would consult again. The nice thing about this, if you didn't like the person it was not a lifetime commitment. The down side, if you liked them you might never see them again.

Iris Phillips disappeared. When police arrived at her house to arrest her, there was no sign of her. The pickup sat out front. The police found a cellar in her backyard. Inside, a dehydrator contained small particles of human remains. On further inspection they also found her son's body in a secret compartment, minus his fingerprints. On the table were petroglyph drawings. After a thorough search of her house, the police lab confirmed human remains in the ashes found in her fireplace. She placed them there herself and made up the story about someone being on her roof. It was assumed by Rachel, Julian and Stella that Phillips sent the untraceable emails with the rock art drawings.

Melinda Delgado Harris had been cleared of killing her grandfather. Her troubles weren't over as she would lose the house if Ozzy's next of kin turned up. If, and until then, she could continue living there. Rachel considered she might be the skinwalker. It turned out she was only practicing witchcraft, not a criminal offense in this century. Rachel felt she wouldn't step out of line at least for the time being. She also thought Melinda unstable and planned to keep an eye on her. Stalking was reason enough. Rachel reported it to the police in case there was ever a need for a paper trail. By the time police questioned Melinda about the stalking, she'd destroyed the evidence.

Julian published the fourth and final part of her story on Old Main. The sidebar told the tale of the riot aftermath. Charges were brought against 50 inmates involved in the massacre. Most plea-bargained with no time added to their original sentences. Seventeen homicides were not prosecuted. Two jury verdicts were achieved. Essentially, the perpetrators got away with murder.

Money was appropriated after the riot to refurbish the old prison and build new ones. It took a federal consent decree to get this much done. Prison reform has occurred resentfully at best. In a 2020 story it was reported that prison guards now had to undergo eight weeks of training. Educational opportunities for inmates have found thirty percent of the prison population taking part. At the time of the report, there had been 26 suicides and seven murders committed in New Mexico prisons since 2007. That leaves prisons susceptible to more violence.

The deaths of Oswaldo Delgado and Olivia Kanteena were filed as unsolved because the method of death remained undetermined. Rachel was certain Iris Phillips shouldered the blame. What demented reasoning she used to sentence them to death, Rachel couldn't presume to understand.

Thanksgiving was Thursday. Rachel, Chloe, Mari-Lynn and Celeste had buffet reservations at La Fonda. Family, the one you choose, is created with common experiences. Rachel felt fortunate to have people she could depend on whatever happened. Julian planned for drinks and snacks on the rooftop Wednesday after the work day – like they would wait until five to begin partying. The staff at the office was in high spirits these days. The magazine had made money and Jules gave everyone a raise. It's amazing how inspiring a five percent increase can be.

Rachel had a lot to be thankful for, including Chile Pod's antics. She made her laugh when she needed it and she especially appreciated her at night. Nights could be lonely but not with her little cat.

She contemplated the horror existing in the world while recognizing the good in people like her friends and new acquaintances. She didn't want to lose touch with Ernesto, Doba or Dave.

The latter surprised her by asking if they might have dinner together. Rachel had to admit she was interested. Because of his mother, Dave seemed to understand what she had been called, reluctantly, to do. That would make a huge difference if it were to evolve into a long-term relationship.

After his question, she replied, "Is this a date?"

And he said, "Why don't we just see what happens."

Rachel picked up Chile Pod and moved to the sofa in the living room. The tortie was in her lap before she could sit down. It was a trick she did perfectly every time. Rachel raised the remote to turn on the news and hesitated. She couldn't help but think about those young men who fought for their lives and lost it all. Rachel took a moment to breathe in what they had been denied: life and freedom.

For now, the *dark wind* had blown its last.

Did you enjoy Skinwalker Medium?

If so, please consider writing a short review for Amazon, Goodreads or
BookBub. Thank you for reading.
G.G. Collins

https://tinyurl.com/yy7v7zsy (G.G. Collins Amazon Book Page)

Check out the blogs:
https://reluctantmediumatlarge.wordpress.com/
https://paralleluniverseatlarge.wordpress.com/

About the Author

As a seasoned reporter and arts editor, G.G. Collins racked up a lot of column inches, a fellowship from the National Endowment for the Arts-American Dance Festival at Duke University and multiple Society of Professional Journalists awards. She learned the ins and outs of publishing at a book publisher. Her books have been reviewed by *Publisher's Weekly* and landed on the *Strand Magazine* reading list.

Working as a journalist is one of the most educational jobs. It's the job of a reporter to ask questions, learn quickly and write even faster about many subjects. In one day, she might cover a fundraiser for cancer research, meet an entertainer in town for a weekend performance and attend a press conference for a local brewery. The next day, it's the new heart center, getting a first grader's take on saving a historical building and welcoming the new sharks at the aquarium.

The result of thousands of interviews, press conferences and performances is that journalists learn a little bit about many things. It was Alexander Pope who wrote, "A little learning is a dangerous thing." He also authored in the same poem: "Fools rush in where angels fear to tread." Both could be applied to reporters, many of whom rush to breaking news sites that could be the location of a terrorist attack, a hurricane landing or a bank robbery.

It's never a dull moment for her protagonist, reporter Rachel Blackstone, who takes more time off to solve paranormal mysteries than she does for vacations.

Bibliography for Further Reading:

The Hate Factory: A First-Hand Account of the 1980 Riot at the Penitentiary of New Mexico by Georgelle Hirliman, 2005

The Devil's Butcher Shop: The New Mexico Prison Uprising by Roger Morris, 1988

"Devastating Penitentiary Riot of 1980 Changed New Mexico and its Prisons" by Phaedra Haywood, *Santa Fe New Mexican*, February 1, 2020

Prison Reforms Ordered After Riot Come Grudgingly in New Mexico" by Wendell Rawls, Jr., *The New York Times*, December 21, 1981

"Navajos Call Them Skinwalkers" by Tony Hillerman, *New Mexico Magazine*, July 1992

The Paranormal Pastor Blog, "The Navajo Skinwalker," by Kyle Germann, Reblogged by Pastor Swope, July 30, 2012

Take a tour of Old Main Prison-New Mexico Penitentiary Full tour, about 40 minutes, via YouTube video. 2017